About the Author

Gary Morgenstern is a career sports television programming executive, and a passionate sports fanatic. During his daily commute by train from Connecticut to New York City, Gary has devoured every title written by his favourite novelist, William Martin. Gary is fortunate to have been encouraged by William Martin to write *The Lombardi Project*, his first novel. He and his wife, Noreen, and four children Kaley, Kendyl, Kamryn and Kellen reside in Sandy Hook, CT.

The Lombardi Project

Gary Morgenstern

The Lombardi Project

Olympia Publishers
London

www.olympiapublishers.com
OLYMPIA PAPERBACK EDITION

A CIP catalogue record for this title is
available from the British Library.

ISBN: 978-1-80439-237-9

First Published in 2023

Olympia Publishers
Tallis House
2 Tallis Street
London
EC4Y 0AB

Printed in Great Britain

Dedication

I dedicate this book to my wife, Noreen.

Acknowledgements

Thank you to William Martin, who encouraged me to write this novel.

CHAPTER 1

He pulled his car around the final bend on the hill, and took a sharp right hand turn into his driveway. His modern, stylish condo was gray and white, and from the street side, looked fairly boring. Just a double garage door and a few nondescript windows. He had planted flowers in the two large pots near the garage doors, but they were neglected and were wilting. He pressed the garage door opener, and pulled his SUV into the right hand bay — the left hand bay was filled with his toys: snow shoes, a kayak, several snowboards, a windsurfer, and a Cannondale racing bike.

He exited the car, and walked through the garage to the door which led to the ground floor entry. He pushed the door open, and that's when it hit him. Within a split second, Jared was lying flat on his back on the floor. He might have blacked out for a fraction of a second as his head slammed against the cement tile floor on his way down. Then suddenly, he was greeted with a new sensation. This one was slightly more pleasant, but not entirely welcome. Pocahontas, Jared's one-hundred-and-twenty pound Newfoundland "puppy" was standing above him, licking his face. Pocahontas often greeted him at the door, but this was the first time she had knocked Jared off his feet. She was growing larger and more powerful.

"Knock it off Poky," said Jared, as he pushed Pocahontas back with his forearm while rolling over on his side to get out of licking range. Pocahontas backed away, then darted up the stairs to the main level of the condo. Jared got to his feet slowly and made his way up the stairs. When he arrived on the main level, the setting sun was beaming through the floor to ceiling windows in the living room, reflecting off a glorious view of the Pacific Ocean. Jared turned and headed toward the kitchen, opened the fridge and grabbed a beer. He popped it open, took a swig and then hit the play button on his answering machine. The electronic voice came on and said, *"Call today at 11.33 a.m., call from phone number: 203-555-4523."* Jared immediately recognized the phone number. He lunged for the answering machine, and hit the stop button. He wasn't ready to listen to the message yet. He needed to process things first. He stood there, thought for a moment and took a long swig of beer. It was a very long swig, in fact, he polished it off. His head was spinning. Jared decided he needed a little more time to process things before listening to the message. He grabbed Poky's leash from a bowl on the kitchen counter, put the leash on her collar, and led her down the stairs. They walked out the door to the garage, Jared pressed the electric garage door opener, then stepped onto the driveway and down to the street. That's when Poky took control and started pulling Jared, with great force, down the road. It was just Poky being Poky.

Jared's mind began to wonder. *"Why would Janey be calling me after all this time?"* Janey and Jared had a history together. They had dated for more than five years. Five years, two months, and eleven days to be exact. That's a figure that Jared had committed to memory. In fact, he could recite the exact number of days they dated — 1,897. He could even recite how many minutes — 2,731,680. He was head-over-heels in love with her. But, not Janey. When she ended their relationship, she just walked away. She simply moved on. Janey moved back to her home town of Fairfield, Connecticut, where she had been a State Senator from 2000 to 2004. At twenty-four years of age, Janey had been the youngest State Senator in Connecticut history (although the minimum age in Connecticut to become a Senator is eighteen). Rumors swirled in political circles that Janey's rise to power was a result of her model good looks, and that might have been true, assuming Connecticut voters marked their ballots based on that criteria alone. In reality, Janey was an extremely bright and hard-working breath of fresh air. She appealed to the people of Connecticut because she was strong on social issues. She was extremely popular with her constituents, regularly made the rounds on the local morning talk shows, shook hands with commuters at the train stations, and used social media to connect with the people of Connecticut before it was the popular thing to do.

In 2004, she attempted to parlay her popularity into a run for the U.S. Senate, but lost a close contest by two percentage points to the incumbent.

After her failed Senate bid, and feeling completely burnt out, Janey moved to California where she met and began dating Jared. She stayed away from politics, opting instead to teach Political Science at USC. The slower pace and reduced stress appealed to Janey. Jared and Janey were active, spending most of their free time at the beach, surfing, waterskiing and kite skiing. They moved in together, and Jared fell deeply and hopelessly in love with Janey.

One would have thought, that with his rugged good looks, Jared would have chalked up many successful relationships in his twenty-six years. But, that was not the case. Jared had never met anyone who truly interested him. In the relationships he had been involved in prior to meeting Janey, Jared had always felt he was simply going through the motions, forcing himself to do things, say things, and even feel things he didn't actually feel. But, from the beginning, it was different with Janey. Jared loved spending time with Janey. And, many of her habits, like ignoring him while she connected with other people on social media websites, would have bothered him if it had been anyone other than Janey. Things were different with her. He found that particular habit endearing and adorable.

Jared often wondered if Janey felt the same way. Janey had always been a free spirit, always in a hurry, and seemingly distracted with a variety of things which always seemed to consume her thoughts. She often said the words "I love you" to Jared, but the words felt hollow — as if she said them because she was expected to.

After spending five years in California with Jared (163,900,800 seconds to be exact), she suddenly announced that she was moving back to Connecticut to take another run at the Senate. Senator Richard Lester, the man who defeated her in the 2004 election, had contacted Janey, and asked her to consider a run in 2010. He was preparing to step away from politics, to take over as CEO of a large international bank. Lester was very persuasive, and Janey was flattered. Janey broke the news to Jared at dinner." "But, why, Janey? I thought you were done with politics." Janey didn't look at Jared as she responded. It's not that she couldn't. She just didn't care enough to. It was that cold, uncaring side of Janey's personality. The side that Jared knew existed, saw many times before, but tried to convince himself didn't really exist.

"I thought I was too," said Janey, "but, I guess not. I guess it's not out of my system. I was devastated when I lost that election. I thought I was done and I never wanted to think about it ever again."

"So, what happened?"

"I don't know," said Janey. "Lester is a good salesman."

Jared stood up from the table and threw his arms up in the air. "And Lester! What's the deal with that? I thought you hated that guy!"

"I used to. I hated him, I really did. But, now he's on my side and he's helping me. It's not personal, it's strictly business." Strictly business? Not quite. Jared could tell things weren't right. How could she be so cold? Didn't she care about him, even a little bit? Janey packed the next morning and flew to Connecticut. For the first few days, Janey called Jared every day to check in. Then, the calls came less frequently, then, not at all. The following Sunday morning, Jared was sitting on his couch in his living room. Pocahontas was sitting at his feet as he read the *New York Times*. He was flipping through the Arts and Leisure section, and there it was. A photo taken at the opening of *Vengeance in Reverse* at the Metropolitan Opera in Lincoln Center. Lester was wearing a stylish tuxedo, his gray hair was perfectly combed across his head, a glass of champagne in one hand, his other arm around Janey's shoulder. The two lovebirds gazed deeply into each other's eyes. The caption below the photo read: *America's Newest Power Couple?* In the years since she abruptly left and cut off all communication with him, Jared received just one email note from Janey. It arrived on the evening of the 2016 Presidential election. The note was quite short. It said, "Can you believe Harp won?" So, why was she calling now? Jared dragged Poky back up the driveway, through the garage and up the stairs to the main level. He removed Poky's leash, placed it back in the bowl on the counter, and slowly approached the answering machine.

Tentatively, he took a deep breath, reached out his hand, and pressed the 'play' button. "*Jared, I'm sure I'm the last person on earth you ever thought you'd hear from, but I really need to talk to you. Don't bother trying to call me — I'm on the move. I'm not the most popular person in Washington right now. Maybe you're aware. Anyway, I will call you back tomorrow around seven. I'm assuming that's still around the time you get home. Anyway, please answer when I call. I beg you.*" I beg you?

CHAPTER 2

Janey exited her taxi cab in the parking lot of the local television station, the local network affiliate based in West Hartford, Connecticut. She entered the building, and approached the reception desk. "Hi, I'm Janey…" The receptionist looked up at Janey as a big smile appeared on her face. "Oh, my dear, I know who you are, Senator Logan. I'm a big fan. I think what you're doing is really wonderful!"

"Thank you, ma'am", said Janey. "That really means a lot to me."

"It is such a travesty. That man is killing America. Someone has to stop him." Just then, a young, baby-faced staffer entered the lobby, introduced himself as Rollie, and led Janey to the green room. After receiving sufficient amounts of make-up for national television, Rollie led Janey to Studio A. The stage manager fitted Janey with a wireless mic, and situated her in a seat at the main news desk. The desk was large, and she sat there alone. That was just fine because the camera would be shooting her close up, as a talking head, during her two-way interview on national television. The stage manager walked Janey through the plan: she would go on live at approximately 7.10 p.m., during the second segment to the Lauren Young Show on PNN (the Politics News Network). He would count her down from ten seconds, then Lauren would toss out her first question. Simple. The stage manager suggested to Janey that she should smile and nod her head while Lauren asked her questions. That always seemed to be the most natural way of doing it. "Five, four, three, two, one."

Lauren: Senator Logan, thank you for joining us tonight.

Janey: Thank you for having me, Lauren.

Lauren: So, fill us in on what you're up to.

Janey: Well, as you know, Lauren, the country is in dire trouble. Unemployment is up around ten and a half to eleven percent. The stock market is in collapse, the American people are frustrated and angry. They're scared. The social programs, which had advanced under President Staley, have all but gone away. Gay rights, equal pay for women, Staley-care — all gone or going away. People are literally dying in the streets without access to affordable health care.

Lauren: But, the people voted for Harp, and they voted for the Republican House and Senate.

Janey: That's true, and we must respect the will of the people. However, things have declined so far in just two years, we have to consider how things will play out during the next two years. Can we afford to sit back and watch it unfold? I feel — as do many of my colleagues, we feel that we must act.

Lauren: And that means?

Janey: Well, that means we utilize all means available to us to make changes on behalf of the American people. As you know, Article II of the United States Constitution states that, "The President, Vice President, and all Civil Officers of the United States shall be removed from Office on Impeachment for, and Conviction of, Treason, Bribery, or other High Crimes and Misdemeanors."

Lauren: So you're talking impeachment. But, what are the crimes? And, with a Republican House of Representatives, how can you succeed? And, what about those who say this will just add to the confusion and state of disarray we already have in

America today?

Janey: I think we can succeed. I believe that we will. The American people will insist that their elected officials be held responsible for their actions. Remember, there are a lot of unanswered questions still revolving around the election two years ago. Questions that need to be answered. And yes, perhaps in the short term, the state of our political system will be more fractured, but we are focused on the long term health of our nation.

Lauren: Can you talk a little about the toll this is having on you personally?

Janey: It's been difficult. I've received death threats. I have been shunned by many of my colleagues in the senate — on both sides of the aisle. The media coverage has been brutal, and it has gotten very personal.

Lauren: Well, Senator Logan, I commend you for what you're doing, and I certainly wish you luck and success. Please come back soon and fill us in on your progress.

Janey: Thank you, Lauren, I will.

Lauren turned to the camera and spoke.

Lauren: Senator Logan and her effort to help repair America. Coming up next, President Harp vows to end food stamps — immediately. What can be done? Colorado GOP Senator Riley Cliff joins us next to explain why he believes this is good for America.

The stage manager removed her wireless mic, but Janey elected to keep the make-up on. She put on her long Burberry raincoat, and even though it was nighttime, she wore her dark sunglasses. Then, she slipped out the side door of the television studio into her waiting taxi cab. She was worried about her safety, and she couldn't be too careful these days.

CHAPTER 3

Jared's 2007 Honda CRV still looked fine, even though the auto maker had replaced it with a newer model several years earlier. But, at ten years old, it ran well and required very few repairs — just tires and brakes. Jared didn't care much about cars, and he always found those people who obsessed over having nice, new, shiny, expensive models both shallow and insane. His ten year old CRV was perfect for his needs — he could fit all his toys right in the back, except for the kayak, which had to ride on the roof. Today, he had the wind surfer in the back, and he was heading down the coast from L.A. to San Diego to meet his brother Erik. Erik was a professor of history at San Diego State and he loved the same action sports that Jared loved. Without a doubt, Erik was Jared's closest confidant, and when he needed someone to talk to, he always drove down to see Erik. It's not that Erik was an expert on relationships. At thirty-one, Erik had yet to have a steady girlfriend. Dates? Yes. But, girlfriends? No. However, Erik was a good listener, and Jared could always count on him to have an opinion. His opinions were rarely well thought out, mind you. They were typically knee-jerk, emotional reactions which generally took Jared's side, regardless of the facts.

When Jared pulled into a parking spot at Mission Bay Park, he could see Erik lying on the grass, his wind sail rolled into a ball, and propped under his head. The park was filled with couples walking on the beach, kids flying kites, and families sitting at picnic tables eating dinner. Jared exited his car, and walked along the path which led to Erik's personal patch of green grass. "Bro, you sleeping?" asked Jared, as he kicked Erik gently in his calf.

Erik bolted upright with a confused look on his face. "Huh? Yeah, I guess so." Jared sat down next to Erik, and placed his igloo cooler on the grass between them.

Jared pulled out two beers, and offered one to Erik. "Bro, you want a brew?" They sat there in silence for a minute, sipping their beers and looking out at Mission Bay and the sun, which was starting to drop into the clouds which framed the horizon. "Guess who called me?" asked Jared.

"President Harp?" responded Erik with a chuckle.

"No, but close. Janey Logan." Erik choked and spit a mouthful of beer back into his bottle. A fair amount of beer dribbled down onto his shirt.

"Janey? No shit! But, how is that close to Harp?" Jared pulled a small towel from his backpack, and tossed it to Erik. Erik used the towel to wipe the beer off his face, and to dab his shirt in an effort to dry it.

"Do you watch the news, read a paper, surf the Internet?" asked Jared. "Janey is at war with Harp — she's trying to get him impeached."

"Why, what'd he do?"

"He's ruining America, Erik. Haven't you heard, the country is falling apart? Aren't you a history professor or something?"

"*History*, bro! Ask me anything about the past, and I got the answer. But, ask me who the Speaker of the House is today, and I have no clue."

"She left a message on my machine yesterday. She sounded really frazzled,"

"No!" yelled Erik in a sharp tone. "That heartless bitch fucked you! Don't you remember? I certainly do."

Jared turned and pulled another beer from the cooler and popped it open. He took a long swig.

When Janey suddenly announced that she was leaving to return to Connecticut for the U.S. Senate run, Jared was heartbroken. He tried to keep his chin up for appearances, but Erik watched as his brother declined into a deep, dark depression. Jared began to drink and eat excessively, gave up all attempts at physical fitness, left his condo only to go to work, and rarely answered his phone. Erik considered conducting an intervention, but decided against it when he realized it would likely backfire. This went on for a full year, and then Jared slowly worked his way out of his funk. Erik vowed never to let his brother get hurt again by a woman, particularly Janey Logan. But, now she was back in the picture, and that made Erik feel very uneasy and suspicious.

"Oh, I remember. But, bro, I'm over her. I'm just…"

"No you're not! Don't you see, she's using you for something? I don't know what. She knows you're not over her. It's like being an alcoholic. You'll never be over her. You have a sickness and it controls you — not the other way around."

"She begged me to pick up when she calls me tomorrow night. You know, she's not with Lester any more. It's over."

"See, she's using you," said Erik. "You don't hear from her for years, then she suddenly calls out of the blue? Bro, there's nothing I can say, I know that. But, do me this favor. The minute you feel she's using you — which I know she is — just hang up the phone. Don't say anything, don't say goodbye, don't try to explain. Just hang up. That way you are in control. You have the power. Can you do that for me?"

"That would be kind of rude, don't you think?"

"Rude?" snapped Erik. "This isn't about politeness, it's

about self-preservation! You can't go back to that place, that deep, dark place she sent you a few years ago."

Jared stared out at the bay for a moment as the sun reached the horizon.

"It's too dark to surf. Want to go get a bite to eat?"

"My sail is torn, couldn't surf if I wanted to," said Erik. "Let's get some tacos and tequila."

CHAPTER 4

Jared had difficulty concentrating at work. All he could think about was the call from Janey at seven p.m. He got in his car at five fifteen p.m., and headed for the freeway. Jared worked at JPL in Pasadena, and lived in Santa Monica. It should have been a pretty straight shot down the 110 to the 10, twenty-five miles (which would translate into an hour and a half — pretty typical for LA traffic). However, Jared forgot that the Dodgers were playing a home game against the rival Giants. So, instead of an hour and a half, it was more like two and a half.

When he walked in the door, he went straight for the answering machine. The light was blinking.

"Shit, she called."

He pushed the button.

"Hi, it's Janey. You probably forgot that the Dodgers are playing tonight. Anyway, I'm at Shutters on the Beach. I'll be at the Living Room on the deck. Get here when you can. Thanks, Jay."

Jay? It' had been so long since Jared had been called Jay. Not that Jared is such a long name, of course. Just two syllables. But, Janey shortened it to Jay, a cute and loving nickname. The Living Room was a casual and comfy bar, and the deck overlooked the Pacific. Janey and Jared had spent many days on that deck back in the day, drinking wine, gazing out at the horizon, and dreaming about their future together. That is, of course, until Senator Richard Lester called and swept Janey away.

The ten minute drive to Shutters was uneventful. Jared saw the annoying smirk on the valet's face when he pulled up in his aging CRV. Jared was wearing jeans and a button-down white shirt with his signature seersucker jacket. He wore Gucci loafers. His long, wavy blonde hair flowed perfectly down to his shoulders. In Los Angeles, in that setting at Shutters, with his unshaven, four day old growth, and with his rugged good looks, you could have easily mistaken Jared for a movie star — not a JPL engineer.

He'd worn that jacket just last weekend to the JPL Summer Picnic — the full seersucker suit with a yellow bowtie. He reached into his jacket pocket and found a business card with the name Molly Reynolds on it. The annual JPL Summer Picnic was a combined family and client event. Molly, an attractive blonde, was a JPL guest from IBM, and someone Jared considered asking out on a date. But, in all the excitement and confusion which occurred since the Janey voice mail (was that just yesterday?), Jared had completely forgotten about Molly. He placed Molly's business card securely back into his jacket pocket — just in case.

Jared entered the lobby, climbed the stairs two steps at a time, and walked briskly to the Living Room. As he entered the restaurant, he looked across the room to the French doors which led to the outside deck. There she was, sitting at a table, her blonde hair flowing in the breeze as she stared at her cell phone. Jared stopped to admire the view. From this distance, Janey looked exactly as he remembered her. In fact, he had met her in this exact spot so many times in the past,— it was as if Mother Nature was playing a trick on him. Was it really five years since he'd last met her on the outside deck of the Living Room, or had it all been a long, convoluted, terrible dream? He could convince himself, he thought, that it was still June 2013, instead of June

2018. He could almost convince himself that Janey still lived with him in Santa Monica, and that she'd never moved to Connecticut to be with that damned Senator Lester. As he approached her table, Janey looked up from her phone, saw that it was Jared and smiled. She jumped up, wrapped her arms around him, and hugged him tightly. He hugged her back, although, not as tightly. After some time, she loosened her grip, leaned back, and looked him in his eyes.

"You look amazing!" she said. "You haven't changed a bit!"

"It's good to see you, Janey."

But, he was lying. Good to see her was a stretch. Strange to see her, would have been more accurate.

They sat down at the table, and the waiter appeared with a glass of red wine. She had arranged that with the waiter before Jared arrived.

They toasted and they each took a sip.

"So, how are you doing?" asked Janey.

Jared took a long sip of wine. In fact, he almost finished his glass.

"I'm okay. I'm a little nervous, to tell you the truth. I've been trying to figure out what this is all about. I pretty much thought about that, and only that, for the past twenty-four hours."

The waiter showed up with another glass of wine for Jared. Janey had worked that out in advance as well.

"So, what did you come up with?" asked Janey.

It would have been nice, thought Jared, if Janey had apologized for putting him through that. But, Janey never apologized. It was as if Janey got some sort of perverse pleasure out of it, for making Jared spend the past twenty-four hours wondering what her call was all about. Like it was some sort of guessing game or something. To Janey, everything was a game.

"Nothing," said Jared. "I came up with nothing."

"Oh, come on," said Janey.

"Ok, I thought maybe you're dying, and you felt compelled to apologize for dumping me and ruining my life before you died."

Janey broke into a laughing fit, first looking up at the ceiling, then resting her head on the table, laughing hysterically. Jared just sat there. After a few more seconds, Janey suddenly got serious.

"Well, no, that's not it," said Janey. "Jared, we are at a grave point in American history. This country is tearing apart at the seams. The American people are revolting against the system, we are in danger. A revol…"

Jared interrupted. "I get it, Janey. I saw your interview on PNN last night with Lauren Young. I heard your speech. Save it."

Janey sat for a moment in silence. Then she spoke, "This is serious, Jared. I know how you must feel about me. I know what I did to you. I would apologize, but I doubt it would do much good. Believe me, coming here — calling you — was a very difficult decision. I wouldn't have done it, I mean, I wouldn't want to do anything that might open up old wounds if I thought I had another option. But, I don't."

"I know" said Jared. "I know this — whatever it is — must be a big deal."

"It is," said Janey. "It involves Pangea. Has there been any change in its status?"

Jared finished another glass of wine, and on cue, another arrived.

"Still in mothballs," said Jared. "Hey, are you trying to get me drunk?"

"Absolutely," acknowledged Janey. "Is it possible that given the nearly ten years since it was last tested, that the system no longer works? Could it just become obsolete somehow?"

"No, I don't think so. Every six months I have to go down to storage at JPL, ensure that all the equipment is in place and accounted for, and that everything appears to be in working order."

"Appears to be?" asked Janey.

"Yeah, visual inspections only. I'm not allowed to power it up or test it. According to the NSA, that would be way too dangerous."

Janey took a sip of wine.

"Jared, I'd like you to meet Vice President Bashoff. Tomorrow."

"Tomorrow?" asked Jared. "The Vice President? Why?"

"As I said earlier, this is a very big deal. The Vice President is very much involved with a plan to take this country back from the lunatics running things in Washington. We want to talk to you about a very high priority, secret project. I think you'll find it fascinating, actually. What do you think? Two p.m. tomorrow right here at Shutters. The Pacific View Suite."

Jared's head was spinning — partly due to the wine and partly due to the magnitude of what Janey was proposing. The Vice President? And, what was that about Pangea?

"I have work tomorrow. I can't make it at two p.m."

"Don't worry, we took care of that with your bosses at JPL. Remember, this is a big deal."

"What?" asked Jared.

"It's been handled at a very high level."

"Okay," said Jared. "Then I guess I'm in."

"Great," said Janey. "And as an added perk, we get the Pacific View Suite tonight for our personal use, that is, if you choose to forego your own room."

Jared and Janey used to watch *The Bachelor* and *Bachelorette* religiously back in the day, when they were together, so he got the reference. But, was she really suggesting what he thought she was suggesting? The two of them, together, after all this time? Well, she was single, Jared was single. The suite was available. That could explain why she was trying to get him drunk.

"Like I said, I'm in."

CHAPTER 5

2008 was a memorable year for many reasons, both good and bad. It was the year that the economy melted down, the financial markets collapsed, the housing market imploded, the too-big-to-fail financial institutions failed and had to be bailed out, and Bernie Madoff became a household name.

2008 was also the year that a community organizer from Chicago became America's forty-fourth, and first African American, President of the United States. After receiving national attention during his keynote address at the 2004 Democratic National Convention, Barack Obama ran for President in 2008, and narrowly defeated Hillary Rodham Clinton, to become the Democratic Presidential Nominee. He then went on to defeat John McCain in the national election.

However, without a doubt, the most significant thing that occurred in 2008 was something that fewer than fifty people in the world were aware of.

Jared Ross, a graduate of the California Institute of Technology in Pasadena, was one of the brightest minds in the field of Gravitational Physics. Hired by The Jet Propulsion Laboratory, Jared went to work on a top priority project which was funded by NASA: how to create artificial gravitational environments for space travelers?

Since mankind began traveling into space in the 1960's, scientists have been studying the impact of low gravity/no gravity environments on the human body. Everyone knows what gravity is — it's what keeps us on the ground, instead of flying off into space. But, gravity is also a signal that tells the body how to act. For example, it tells muscles and bones how strong they must be. In zero gravity environments, muscles waste away quickly because the body perceives it does not need them. The muscles in our body which are used to fight gravity — for example, those which allow us to maintain our posture — can lose up to twenty percent of their mass if not used. Therefore, while traveling in space, or while on a low-gravity planet for an extended period of time, it will be important for space travelers to live and operate in an environment that replicates earth's gravitational forces for as much time as possible.

While working on this problem, Jared built a gravity generator, intended to create a personal, artificial, gravitational field in a small space (a bedroom, an automobile, or a bathroom). The design was actually pretty simple. The apparatus consisted of a twelve-foot diameter copper hoop, a laptop computer, and a tiny nuclear reactor comprised of a five-inch lead test-tube-sized cylinder of uranium. The reactor created a powerfully focused, artificial, gravitational force. By precisely controlling the gravitational force radiating around the hoop, which was easily controlled via the laptop computer, the degree of the gravitational force could be managed. However, during testing, Jared was shocked to learn that what he created was actually an artificial black hole.

Without knowing what would happen or how dangerous it might be, Jared decided to step through the hoop while it was powered on. But, when he did, he found that he had transported himself to another place. It appeared that he was still in his lab, however, it looked completely different. Everything was different, except for the size of the room. The furniture was different, the wall paint was different, the lighting fixtures were different, and the desks, tables and chairs were different. However, what was most shocking was there was a stranger in the lab with him — someone who hadn't been there a few seconds earlier, and someone he didn't know or recognize at all.

"Where did you come from?" asked a tall thin man with gray hair and a British accent? "You need security clearance to be in here. We're conducting very sensitive experiments. May I see your ID?"

"My ID?" asked Jared. "I don't believe... who are you?"

"I don't believe this!" said the man. "You'd better leave. I suggest you leave immediately, and take that damned hula hoop with you!"

Jared, who was trembling, turned and stepped back through the hoop. He was immediately transported right back to where he started — in the comfortable surroundings of his own lab.

So, that is how Jared Ross became the father of time travel, and became the world's first time traveler.

During the subsequent weeks and months, Jared conducted extensive testing, in secret. He was completely mesmerized by what he invented and wanted to share it with others. However, he was concerned that the 'powers that be' at JPL would shut the project down before he had a chance to fully understand the details of what he discovered.

Jared learned that he could control the distance back in time he traveled by managing (via the laptop computer), the force of gravity radiating around the copper hoop. Only in retrospect could he determine that, on that very first trip, he had traveled twenty-one years into the past to 1987. And after some research, he learned that the gray haired man he was speaking to was Dr Reginald Leach, a JPL employee working on early drone technology. Dr Leach passed away in 2001 of a heart attack, so Jared would not have an opportunity to say hello and see if the Doctor remembered the incident.

Testing also proved that the exact date and time of the travel target could be pinpointed to within approximately two minutes. Passing through the hoop was easy and safe, and after extensive testing on humans (Jared), it had not been shown to cause any health-related issues. And best of all, Jared had built the hoop constructed of twelve copper arches (each, one-foot long) which fit together like a giant Lego set, so when dismantled, the entire portal apparatus fit easily into a medium sized duffle bag.

Jared's testing had revealed the following laws of time travel:

1)   Time travel is a one way street. Travel is only possible into the past, not the future

2)   Once you travel into the past, you can return to the exact place you originated from — but cannot advance further

3) When you return to the place you originated from, you will arrive at the exact moment in time that you left. No time will have actually passed

4) You must travel from the exact geographic location through the hoop to the location you want to travel to.

Having tested the system rigorously and having accumulated sufficient knowledge about how it worked, Jared decided it was time to share the technology with his supervisor, Jason Downey. Jared knew Jason would be angry that he hadn't come to him earlier with it. That was just how Jason was about everything. As Jared's superior, Jason hated when Jared knew something that he didn't. A classic case of insecurity, spurred on by Jason's realization that Jared was smarter than he was.

As expected, Jason was both astounded and angry, but he let

the anger pass. Now that someone else knew about Pangea, it gave Jared an opportunity to test the impact of seeing someone in the past, and determining if that person would remember the encounter. Up until that point, Jared was careful not to see or interact with anyone he knew. Jason had chosen completely random moments and locations to travel to. He would often set the hoop up in the living room of his condo, and travel a year or two into the past. Then he'd check his laptop for the exact day and time, and by calibrating results, he was able to accurately pinpoint the gravitational force required in order to arrive precisely at desired dates and times.

As the travel dates and times became more precise, he began traveling minutes and hours into the past, rather than years. On the day he demonstrated the system for Jason for the first time, Jared had set the apparatus up in his lab, and set the destination to twenty minutes earlier. When Jared stepped through the hoop, he saw the lab as it was twenty minutes ago. There was Jason. There was Jared! How odd. There he was, staring at himself (his "other" self) as he conversed with Jason on the other side of the lab. Jared was careful not to interfere in any way with what occurred in the past. It was unclear what would happen, and it was unknown if there would be some sort of ripple effect that impacted his life or other events on earth.

Jason stepped back through the hoop to the exact moment that he left. While no time had passed for either of them, Jason recalled seeing Jared step through the hoop twenty (make that twenty-one) minutes earlier.

"That was fucking amazing!" yelled Jason.

"I know," responded Jared. It was so strange to see myself. It was like some kind of out of body experience. It was like I was a ghost. It really creeped me out, but it answered two huge questions I've had. Would I see myself if I went back in time, and would the people I interact with remember it later on? But, now I wonder,— did that experience really occur in the past, or on some other, parallel plane?

The presentation to the U.S. government didn't go over very well. They were amazed, of course, but they were also terrified. The conference room at the Pentagon included officials from the CIA, FBI, NSA, and the White House. Officials were careful to keep the number of attendees to a minimum — and of course, at a very high security level.

The NSA was ultimately given oversight of the technology, and the group determined that the technology was far too dangerous to publicize. Including Jared and Jason at JPL, NASA's Executive Director, a CalTech official (together, NASA and CalTech managed JPL), the President of the United States and a few other high ranking government officials, less than fifty people in the world were aware of the existence of the technology.

The NSA dubbed the project Pangea (a suitably innocuous name), and decided to lock it away in a closet. While stunning, the technology was deemed far too dangerous to play around with. There's no doubt it could've proven to have valuable uses. Imagine using the portal to stop the 9/11 terrorist attacks, or the Pearl Harbor attacks during World War II. How about stopping the assassination of John F. Kennedy, or the massacre of twenty children and six adults at Sandy Hook Elementary School in Connecticut? But, where would it end? Which horrific moments in history would make the cut, and which wouldn't? Who would make that decision? Perhaps the biggest question was would there be the ripple effect of any of these decisions on world events?

In the end, it was decided that messing with Mother Nature, with unknown and potentially disastrous results, would be far too great a risk. And so, the apparatus was locked away in a storage vault at JPL, and Jared was assigned the task of checking on its status and filing a report every six months.

CHAPTER 6

When Jared opened his eyes, he had no idea where he was. Then it hit him — he was in the suite at Shutters. It was very bright in the suite. Everything was white — the walls, the furniture, the curtains, the bedding. The curtains were pulled open, and when Jared looked over towards the sliding glass doors, he saw that they were open, a slight breeze blowing in. He saw Janey sitting outside on the veranda reading a newspaper. His eyes slowly adjusted to the light, but then he realized his head was pounding with a first class hangover. Jared let out a loud roar and rolled over. Then he buried his head under a pillow.

Janey heard the guttural sound, and made her way from the veranda into the bedroom. She jumped on the bed and proceeded to crawl up onto Jared's back.

"How are you feeling, sleepy head?" she asked.

No reply. Janey bounced up and down on Jared, like a seal bouncing in the waves.

"Terrible," said Jared. "I feel terrible, what do you expect? You took advantage of me! I was a poor helpless soul, and you kept feeding me wine. Now I'm hungover!"

"Just because your glass was full didn't mean you had to drink it. That was your choice."

"Good argument, Counselor," said Jared. "What happened last night? Did we…?"

"Ouch!" said Janey. "You sure know how to hurt a girl's feelings."

"Sorry, I just don't remember much. I don't remember getting in bed, let alone anything that might have happened afterwards."

"Newsflash, Jared! You didn't get into bed, and nothing happened — because you passed out!"

"I did?" asked Jared.

"Yup, you passed out on the bathroom floor while I was taking a shower. I lifted you, as best I could, dragged you into the bedroom, and pulled you up on the bed."

"Thank you. Sorry about that. Did you undress me as well?"

"I did."

"Thank you for that too," said Jared.

"You're welcome. Now I suggest you get yourself in a shower and dressed. The Vice President will be here in less than an hour."

The knock on the suite door came swift and hard. If a knock on a door could sound official, this one did. Janey was still in the bathroom drying her hair, so Jared opened the door. Two tall secret service agents stood in the hall and flashed their badges. They identified themselves as Secret Service Agents, and explained that they needed to "sweep" the suite before the V.P. could enter.

"Sweep the place?" joked Jared. "Oh, no need, housekeeping will clean the room later"

The two Secret Service Agents moved quickly and precisely through the suite, using some sort of detector wands on the couches, the beds and the furniture. It's unclear what those devices were checking for, but the agents took the task very seriously. One of the agents spoke quietly into his wrist, and within ten seconds, the other agent opened the door as Vice

President Bashoff entered the suite.

Bashoff walked directly up to Jared and extended his hand.

"David Bashoff," said the Vice President, as he shook Jared's hand.

"Jared Ross, so nice to meet you Mr Vice President."

Just then, Janey entered the room, her hair flowing. She looked like a model on a photo shoot.

"There she is," said the Vice President. "Wonderful to see you, Janey my dear."

Janey shook the Vice President's hand, and said, "So, you met Jared Ross?"

"Yes, I did."

Turning to Jared, the Vice President said, "Thank you for taking the time to meet with me, Jared. I'm not sure how much Janey has shared with you, but we have reached a critical point in the history of our country. Last night, about three thousand Mexican nationals attacked the wall President Harp is constructing along the Texas-Mexico border. When I say attacked, the Mexican people used all sorts of rocket ordnances and other advanced weaponry. This means, the Mexican government was involved. Now, this morning, large-scale gay and lesbian rights rallies are occurring in more than a hundred major U.S. cities, as they protest the repeal of gay marriage rights. Tomorrow, we are looking at a million person march in Washington, protesting the repeal of the Affordable Care Act. This country is literally tearing apart at the seams. We need to do something."

"It seems obvious to me that the direction President Harp and the Republican Congress is moving the country, is at the root of the problem," said Jared. "Your party is driving a wedge between people."

Jared looked over at Janey, terrified. As the words came out of his mouth, he realized that what he had just said would likely be offensive to the Vice President. And who was he to be hurling statements at the Vice President like that? However, Janey just smiled.

"You're absolutely correct, Jared," said Vice President Bashoff. "I don't agree with where my party is headed. I don't agree with many of the policies President Harp has enacted. I don't agree with his Supreme Court nominees, or how he has stubbornly attempted to embarrass and offend the Democrats. I have even considered stepping down, but I really feel that I have an obligation to this country to try to find solutions. I feel I can have a bigger impact from my current seat, than I would on the outside."

Jared walked towards the kitchenette to grab some sodas or juices from the fridge, but a Secret Service Agent stepped in front of him.

"Sorry," said Jared. "I was just going to offer the Vice President something to drink."

"I'll take care of it," said the agent.

"So, Mr Vice President," said Jared, "What do you intend to do?"

"It's a good question," said the Vice President. "Janey and I have spent a long time asking one another that same question. We considered an impeachment proceeding. However, success would be highly unlikely with the Republican Congress. And, truth be told, even if we're successful, I'm not sure it would change much. I believe, as does Janey, that we need to change the mindset."

"The mindset?" asked Jared.

"Yes," said the Vice President. "We believe that, as a whole, the American people are not thinking like Americans at this point in our history. America was founded on principles of fairness, and goodness. The right to life, liberty and happiness for all Americans, not just the super wealthy. We have a history of welcoming the poor and the oppressed. We have a history of helping our neighbors, of caring for the sick and less fortunate. Does that sound like the America we see all around us today?"

"No, not at all," acknowledged Jared. "But, like I said, what can you do about that?"

"Well, we have an idea," said Vice President Bashoff. "But we need your help."

One of the Secret Service Agents approached with a tray holding an assortment of sodas and juices. If he were wearing a bowtie, you'd swear he was a waiter. Jared grabbed an apple juice container from the tray, and dropped down onto the fluffy white couch.

"And, you need my help?" asked Jared.

"Yes, we need your help and we need Pangea."

CHAPTER 7

The Pacific View Suite at Shutters on the Beach in Santa Monica became ground zero for The Lombardi Project. On this day at ten a.m., the first official meeting among the five members of the Lombardi Team was set to begin. The team sat at a long table in the dining area.

The Vice President spoke first.

"Thank you all for being here, and for your commitment to our cause. As you know, this project is top secret. You cannot speak of anything that is discussed among members of this group, to anyone outside the group. Stage one of this project is to acquire our target. In order to accomplish this task we will be employing a technology called Pangea. Jared, please fill the group in on the details — broad details please — of Pangea."

A photo of the Pangea apparatus appeared on a screen on the wall at the far end of the room, above the long table.

"Pangea is a time travel portal which can transport humans to specific dates and times in the past. It is a relatively simple concept which uses a super strong gravitational field to create a contained, artificial black hole. By passing through the hoop, and by controlling the strength of the gravitational field, we can pinpoint the distance of the trip into the past. The hoop must be placed in the exact location you want to be transported to. When you're gone, no time will actually pass at your departure location. At your arrival location, it is real time. People will see you, talk to you, and they will recall seeing you. The things you interact with are real — people, objects, moments. Every precaution must be taken to ensure that the impact on history is kept to a minimum. This is dangerous stuff."

"Thank you, Jared" said the Vice President. "Jared is correct, this is dangerous stuff. What Jared neglected to mention due to his humility, is that he, and he alone, invented the Pangea Portal technology. He also failed to mention that the U.S. Government deemed the technology so potentially dangerous, that they locked it away behind doors for the past ten years, hoping no one would ever find out about it."

An architectural map of a building appeared on the big screen, replacing the photo of Pangea.

"Mr Corkoran, please fill the group in on how and when we will acquire the Pangea apparatus."

Don Corkoran stood, and walked to the head of the table. Corkoran was in his mid-sixties, and walked with a limp. He looked military, and in fact, he fought in the Vietnam War. Following the war, he worked for the NSA in counterintelligence. He held a long wooden pointer, and used it to point to the map.

"This is JPL headquarters. This corridor and the room at the end, are located on the sub-basement floor S-3. The room is what they call 'the locker', which houses many of the most secretive or sometimes dangerous items the government controls. Luckily for us, Jared Ross has entry access to the room, for a length of thirty minutes, on a set date every six months. We will utilize Jared's access to retrieve Pangea. As is standard operating procedure, Jared will be notified of his scheduled access two days prior, however, based on prior history, we expect that it will be on June 25th or 26th. Jared will be accompanied by a guard from the JPL, so we will have to come up with a scheme to distract the guard, so that we can get the Pangea apparatus into a carrying case, and out the door. Leave it to me, I will devise a plan."

"Thank you, Mr Corkoran," said the Vice President. "Our target travel date is early July, so assuming we retrieve Pangea in late June, we should be in good shape."

"Mr Snyder," said the Vice President. "Now the fun part. Please share some details with the group with respect to our target. Not too much detail, please. There will be time for that later."

Charles Snyder stood and walked to the front of the room. Snyder looked like your typical college professor, and with good reason. Snyder was a professor of American History, and head of the American Studies Department at Princeton University. Snyder was the foremost living authority on the American Revolution, had written nine books on the topic, and had been a speech writer for two former U.S. Presidents.

"Good morning, everyone. I'm happy and excited to be part of this project. This is a tumultuous time in American history to be sure, and we are undertaking a truly historic effort. The man we are targeting is a hero of mine, and I can hardly believe I will have an opportunity to meet this great man. I am shaking right now as I think about it."

Snyder raised his hand, pointed the remote towards the screen, and clicked. In the place where the map of the JPL sub-basement S-3 map had been, a new picture took its place. The picture was of a well-known painting by George Wilson Peele. The man in the painting was standing. He was wearing a colorful military uniform, and leaning with one hand on a walking-stick, the other hand was tucked into an opening in his vest. A sword was attached to his pant leg. The man had an all-knowing smirk on his face. He looked confident and a bit self-important. It was a portrait of General George Washington.

There was a gasp from the people around the table. George Washington? The almost mythical man who stands for all things America?

"I know you're probably wondering why we're going to bring George Washington here to the twenty-first Century," said Vice President Bashoff. The reason is quite simple. Sometimes it's impossible to truly know the depths of your situation when you're standing in the middle of it. Sometimes, you need the benefit of hindsight to accurately assess that picture. My friends, we do not have the luxury of hindsight in this case. I believe we must act now if we want to save our nation. Experts, people like Charles Snyder, have an ability to size up a situation, even while in the midst of it, better than most. You've heard it said — 'to know your future, you must know your past'. Experts who know have indicated these are dangerous times. We need to act. Our plan is to bring George Washington here to 2018, and to have him stand before the American people, and to implore them to unite with one another, and to demand that their political leaders unite for the common good of this country. We need to return to the ideals which were set forth by our forefathers. We need to do this now, because this may be our only opportunity."

Stunned silence. No one spoke. It would take time to digest what seemed like a completely insane idea.

"If we're successful, who will believe that this man is George Washington?" asked Jared. "I mean, are we breaking the news about Pangea? Even if we did, would we be able to prove that the man is actually George Washington, or will it simply come off as some ridiculous PR stunt?"

"Great question," said the Vice President. "Don't worry, we have that covered. I promise you. We will be able to prove it."

CHAPTER 8

Funds from the Lombardi Project would have covered first class seats on the commercial flight from LAX to JFK, however, Jared, Janey and Snyder needed to sit together. So, that meant three seats together on the 757 in coach. And so began Jared's history lesson.

"Following the Americans' victory during the siege of Boston," said Snyder, "Washington moved the troops to New York. They left Boston in mid-March, 1776, and arrived in Manhattan about a month later."

"Wow," said Jared. "It took them a month. Today we're traveling from LA to New York in six hours."

"That's right," said Snyder. "These are the things I'm excited to share with General Washington. It will be so fascinating to see how he reacts to the modern world. I can't wait. Anyway, after their defeat in Boston, the British retreated to Halifax, Nova Scotia to await reinforcements and to plan their strategy. Washington predicted correctly that the British would attempt to take New York, due to its deep harbor and strategic importance."

"How do you defend a city like New York?" asked Janey.

"Not easily," admitted Snyder. "What made it especially challenging, was that Washington was convinced that the British would attack Manhattan, while his top men, Putnam and Sullivan, believed they'd attack Long Island. So Washington split his troops, stationing men on both Manhattan and Long Island. The result being, an undermanned army in both locations. And when you consider the massive number of troops the British had assembled — close to forty thousand, the prospects did not look good for the colonists."

"So, who was right? Where did they attack?" asked Jared.

"The British attacked on Long Island. They came ashore on August 22nd at Gravesend Bay in southwest Kings County — what is now Brooklyn — across the Narrows from Staten Island. After waiting at Gravesend Bay for five days, the British attacked the Americans at Guan Heights. Unknown to the Americans, however, Howe had brought his main army around their rear and attacked their flank soon after. The Americans panicked, resulting in twenty percent losses through casualty or capture, although a stand by four hundred Maryland troops prevented a larger portion of the army from being lost. The remainder of the army retreated to the main defenses on Brooklyn Heights. The British dug in for a siege, but on the night of August 29—30, Washington evacuated the entire army to Manhattan without the loss of supplies or a single life."

"So, we're going to get to General Washington before the battle?" asked Janey.

"Exactly," replied Snyder. "We know where General Washington was headquartered prior to the Battle of Brooklyn. By the way, they also refer to that battle sometimes as the Battle of Long Island, and the Battle of Brooklyn Heights. I probably interchange those names sometimes myself."

"Yes, you do," said Jared.

"Anyway, we are heading today to Prospect Park in Brooklyn. We think that would be a good place to 'land'. Prospect Park didn't exist as a park in Revolutionary times, of course. The Park was built around the mid 1800's. But, the Battle of Long Island was fought right there, in what is now Prospect

Park."

Snyder pulled out a topographical map showing a string of hills which cut across Prospect Park.

"These hills were formed as a result of the terminal moraine of the receding Wisconsin Glacier about seventeen thousand years ago. It's basically the debris that the glacier pushed ahead of it as it progressed south. When the glacier receded, it left these hills in its place."

Snyder pulled a pen from his jacket pocket and pointed to the map.

"This is Lookout Hill. Here is Sullivan Hill and Breeze Hill. Over here is Prospect Hill. At about two hundred feet, it's the highest point in the Park. We believe it's the ideal spot to 'land'. From there, you will be able to look towards the west and see Manhattan Island, and the Palisades of New Jersey beyond it. Most importantly, you will be able to see the East River ferry dock on the Brooklyn side, which will be about three miles away."

"How will I know where I'm going?" asked Jared. "There won't be any roads or street signs, will there?"

"Good question," replied Snyder. "You will be traveling with a pack of necessities — some items will be used to help you navigate and survive — a map, a compass. Other items will be used to convince General Washington who you are, what you're doing, and why you need his help. We're going through those details now. We will share them with you in due course."

"Okay, so when am I going?"

"Here's the plan as we've designed it to date. You will travel to New York on Sunday, July 8th. We will scout the location at Prospect Hill over the course of the next several days. We want to make sure we can do what we need to do without any interference from authorities or citizens in the Park. The following day, Monday, July 9th, will be your travel date. Upon arrival in 1776, you will have to break down the hoop and other equipment, pack them into the duffle we will provide, and stash it somewhere."

"Stash it?" asked Jared.

"Yes, absolutely. You can't lug that around with you. Sentries might check your bag along your route. Imagine if they saw the apparatus. What would they think?"

"Good point."

"So, you will need to hide the duffle," said Snyder. "Perhaps, you can bury it. We can include a small shovel with your equipment. One way or another, you will need to leave it somewhere in the park. The key is not to be seen by anyone at your destination. Then, as I mentioned, we will provide you with the compass and a map based on info we are accumulating from that era. We're thinking you will leave early in the morning — five or six a.m. You'll take Battle Pass, an opening in the terminal moraine where the old Flatbush Road passed from Brooklyn to Flatbush. You'll follow the Old Flatbush Road down to the Brooklyn ferry dock. It should take you under two hours with some rest along the way. That should get you to the ferry at about one p.m. We will supply you with some colonial currency — even some silver and British coins. You'll pay your fare for the ferry across the East River to the Great Dock on the Manhattan side. The dock was located one block south of the canal — an actual waterway which was located at what is now Broad Street. You'll head west towards the fort, at which point you'll see the Bowling Green, and Broadway. Washington's headquarters was at Number 1 Broadway, a stately mansion and a famous New York landmark. The home was owned by Captain Archibald

Kennedy of the Royal Navy, until his departure for England. Your challenge will be to get an audience with Washington, but we are working on a few ideas."

"I'm nervous just thinking about it," said Jared. "I'm going to have an audience with George Washington!"

"Pretty amazing, right?" said Snyder. "But don't worry, we will prep you to such an extent, it will be easy. Anyway, we expect it will take several meetings and several days to convince him to join you — that's assuming, you can convince him at all. We are targeting a return trip no later than Monday, July 16th. That gives you a full week. That will give him five weeks before the British land at Gravesend Bay — remember, he'll arrive back in 1776 at the exact moment he left, so no time will be lost there."

"And I'm assuming he will have a full agenda here in 2018, right?"

"Oh yes," said Janey. "He will be quite busy with work and some fun, touristy stuff."

CHAPTER 9

Even though sixty percent of the Lombardi Project Team members were on their way to New York, the daily meeting was about to start with the two members currently on the west coast. Vice President Bashoff took his seat at one end of the long table in the Pacific View Suite, while Don Corkoran took a seat at the other end.

Don Corkoran and Vice President Bashoff had a long history together. They attended West Point together in the late sixties, and while Corkoran was a lifelong military guy, Bashoff was not. Bashoff wanted to be a lawyer, and free tuition in exchange for some active service duty upon graduation was a great deal. As soon as he could, Bashoff applied to Harvard Law, and headed to Cambridge.

Corkoran rose to the rank of Captain, before moving over to the NSA. There, he rekindled his friendship with Bashoff, and the two had been almost inseparable ever since. Their wives were friendly, their youngest daughters (each fifteen years old) were friends, and they played golf together whenever they could squeeze in some free time.

"Donny, I want to talk about two items today, that's all I have," said the Vice President. "First, where are we on the plan to get Pangea out of JPL?"

"As you know sir, when Pangea was tested in 2008, it was deemed very dangerous. A decision was made to have the unit locked away in storage at JPL. Only the President can authorize testing and removal of the unit, which I considered attempting to get. I thought we could claim that we felt it made sense to test it every ten years. However, I think that would be a mistake. I don't think we even want to mention Pangea — not to anyone. Very few people know that Pangea even exists. Fewer remember it exists, and I would venture to bet that virtually no one thinks about it at all. I'd prefer to keep it that way. After doing some research, I discovered that the guard who accompanies Jared to the storage room is guy named Perchup. Let's just say the man is not too sharp. I think I can come up with a plan to 'drop and switch' another duffle in place of Pangea. I'll have something to demonstrate within a week or so."

"Excellent, Donny. Sounds good. Now, here's the one that keeps me up at night. As long as Washington is in the 1700's, he's fine. History tells us that. But, when we have him here in 2018, we are responsible for his wellbeing. What if something happens to him? It could have a disastrous impact on history, on the very existence of the United States of America."

"But, can history be altered?" asked Corkoran. "I mean, perhaps nothing <u>can</u> happen to Washington while here's here, because history says he fights and wins the war."

"There's a name for that," said the Vice President. "It's called the 'Grandfather Paradox', and frankly, no one knows what would happen. In fact, many people used the paradox as proof that time travel could never happen. There are many theories, but no one really knows. All I know is we must find a way to ensure Washington's wellbeing."

"We can't call in the Secret Service," said Corkoran. "Not in advance, anyway. If we do that, everyone will know what we're up to. The surprise will be lost, the President will object, and the entire effort will be sunk. But, I could create our own small, private Secret Service unit. We would operate covertly. As our plan proceeds, it will become public and the Secret Service will take over."

"Okay, I guess that's a workable solution," said the Vice President. "I guess the key is to limit the amount of time from Washington's arrival, to his address to congress. Once we do that, we'll have the Secret Service's support. We can schedule his grand tour after his public address."

"Do we have a budget for this?" asked Corkoran.

"Whatever you need," said Bashoff. "So, what do you say, want to play nine?"

CHAPTER 10

Their plane landed at JFK at 8.35 a.m., and while they didn't sleep at all during the flight, they each marveled at how awake and alert they felt. They chalked it up to adrenaline. JFK airport is operated by the Port Authority of New York and New Jersey, and if you've never been there, you'd likely be surprised by the look of the place. New York is the center of the world from a financial, arts, and fashion perspective. The United Nations is located there. Yet, the airport is dated and very unimpressive. LaGuardia is even worse.

As they walked through the terminal and headed for baggage claim, there were protesters standing in groups with signs stating that they were on strike. Certain security personnel, baggage handlers, garbage collectors, and wheelchair attendants were currently on strike, demanding pay increases and improved working conditions. This had been a common sight since President Harp was elected two years ago. Garbage bags had been lined up along the corridor, and garbage bins had been filled to the brim, overflowing with cups, plates and other trash.

"This is ridiculous" said Snyder. "The unions are fed up. So are the workers."

"I've never been a fan of the New York airports, but this is crazy," said Jared. "It looks terrible. Pretty soon, this place will be rat infested — if it's not already."

"That's what I'm talking about," said Janey. "This is the new normal under President Harp. New Jersey Transit workers are on strike, so is the New York City Teachers Union, garbage collectors in Buffalo, and the State Troopers in Albany and Syracuse. And, that's just New York State. This country is falling apart. That's why this project is so important."

As they descended the escalator to baggage claim at the American Airlines terminal, they could see that the place was packed. People were crowded twenty deep in front of the baggage claim conveyor belts. People were crowded everywhere. An American Airlines worker was ushering people off the escalator, and driving them back toward the far wall so that people could exit the escalator. If not for this lone worker, people would be crashing into one another at the bottom of the escalator, without any open space to flow into.

Signs were posted on walls and on pylons throughout the baggage claim area, warning travelers of long delays and asking for their patience. But, it was clear that the hundreds or maybe thousands of travelers in the baggage claim area were out of patience.

"This is insane," said Janey. "Let's head out to the curb. There should be a car waiting for us and I'll ask the driver to come back for our bags."

Big smiles appeared on the faces of Jared and Snyder. One of the benefits of traveling with a U.S. Senator — people at their service.

Out at the curb, the mayhem was equally bad. All those people in their cars waiting for their friends and relatives had nowhere to go as they waited an hour or more. However, right in front of the main entrance to the terminal stood a very large, black SUV. As they made their way to it, a well-dressed man in a black suit popped out of the passenger side and approached the three weary travelers.

"Senator Logan," said the man in the black suit. "My name is Hartwell. I work for Mr Corkoran. Right this way, please."

They followed Hartwell to the vehicle, and slid into the second and third rows in back. The thick leather seats were plush and comfortable, and the SUV smelled rich. Hartwell got into the passenger seat next to the driver.

"No luggage?" asked Hartwell.

"We couldn't wait for it," said Janey. "We couldn't get anywhere near the belts."

"Oh yeah, that's right, the strike," said the driver. "Give us your claim tickets and we'll go back for them."

New York usually begins to look nicer around this time of year as the season transforms from winter to spring. Buds on the trees, perennials popping through the soil, bright blue skies with white puffy clouds. However, New York just wasn't looking so great these days. Garbage piled up on the sides of the expressway, pot holes which developed over the snowy winter months, still unfilled. Even the air, which normally begins to smell of sea salt from the Atlantic, was stale and nasty.

The driver took Linden Boulevard West from the airport, passing into Brooklyn along the south shore of Long Island. When they hit Flatbush Avenue, he turned right heading north along the eastern boundary of Prospect Park.

"Stay on Flatbush until we reach the Library," said Snyder to the driver.

When they reached Empire Boulevard, they entered the park.

"Most people don't know this, but these are two different parks," said Snyder to Janey and Jared, pointing first to the left, then to the right. "On the left is Prospect Park, to the right is Mount Prospect Park. Vaux and Olmstead, who designed Central

Park in Manhattan, designed Prospect Park. Originally, Mount Prospect Park was to be included in Prospect Park, but because of this road, which bisected the two park areas, they felt Mount Prospect shouldn't be included."

"Flatbush Avenue was here in the 1700's?" asked Janey.

"It was," said Snyder. "It was originally an old Indian Trail which took advantage of a low point in the terminal moraine left by the Wisconsin glacier. It was the main road from Flatbush to Brooklyn. In the 1920's it was straightened, but it roughly followed the same course it did then. In fact, you're going to follow Flatbush down to the Brooklyn ferry dock once you land in 1776."

The SUV pulled alongside the Brooklyn Central Library. Ground was broken for construction in 1911, but due to political in-fighting, the Great Depression, and the onset of World War I, the building wasn't completed until 1941. The design of the building was modified, the end result being, one of the greatest Art Deco buildings in America.

"You can pull over right here," said Snyder to the driver.

The SUV stopped right in front of the main entrance to the library on Eastern Parkway. Snyder, Jared and Janey exited the car, each with their phones and a water bottle in hand.

"We'll head back over to JFK to retrieve your bags," said Hartwell. "What time would you like us to meet you back here?"

"Well, it's ten thirty a.m. right now. How about one p.m.?"

The driver nodded and drove off. The three Lombardi Project team members walked along Eastern Parkway, just past the end of the Central Library building. They turned right and ascended a curved flight of stone steps up to the top of Mount Prospect. At the top of the stairway, they found a large grassy field. In 1856, the City of Brooklyn built a large reservoir at the top of Mount Prospect. The reservoir stood until 1940, when New York's water supply was shifted to Upstate New York. They walked a little further until they came to another set of stone steps — these were much shorter.

"This is The Lookout," said Snyder. "It's the highest point in the Park, and it provided the Continental Army with sweeping views of Manhattan, Brooklyn, Staten Island and New Jersey. This is where we will set the Portal."

"There's no one here right now," said Jared. "But, what if there are people around. Won't they see what we're doing?"

"I'm not too concerned," said Snyder. "First, you will be traveling very early in the morning on a Sunday — we're thinking six a.m. or so. Plus, this is New York. No one really pays too much attention, and we'll surround you with people — we'll block you."

"What about on the other side... in 1776?" asked Janey. "There will be no one to block him there."

"That's true," said Snyder. "But, the Colonial Army won't be up on Mount Prospect in late May. And, the six a.m. hour will likely mean no stragglers up here either. The key is for Jared to break the hoop down, pack it in the duffle, and hide it as quickly as possible."

"No problem," said Jared. "But, even if you block people from seeing me here on this side, the hoop is twelve feet high, and when I step through it, the thing will just vanish. It follows me through the artificial black hole. It's unclear why, but it does. People will see the hoop disappear. It's an astonishing sight. I've only seen it on video, taken by the JPL team, but it's really weird. One second it's there, then a flash, and the next second it's not."

"Don't worry, Jared," said Snyder. "I'll handle it. You just worry about hiding the hoop when you get there."

"Okay," said Jared. "What's next?"

Snyder handed Jared a small, nylon sack with a zipper.

"You'll need this. It's a compass. It's the one you'll take with you. Turn and face Flatbush Avenue, and see where the needle is pointed."

"North, north west," said Jared.

"Make a mental note," said Snyder. "Remember it. This is very important. It will take your brain several days to adjust to 1776 — that is, if it ever does. It will be as hard for you to adjust to life in that era, as it will be for Washington to adjust to ours. Your brain has a fixed understanding of what the world looks like. You will be standing right here in this spot, and nothing will look at all familiar to you. The tree line will look different. The views will be completely different. There will be no stairs down to the road. Flatbush Avenue will be unrecognizable. It will not be paved, it will be narrow, and it will wind back and forth around small hills and trees. You will be able to look towards the west and see Manhattan, but you won't recognize it. No skyscrapers, no bridges. It will be just a little village with a few low buildings and a fort at the southern tip. The rest will be forested and hilly. Without this compass, you may panic as your brain tries to make sense of it all. If it comes to that, it will help you determine which direction to head."

"Got it," said Jared. "Where will I change clothes? On this side or that side?"

"You'll change here. We can't risk anyone seeing you in 2018 garb. Then you'll make your way down to Flatbush Road, turn west, and start your trek towards the Brooklyn ferry."

The three Lombardi Team members descended the steps back down towards Flatbush Avenue. They passed an old gray haired woman walking her dog.

"That's the first person we've seen up here and it's eleven thirty a.m.," said Snyder. "I seriously doubt we'll run into anyone on a Sunday morning at six a.m."

When they reached the bottom of the stone steps, they turned left and headed west towards Manhattan.

"How about sexual relations?" asked Jared. "Can I partake?"

Janey elbowed Jared in the ribs, hard enough to cause him to yelp.

"I'm serious," said Jared. "It would be fascinating. It would be interesting to see how it was done back then. There'd certainly be no joy in it for me. Dr Snyder, surely there'd be some scientific value — strictly educational, of course. No?"

Janey rolled her eyes and gave Jared a stiff hip check this time, hard enough that he tumbled into Snyder who slipped off the curb and into Flatbush Avenue.

"Easy, you two," said Snyder.

"Sorry," replied Janey and Jared in unison. They were both blushing like school children.

They reached a corner and stopped at a red crosswalk sign.

"They'll be none of these," said Snyder, pointing at the cross walk sign. "And, there'll be no sex. You won't get a respectable woman, and you won't want to go near any of the other women without a condom. The problem is, the latex condom wasn't invented until 1920. Back then, they used lamb intestines. However, you'd probably have to search pretty hard to find one. And, I'm not sure how well they worked. You can't leave a child behind in 1776, and you really don't want to catch some sort of ancient sexually transmitted disease. Anyway, I'd prefer you stayed focused on the task at hand."

"Sorry," said Jared. "I just wanted to help with your understanding of history. Just offering my services," he said with a wink.

They trekked about a mile down Flatbush Avenue, and the team decided to stop at a hotdog stand for some nourishment.

"The best hotdogs in the world, boiled in the best dirty water on earth," said Jared. "Too bad they won't have these on the other side."

The vendor selling the hotdogs was Pakistani, and spoke little English. They bought six hotdogs and three bottles of water. Apparently that was enough for the vendor to throw in three knishes at no additional cost.

They passed the Navy Yard and approached Vinegar Hill. They could see the riverfront and Manhattan across the East River. They stopped walking.

"We're not exactly sure where Flatbush met the River in '76, but we know it ends at the dockyard. Anyway, you'll have some currency to purchase your fare across to Manhattan."

"What if I'm questioned by authorities along the way or at the ferry dock?"

"You will have a letter in your possession. It's a letter you will say was given to you by General Horatio Gates in Saratoga, with explicit instructions to deliver it by hand, personally to General Washington. That is the same story you will tell when you arrive at Number 1 Broadway. That is how you will get an audience with Washington."

The Lombardi team turned around and began walking east back towards Prospect Park. It was twelve thirty p.m. and they wanted to be on time for their rendezvous with the men in black with the big, comfy black SUV.

CHAPTER 11

They had forgotten to close the shades when they went to bed, so on this bright, late spring morning, the rays of the sun woke them early.

They had arrived at the Grand Hyatt Hotel during the early evening the night before, following their tour of Prospect Park and Flatbush Avenue. The red eye from LAX had finally caught up with them. Snyder had retired to his room, while Jared and Janey shared theirs. They ordered room service, which included a bottle of Champagne, and the conversation began.

"Janey, why'd you do it?"

"Haven't we been over this already?"

"No, not really," said Jared. "At least not to the point where it actually makes sense to me. One minute we're happy living a nice life in L.A. Next thing I know, you're packing and you're gone. And, within minutes, you're in a relationship with—"

"I was happy. I wasn't looking for it, but when Lester contacted me, something just clicked inside me. I wasn't over that loss to him. I didn't know it, but there was something deep down inside me that wasn't done."

"And your relationship with Richard Lester? What was that all about?"

Janey walked over to the window. She looked down at the darkened New York street, a spot in which sunlight was unable to cut through the canyon of skyscrapers. She took a sip of coffee. She stared blankly, not focusing on anything. She spoke in a monotone.

"I don't know. It was just something that happened. Like going down a water slide and ending up in the pool. It was just inevitable. It wasn't emotional for me."

Janey and Jared showered, then headed down to the lobby for a bite to eat. The old Commodore Hotel, which stood on the spot adjacent to Grand Central Terminal, was the essence of luxury and opulence when it opened in 1920. Over the years, it became worn and dated. Then, Donald Trump purchased the hotel, modernized it, and in 1980, it reopened as the Grand Hyatt. With miles of marble, cascading waterfalls, and many levels of luxury, the lobby is a sight to behold.

On this typical weekday morning, the business men were sitting at tables, meeting with clients, downing gallons of coffee. In this place, you wouldn't know that America was on the brink of collapse. The Grand Hyatt lobby hummed along at a frenetic pace.

"Things seem pretty good here," observed Jared.

"Don't let it fool you. Typical New York and typical New Yorkers. They're a hardy bunch. They just go on making money, chasing the American Dream. Oh, they're worried. Many are angry. Many are suffering. But, these are the direct descendants of JP Morgan and the Vanderbilt's. Maybe not blood relatives, but in spirit. They never stop or take a rest — it's not in their DNA. They forge ahead at full speed with blinders on."

Just then, Snyder arrived, coffee in hand and looking well rested.

"Ready to go?" asked Snyder. "We're heading downtown."

Grand Central is one of several transportation hubs in Manhattan. They walked through a narrow door which connected the hotel to Grand Central Terminal. The place was alive with thousands of commuters who arrive here every morning from the northern suburbs of West Chester County, Duchess County and Connecticut. They passed the central rotunda with its famous clock and star-studded ceiling, and followed a corridor leading to the subway lines.

They descended down a long escalator to the turnstiles, where Snyder handed them each a metro card ticket.

They took the stairs down to the four and five line downtown towards Brooklyn. On the platform, two homeless men were sleeping on a wooden bench. The platform had an odor of old garbage and stale urine. The lights above the platform were burned out, and the concrete platform was crumbling and in severe disrepair.

"More signs of Harp's government failing," said Janey, pointing to a pile of rubble near the edge of the platform, where work had begun on repairs to the concrete, but had come to an abrupt halt when Harp entered the White House.

A homeless man, wearing battered clothes and a rancid brown ski cap, approached the three Lombardi Team members and asked for change. All three reached into their pockets to retrieve some money, but only Snyder came out with some change. The homeless man was grateful. The man smiled, grunted some intelligible words, and walked off.

They jumped on the express four train downtown. The express made only four stops before arriving at Bowling Green Station. They walked to the end of the platform, and ascended the stairs to the street. They exited on the south east corner of Bowling Green. The sun was bright, and the sky was vivid blue, with just a few puffy clouds in the morning sky. Directly in front of them was a large and impressive building in the Beau Arts style, with a grand stone staircase, and four large stone statues in front.

"This is the Alexander Hamilton U.S. Custom House," said Snyder, pointing to the building. "It was built in the early 1900's on nearly the exact spot where Fort Amsterdam stood. Jared, when you arrive here in 1776, you'll see the Fort. You can use that as your primary reference point."

Snyder turned to his right, and pointed to a building directly on the other side of Bowling Green, on the corner at the end of Broadway.

"That's the International Mercantile Marine Company Building. It was built in 1882 on the site of the Archibald Kennedy Mansion. It is at Number 1 Broadway, and it's where Washington made his headquarters during the Battle of Long Island. It was a solidly built, two-storey home, surrounded on the two open sides by a wrought iron fence. It will look pretty secure when you see it, with Continental Army Sentries likely on duty outside. You will see four steps leading to a small front porch. Your goal will be to talk your way into the building. Once again, the letter from General Gates will serve as your entree. Don't worry. We have several examples of his letters, so we will be able to perfectly recreate the style of the day, as well as Gates' seal."

Jared looked around. The distance from where he was standing near the entrance to the subway on the southeastern side of the Bowling Green, to the front entrance of Number 1 Broadway, couldn't have been more than a couple hundred feet. He wondered how similar and familiar things would look and feel in 1776.

There was a mix of business people and tourists walking the streets in this area. There was a guy playing guitar standing at the northeast corner of the Alexander Hamilton Custom House. His guitar case was on the ground in front of him, opened and filled with some change and a few dollar bills. He was surrounded by approximately ten people, who appreciated his rendition of Van Morrison's "Brown Eyed Girl".

There were three tables with umbrellas next to the guitar player. The tables were covered with various items for sale — sun glasses, post cards, children's books, miniature Statue of Liberty, Empire State Building, and Freedom Tower models. There was a moving truck in front of No. 14 Broadway. Three mothers pushed baby strollers along the eastern side of the Customs House sidewalk. It was busy this morning, but likely not any busier than your average Tuesday morning. What would the scene look like in 1776? Would Jared stand out, or would he mix right in? He was both curious and a little nervous.

The group began walking uptown along Bowling Green. The park was small and teardrop shaped, and surrounded by a black, cast iron fence.

"This park was here in 1776, so was this fence," said Snyder. "When you get here, you'll notice a large statue of King William. But, it won't be there for long. The Declaration of Independence was read publicly to the Colonists for the first time on July the 9th, and it started a riot of sorts — I guess you could call it a celebratory riot. The Colonists toppled the statue, removed the king's head, and mounted it on one of these cast iron fence posts. They also sawed off the cast iron fence post finials, which were shaped like British crowns. Then they brought the rest of the iron statue up to Connecticut, where it was melted down and turned into musket balls."

A man in a business suit approached the group. The man had a smile on his face. He was in his mid-forties, dark hair — which was graying at his temples, and thick, black eye glasses. He walked straight up to Janey and extended his hand.

"Senator Logan, what a pleasure it is to meet you. My name is Ryan Kelly. I can't tell you how grateful I am that you're willing to take on Harp! That man must be stopped. The country is in shambles. Thank you."

Janey shook the man's hand. She stopped walking and put her hands on her hips.

"Thank you, Mr Kelly, I appreciate your thoughts. May I ask what you do for a living?"

"I'm in investments at Merrill Lynch. What a disaster. American's have lost confidence. The stock market is in free fall. People are afraid. The future is murky, we're all scared."

"Rest assured, Mr Kelly. We are working on solutions. We will restore this country to its proper place in the world. In the meantime, do what you can, spread the word. This administration and the majority in the house and senate are ruining everything America stands for. The good people of America must make their voices heard. That's how real change will get done."

They shook hands again, said goodbye, and walked on. They stopped at a Shake Shack, New York's answer to In and Out Burger on the west coast. Even with the country falling apart, and even with the problems so evident all around them everywhere they looked in New York City, Shake Shack still had a way of raising their spirits.

They continued their trek north to Wall Street. On the west side of the street, Wall Street came to an end at Trinity Church.

"This is Trinity Church," said Snyder. "You will see it, right here on this spot when you get here. But, it won't be this version of the church, it will be the original version. It was a modest rectangular structure with a gambrel roof and a small porch. That church was destroyed in the great New York City fire of 1776. A second Trinity Church was built in 1790, but was torn down after being damaged by snow in 1840. This version of the church was built on the same spot as the first two, and opened for worship in 1846."

"Why did they build the church at the end of Wall Street?" asked Janey. "Why didn't they continue the street across the island to the Hudson?"

"It did end at the Hudson," said Snyder with a chuckle. "Manhattan Island ended in those days one block west of where we're standing right now, just past Greenwich Street. Over the years, the island was widened and lengthened with landfill — east towards the East River, south into the Harbor, and west into the Hudson. The World Financial Center, where the Twin Towers once stood and where the Freedom Tower stands today, sits on landfill, all made from earthen materials excavated while digging the foundations of those huge skyscrapers."

The group turned left on Wall Street, and headed east. They stopped in front of Federal Hall which stands on the north side of Wall Street.

"There's our man," said Jared, pointing to the huge bronze statue of George Washington mounted on a tall pedestal.

"That's him all right. The statue was erected in the spot where Washington stood, on a second floor balcony of the original Federal Hall building, when he was sworn in as America's first President. The original Federal Hall was demolished in 1812, and this new building was opened in 1842. Part of the railing and floor from the second floor balcony of the original Federal Hall is on display in the current Federal Hall building."

The group continued north, then cut across Vesey Street towards the Freedom Tower. Snyder felt it would be a good idea to get a bird's eye view of lower Manhattan and Brooklyn to help put the scope and scale into perspective. There was a line of tourists wrapped around pylons, awaiting their scheduled time to enter the building for their elevator ride to the 102nd floor observation deck.

The group avoided the tour entrance, and instead went to the main employee entrance. At the security desk, Janey flashed her government issued Senate ID, and asked to speak to the head of security. The head of security was excited to have such an important dignitary visit the building, and quickly ushered them to the observatory elevators. As they ascended, an interesting history of New York played on the elevator walls, showing the evolution of the cityscape across the decades. Scenes depicted the pastoral days of the Native Americans in Manhattan, to the Arrival of the Dutch, the colonial era, and the rise of the city's urbanization.

"Paying attention, Jared?" asked Snyder. "Everything you need to know is right there."

They exited the elevator, and headed to a stairway which took them one flight down to the 101st floor observation deck. There, the floor to ceiling windows offered jaw dropping panoramas of the city. The Statue of Liberty, standing so proudly in the Harbor, and the irregular and winding streets of lower Manhattan right below. They could see the Alexander Hamilton Customs House and Bowling Green sitting side by side, and the East River, with Brooklyn just beyond.

"When I look out there," said Snyder, "and think about Washington retreating with his troops in the middle of the night during the Battle of Long Island, right there," he said pointing. "It really happened, two hundred and forty years ago, right there in that place. It takes my breath away."

"I never thought of it like that," said Janey. "Sometimes

history seems so flat, somehow not real at all. But, when you say it like that — those men fighting for their country, fighting for their lives, scrambling to keep their dreams alive. And it happened, as you said, right there."

Janey wiped a tear from her eye.

"It was a defeat for the Americans, to be sure," said Snyder. "But make no mistake, the retreat was a brilliant tactical move by Washington. Maybe he was lucky, or perhaps a genius. But one thing is for sure — had they not retreated safely, it could have been the end of the Continental Army. The Revolution might have ended that night."

The group gazed out towards Brooklyn. They could see Prospect Park, and the path of Flatbush Avenue, as it cut its way towards the East River.

Janey texted Hartwell, '*We'll be down in ten minutes*'. Then she bought a bottle of water from one of the concession stands. Jared took one last look out towards Brooklyn, trying to lock the image of Prospect Park in his mind. Snyder gazed out at the Harbor, the rays of the setting sun bouncing off the water.

The trio made their way to the elevator, and exited the building. The big black SUV was waiting for them at the curb, and they climbed in.

"Your bags are in your rooms at the Grand Hyatt," said Hartwell.

"Great!" said Jared. "Please take us to our bags."

CHAPTER 12

The Vice President was sitting in his hotel room at Shutters on the Beach, watching a movie on TV. He reached for his cell phone and typed a text to Don Corkoran.

'Donny, remember Jon Arvan who worked at the CDC? I think he lives in Del Mar. See if you can get him to meet us tomorrow at eleven a.m. for our daily Lombardi Team Meeting. Thx.'

This Lombardi Team Meeting was notable in that it welcomed its first ever guest attendee. The Vice President and Corkoran were already in the Pacific View Suite when Jon Arvan knocked on the door. The Vice President answered the door, and welcomed Jon inside.

"Jonny, thanks for coming up on such short notice," said the Vice President, as he shook his hand and gave him a stiff pat on the shoulder.

Jon Arvan was in his mid-sixties, a full head of thick gray hair, and a dark tan. He wore a navy blazer and yellow tie. At just five foot nine, he was considered short. However, Arvan was thin and in excellent shape.

"My pleasure, David," said Jon. "Donny, nice to see you as well. You two are still inseparable I see."

The men walked to the long meeting table and took their seats.

"David, my son and his family are coming into town today

from Chicago," said Jon, "so if you don't mind, I'd like to get right down to it — whatever 'it' is."

"Of course," said the Vice President. "This shouldn't take long. I was watching a movie on TV last night — it came out a few years ago — perhaps you remember it. A woman and her son were locked in a room for years, and when they finally got out, the boy wore a surgeon's mask. I'm assuming the mask was intended to protect him from germs. Anyway, I was wondering, if a human travelled from the past to the present time, would he or she be in danger of getting ill from the germs that exist today?"

"Yes, I remember the movie," said Jon. "May I ask what you guys are up to? Time travel?"

"Not exactly," said the Vice President. "I was asked to Chair a committee on cloning. We are trying to assess the risks, dangers, morality, and other considerations. Scientists uncovered a large amount of viable human tissue and DNA from around two hundred years ago in Washington State, and we're trying to determine if germs and health should be one of our considerations."

"I see," said Jon. "Well, if you recall, in the movie, the boy wore the surgeon's mask, not his mother. That's because he was born in the room, never left the room, and never developed natural immunities. The mom, on the other hand, lived in the outside world, and had an opportunity to develop immunities over the course of a number of years. Likewise, if someone from two hundred years ago was suddenly dropped into the world of 2018, you could assume that the individual had developed immunities over the course of his or her lifetime, and that he or she would be fine. The bigger issue would be food and water. Like going to other countries today, the most common cause of water-borne illness is bacteria, such as E. coli, cholera and salmonella. In many cases, travelers become ill simply because the pathogens in the water are foreign to their immune systems, while locals have adapted to the water supply and can drink it without any problem. The key is to be mindful of what that person is putting in his or her mouth."

"But, there's nothing potentially life threatening?" asked Corkoran.

"No, I don't believe so," said Jon. "However, any cloned organism, regardless of where or when the DNA was formed, would be a product of the current time. David, are you sure you didn't already know that?"

The Vice President cracked a half-smile and took a sip from his water bottle.

"It's okay, David," said Jon. "You don't have to tell me what you're working on, but I'm sorry you felt you had to make up that story about cloning. It's none of my business."

The Vice President wiped his mouth with his napkin, then he cleared his throat.

"I'm sorry, Jon. That was dumb, I know. I can't share details with you right now, but it will all become clear in the very near future. Thank you again for coming up."

The men stood up from their chairs and moved to the door.

"I'd ask you to join Donny and me at the driving range, but I know you said you have to get back."

"Tempting offer, but I'll take a rain check."

Jon saluted as he walked out the door. As the door shut, the Vice President and Corkoran burst into laughter.

"Cloning?" said Corkoran. "Nice try!"

CHAPTER 13

The flight home on Wednesday was uneventful. Jared asked to be dropped at his condo in Pasadena, Janey went to the Pacific View Suite at Shutters, and Snyder was dropped at his hotel downtown. Jared wanted to grab his mail, messages, and check in on Pocahontas, who was staying with his next door neighbor. More than anything, he wanted to take a break from the madness (and Janey) for a few hours. He planned to sleep at the condo, and meet at the Pacific View Suite the following morning at ten a.m. for the daily Lombardi Team meeting.

He entered the code on the keypad on the side of the garage, and the right hand bay door opened. His CRV was sitting in the garage, right where he left it. He went through the door and into the lower level. The only piece of furniture on this level, a twelve by eleven foot drab room with beige tile, was a tan couch which sat along the far side of the room along the wall. There was a light switch near the entrance from the garage, and a light bulb, with no fixture covering it, in the center of the ceiling. The fixture had fallen and broken a few weeks ago, when Pocahontas knocked him over, and he fell hard onto the floor above. The couch, which used to be in his living room upstairs, was sent down to lower level when he bought a new sectional, and still remained there simply because he was too lazy to figure out how to dispose of it. But, as he looked at the ugly couch, he realized it wasn't centered along the far wall as it usually was. It was a few feet off to the left. He thought that was strange.

When he arrived upstairs, he noticed several things were slightly out of place. Nothing drastic, and if he had a wife or kids, he'd never have given it a second thought. However, because he lived alone and didn't have a housekeeper, he knew precisely where everything went. He knew the only way things would be moved to a different position was if he had done it himself.

For example, the three bar stool chairs which sat at the breakfast counter were always perfectly centered under the counter, and the distance between one another was also perfectly slotted. But now, they were bunched together and off center in a way that perhaps only Jared would notice. In addition, the throw pillows on his sectional couch in the living room were out of place — again — in a way that only Jared would recognize. The floor lamp in the corner near the bookcase was pushed in towards the wall, in a manner in which Jared would never leave it. There were many more examples, all leading to an obvious conclusion: someone had been in the condo while Jared was away.

He grabbed his sweater and went next door to the Turner's' condo. He went up the stairs to the porch and rang the bell. Jennifer Turner answered the door. Jennifer had sandy brown hair down to her shoulders, a nice California tan, brilliant blue eyes, sparkling white teeth, and a thin athletic surfer's body. Had Jennifer not been married to Brad, Jared would have certainly pursued her.

"Hi, Jared," said Jennifer as she opened the door. "Brad's in San Fran on business until Friday, but I've been taking care of Poky for you."

"Thanks," said Jared as he walked into the condo. He could hear Poky's breathing before he could see her, which was a good thing. Within seconds, Pocahontas had turned the corner into the entryway, leapt through the air and tackled Jared. Jared fell violently onto his back, unable to break his fall at all. It hurt, but he played it cool in front of Jennifer.

"Hey, girl!" said Jared, with an upbeat tone. "Wanna go for a walk? Do ya?"

Jennifer handed him her leash, he put it on her collar and they headed out.

"Good luck!" yelled Jennifer after them, as they headed down the steps.

Silver Lane, the narrow, winding street on which Jared lived, was quiet that evening. A man who lived a few condos down was getting his mail from the communal mailbox unit which stood at the end of the driveway which was shared by all residents of the building. Jared waved, and the man waved back. The street lights were on as the remaining natural sunlight was just about to be extinguished. Pocahontas was pulling Jared down the road as she normally did, but with even more energy than normal. Why was she always in such a hurry, and where did she think she was going? Jared pulled his cell phone from his pocket and dialed Janey's cell. He didn't want to use the landline in his condo — maybe it was bugged. Or more likely, perhaps he was just paranoid from watching detective movies and TV shows. Janey answered on the first ring.

"Hi, Janey, it's me," said Jared.

"I know, your name comes up on my phone, dummy. What's up?"

"So, I walked into the condo, and I'm not sure, but I'm pretty sure someone was in there while we were in New York. It's not that noticeable, but things are out of place. You know me, I notice everything."

"Yes, I know," said Janey in a sarcastic tone. "Did you call the police?"

"No, I'm not sure what to do. Like I said, nothing seems to be missing, nothing is broken. If someone was in there, it seems like they might have been looking for something. But whoever they were, they were careful to not make a mess. Do you think it's connected to Pangea? Could anyone know, outside of our little group, what's going on?"

"I don't know. Where are you now?"

"I just picked up Poky from Jennifer's. Now Poky's pulling me up the road."

"Jennifer, huh? That girl you have the big crush on?"

"I wouldn't call it a crush. I'd call it an appreciation of her natural beauty. She's married, remember? Brad's in San Fran."

"How convenient," said Janey. "Here's what I think you should do. See if your 'home-alone' friend with all that natural beauty will take Poky for one more night. Then come over here and stay with me. Might be a good idea to stay out of the condo if it's a crime scene. The Vice President went back to Washington today, but he'll be on the phone tomorrow morning for our daily Lombardi meeting. We'll get his opinion."

"Good idea. I'll be there in an hour," said Jared.

"An hour, huh? Interesting."

"What's interesting about that?" asked Jared.

"An hour is just enough time to do the 'deed' with your married, home-alone, natural beauty friend," said Janey.

Then she hung up.

When Jared arrived at Shutters on the Beach, he went up to the Pacific View Suite and knocked on the door, but there was no answer. He knocked again. Still no answer. Jared pulled his card key from his wallet, and let himself in. The TV in the living area was on and tuned to MSNBC. The remains from a room service salad were on the dining table, a bottle of wine was opened, and half a glass of Cabernet was sitting on the counter. Where was Janey? For a moment, Jared was feeling a bit worried, but then he heard it — water from the shower running in the bathroom. Jared went to the bedroom, stripped off his clothes, and made his way to the bathroom. He opened the bathroom door, and tiptoed in as steam from the hot water clouded the mirror as well as the glass on the shower stall. When he pushed opened the shower door and stepped inside, Janey turned quickly and was startled. When she realized it was Jared, she smiled and put her arms around his neck.

"That was quick," said Janey. "Am I your dinner or dessert?"

"You're both," said Jared.

She kissed him and they enjoyed the rest of the evening together.

The conference table seemed extra-large for the Daily Lombardi Team Meeting without the Vice President in the room. Although, in a sense, he was in the room. His face appeared on a large screen on the wall. He promptly called the meeting to order.

"Let's start with Don. Any progress on the Pangea 'drop and switch' plan?"

"I'm thinking we'll use a sports equipment duffle. Jared, do you play any sports?"

"I play hockey," said Jared. "I have an extremely large CCM hockey bag — it even has wheels."

"That's perfect," said Corkoran. "Can you bring it with you tomorrow? We have a mockup of the Pangea apparatus. We can see how everything fits in your hockey duffle."

"Great," said the Vice President. He turned to Jared. "Jared, I hear you had a little scare when you got home last night. Please fill us in on the details."

Jared pulled the remote keyboard toward him on the conference table. He hit a key and the Vice President's face shrunk into a small box in the upper right hand corner of the screen. He hit another key and a photo of Jared's couch on the lower level of his condo filled the big box.

"I was in New York for two nights and arrived home last night. This couch in the photo is always situated in the center of the wall. When I got home, it was there — off center to the right. I live alone, I'm very meticulous. I noticed this immediately."

"Anyone else have a key to your place? Did you authorize anyone to enter your home while you were away? To water flowers, walk your dog?"

"His girlfriend walked his dog," said Janey, chiming in.

"My neighbors had my dog at their place. My flowers are fake. No, no one has a key but me."

"I used to have a key," said Janey, "but I lost my key privileges."

Jared pressed another key, a new photo popped up, and he first described what he found with regard to the throw pillows on his couch, then the chairs at the breakfast bar, and the floor lamp.

"Donny, what do you think?" asked the Vice President.

Corkoran thought for a moment and removed his glasses. He leaned back in his chair, legs crossed as he rubbed his eyes, deep in thought.

"It's troubling," he said. "I believe Jared is probably right, someone was in there. But who? And why? I couldn't say. Does it have something to do with Lombardi? Not necessarily, but possibly. Is someone on to us? It seems to me if someone actually were on to us, one of us would have to be the leak. Who else knows?"

Corkoran asked that question while looking around the table.

No one looked away as Corkoran made eye contact with each team member, one by one. No one said a word.

Then the Vice President spoke, "What about Jon Arvan?"

No one, other than Corkoran, had ever heard of Jon Arvan. They all looked blankly at the Vice President.

"I'll bite. Who's Jon Arvan?" asked Jared.

"He's a friend of ours," said the Vice President. "Don and I worked with him when he was at the CDC. Good guy, close friend — or so I thought. We invited him to the Pacific View Suite yesterday. We had some questions about health risks for a time traveler. Turns out the only real dangers are eating and drinking, but they're not life threatening."

"You had him in here?" asked Jared. "You asked him about time travel? Was that a good idea?"

"Yeah, maybe that wasn't so smart," said the Vice President. "I'll take full responsibility for that. But, we asked the questions under the guise of a secret cloning project. It was pretty thinly veiled, and Arvan didn't buy it, but…"

"We need to calm down," said Corkoran. "We have no proof of anything." He turned to Jared. "Do you own the place, Jared, or do you rent?"

"I'm renting."

"For all we know, your landlord went in to check on things."

"No, my landlord doesn't live in…"

Corkoran put up his hand to stop Jared mid-sentence.

"My point is, we just don't know. I will send in some guys this afternoon to do a sweep. They'll check for foot prints, finger prints, bugging devices. We'll get to the bottom of it. In the meanwhile, stay out of your condo until I give the all clear."

Jared smiled as he thought — more dinner and dessert with Janey tonight.

"Guys, we're done here," said the Vice President. "Switch over to CNN. Scary stuff, guys, this plan better work. See you tomorrow."

The screen in the suite switched from Vice President Bashoff's face to CNN. President Harp was standing at a podium in the Rose Garden at the White House. "As you know, I promised to build a wall along our border with Mexico. The wall is almost completed. The Army Corps of Engineers told me yesterday the wall is ninety-four percent completed, and will be finished by August 1st. That's great news, and I thank all of those who worked tirelessly to get it done. Now that our southern border is secure, I am here today to announce the VDP and UDP plan and timeline. Beginning July 1st, those illegal aliens who elect to register with the U.S. Department of Citizenship and Immigration Services and select the Voluntary Deportation Plan — it's sometimes called the self-deportation plan as well — will be first in line to get a legal opportunity to return to this country and become a legal citizen. For those who remain here, we will begin the process of forced deportation for five hundred thousand illegal aliens per month beginning August 1st, until all thirteen million illegals have been sent back to the country from which they came. Those who do not opt for the VDP, will have a longer wait, and a much harder time returning to this country — if at all. It's your choice."

"Shameful," said Snyder as he flipped off the TV.

CHAPTER 14

The Presidential Gym at the White House was state of the art — not lavish but very nice and well equipped. The room was open and available to all staff and full time government employees based at the White House. During lunch hour, the place was often packed. However, at six a.m. on this Thursday morning, the President was alone.

President Harp sat on the workout bench, a ten pound dumbbell in each hand. He raised the dumbbells over his head in unison, then back down, up and down. When he was done, he walked over to the mirror on the wall and flexed his forearms. He saw someone behind him in the reflection from the mirror. He turned.

"Oh, Mark, I didn't see you come in," said the President.

Mark Donahue, Deputy Director of the FBI, was leaning against a post, watching as the President went through his daily morning workout routine.

"My apologies, sir, I didn't mean to startle you," said Donahue.

"No problem," said the President, as he walked toward Donahue, still flexing. "How do I look?"

The President was wearing navy Nike shorts, a white tee shirt with the Presidential seal on the front, long tube socks and slippers. The President's arms looked thin and frail, but his legs looked strong and muscular.

"You look great, sir. Very impressive."

The President sat at the leg press machine, and started pumping away. The weight was clearly heavy for him, and he was struggling. His jaw was clenched, and his neck muscles were tightened. But, he pressed on. When he got to ten, he stopped and took a long breath.

"It's all about the legs," said the President. "My father walked with a cane late in life, then was relegated to a wheel chair at the end. I never want to be stuck in a wheel chair. You want to be in a wheel chair, Donahue?"

"No, sir. No, I don't."

"Of course not," said the President. "That's why you have to work on the legs. So what's up? Rioting about my deportation plan? Eff them."

Donahue walked closer to the President and sat on a large workout ball. He leaned in and spoke softly.

"Mr President, we followed Senator Logan to Los Angeles. She'd been there for about a week. Then she flew to New York for a couple of days, we're not sure why, but now she's back in L.A. We did some checking, and her name is on a lease for a condo in Pasadena, on Silver Lane. Another name is on the lease as well, Jared Ross. We don't know who he is, but we're checking. We stopped over there a few days ago to check it out. Not much to see. We placed a few monitoring devices in the apartment — the usual stuff. Hopefully we'll learn what she's up to."

"Well, stay on her, God damn it!" said the President. "That piss ant thinks she's going to run me out of office. Well she's got another thing coming. Stay on her and keep me posted."

"Will do, Mr President. I have our best people on the case."

CHAPTER 15

Snyder drove his Audi TT convertible as Jared sat cramped in the passenger seat. At six foot three, Jared often felt cramped in cars, but this one was worse than most. Snyder exited the 405 Freeway at Culver Boulevard, and made a left into the Sony Pictures Lot. They passed under the arches, stopped at the security booth and gave their names. They were there to meet with Deborah Lynn Scott. They received directions to the costumes department and parked in front of the building.

"We're meeting with Deborah Moreland today," said Snyder. "She won the Academy Award in 1998 for Best Costume Design for the film *Quest for Liberty.*

Deborah met them at the front door and introduced herself. She walked them back to one of the many 'closets', which in reality, were each the size of a basketball court. The closet they were in was marked "Military" on a plaque on the door. As they walked in, they saw everything from World War II uniforms and artillery, to Nazi uniforms, Japanese, and Civil War uniforms. In the far right hand corner of the room he saw a section with a sign hanging above it by a wire: "Revolutionary War".

There was a small card table with folding chairs nearby, so the group sat down. Deborah opened her notebook, ready to take notes.

"Thank you, Deborah, for taking the time to meet with us" said Snyder. "Vice President Bashoff told us you were very busy, and he made us promise not to take up too much of your time."

"Oh, that's all right," said Deborah. "I've only met David once, but I know his wife Charlene very well. She works tirelessly to support my Breast Cancer Awareness Charity — I could never fully repay her for her help. So, tell me, what kind of role is this?"

"It's pretty simple, actually," said Snyder. "However, authenticity is of the utmost importance. All styles and materials must be absolutely accurate. Even the undergarments."

"Well, that's a new one," said Deborah.

"Jared will be playing a Continental Militia Man from Connecticut. It will be 1776, of course, so the uniforms weren't standardized — we know that. He should wear something that would have been worn by someone from Connecticut, but it should be on the nice side — at least for a militiaman."

"The clothing worn by the Patriots during the first year of the American Revolution was simply a cross section of the different fashions and styles of civilian clothing worn by New Englanders, with all levels of society being represented," said Deborah. "Some uniformity did exist in the more affluent militia companies, and some attempts were made to uniform the Patriot forces. Because the New England militia and minutemen of 1775 and 1776 wore civilian clothing, in reality, they wore clothing no different from any other New England males at the time."

Deborah unrolled her measuring tape and began taking Jared's measurements as he stood in the middle of the floor.

"Men's clothing during the American Revolution was extremely form fitted and individually tailored to fit the wearer's body," she said.

She took a light brown waistcoat from a hanger and held it up in front of Jared.

"The waistcoat was the part of a man's clothing worn over

the shirt and under the coat or jacket," said Deborah. "Waistcoats were made with and without sleeves. It was considered a social taboo in the eighteenth century for men to go out in public showing their shirt sleeves. Men would almost never be caught in public just wearing a shirt and a waistcoat with no coat or jacket worn over it. Here, try this on, Jared."

Jared pulled the waistcoat on and looked at himself in the full length mirror. He turned to one side, then the other.

Deborah turned to Snyder.

"What do you think?" she asked. "It obviously needs to be lengthened."

"I like it" said Snyder.

Deborah began marking the waistcoat with chalk for length and fit.

"The Patriot militia and minutemen would never have reported for military service wearing only an unsleeved waistcoat with no jacket worn over it. Waistcoats were constructed of wool, linen, velvet, silk, or fabric blends. In a suit of clothing, typically the buttons on a waistcoat matched that of the coat. Common buttons on waistcoats were cloth covered, thread wrapped, metal, leather, or horn."

Deborah went through the same process for the rest of the uniform. Knee breeches, shirts, neck coverings, jackets, stockings, shoes, undergarments, and head gear. Her detailed knowledge of each of these items was comforting.

"What time of year will it be?" asked Deborah. "And how many sets of uniforms will be needed?"

"It will be set in early summer," said Snyder, "and we will need just one set. It is important that the uniform look nice, but it must look worn as well. Can you help us with weaponry?"

"Absolutely," said Deborah as she slid open the door to a

huge metal closet. "In addition to a musket, a militia man carried a leather or tin cartridge box on his right side that held twenty to thirty rounds of ammunition, a musket tool, and a supply of flints. On his left side, he carried his bayonet in a leather scabbard attached to a linen or leather shoulder strap. Each soldier had a haversack, usually made of linen, to carry his food rations and eating utensils. The utensils usually included a fork made of wrought iron, a pewter or horn spoon, a knife, a plate, and a cup. He also had a canteen of wood, tin, or glass to carry water. A knapsack held extra clothing and other personal items such as a razor for shaving, a tinderbox with flint and steel for starting a fire, candle holders, a comb, and a mirror. Soldiers also often carried a fishhook and some twine so that they could catch some fish when they were near a lake, creek, or river."

As she pulled each of these items from the closet, she placed them on Jared.

"This is really heavy," said Jared. "Did those men really carry all of this stuff?"

"A well outfitted militia did," said Snyder. "You'll have to get used to it."

"Are the weapons functional?" asked Snyder

"Yes, they are," said Deborah. "I suggest you spend some time practicing if you intend on firing them during the show. Also, no facial hair. It was considered a societal taboo in those days."

Snyder stood and extended his hand to Deborah.

"We really can't thank you enough, Deborah. What's the next step?'

"It's my pleasure, Charles. We will get working on altering all the clothing immediately, and will test and shine the weapons tomorrow. I'll give you a call when we're done so you can pick everything up. Should be in a week or so. Probably next Friday, June 27th."

"That's perfect, thank you," said Snyder.

Deborah walked Jared and Snyder to the door, and the two men got back into the car. As Snyder was about to back out of the parking spot, Jared turned to him.

"I just got the text from JPL," said Jared. "My six-month Pangea survey is set for ten a.m. on June 25th. That's four days from now. I hope Corkoran is ready."

"I'm sure he is," said Snyder.

CHAPTER 16

FBI Director, Mark Donahue, was sitting on an ornate jeweled settee in the waiting area outside the Oval Office.

"Would you like a bottled water while you wait, Director Donahue?" asked the young, attractive administrative assistant who was sitting at the desk.

"No thank you, I'm fine."

"The President will just be another few minutes, he knows you're here."

While Donahue was sitting there in the waiting area, he could hear loud noises coming from inside the Oval Office. Cheering and clapping. Even some hooting and hollering. Donahue tried to make sense of what he was hearing. Is there a studio audience set up inside the Oval Office, and could they be cheering a Bill the President just signed? Talk about great reality programming! That show would be a hit for C-Span. Just add some air horns and confetti.

The doors opened and then it all made sense. The U.S. National Women's Hockey Team, who won the Gold Medal at the 2017 World Championships, got their day at the White House. They had taken pictures earlier on the porch, and now they were in the Oval Office for another photo op. Group photos, individual photos, even photos of each player sitting in President Harp's seat behind his desk. What a thrill it must be for these women, he thought.

President Harp shook each player's hand, waved goodbye,

and then they were gone.

"Mark, come on in," said the President. "I do so many of those a year, I really should get paid extra for that. Anyway, sit down."

Donahue sat down on a fluffy white couch, and Harp sat down across from him on a matching couch. A gold medal sat on a coffee table between them, set in a small Lucite trophy case.

"That's a gold medal from the Women's World Championship. It was a gift to me. What am I going to do with it? You want it, Mark? Do they have a trophy case down there at the Hoover Building?"

"No thank you, sir."

Harp made a face, picked up the gold medal case from the coffee table and threw it about ten feet across the room. His throw fell short, missing the decorative garbage can by about two feet. The Lucite case hit the floor, and smashed into pieces. The gold medal fell to the floor, twisting around the colorful nylon lanyard. The President looked at Donahue and laughed. Donahue didn't find it funny, but smiled back out of respect for the President.

"So, what do you have for me?" asked Harp.

"Sir, we did some follow up on the other name on the condo lease in Santa Monica. It seems the Senator had a relationship with, and lived with Jared Ross."

The President frowned.

"Who's Jared Ross? Am I supposed to recognize that name?"

"No, not necessarily," said Donahue. "We don't know much about him"

"So?' said Harp.

"Well, it may be nothing. But, we checked with JPL, and Ross was recently put on sick leave for health reasons."

"Again, so? What's the significance?"

"Maybe nothing," said Donahue. "But, there's definitely some interesting aspects. Ross and the Senator lived together in the condo several years ago. She moved back to Connecticut to run for Senate. Last week, we followed her back to L.A. where she seems to be living with Ross at Shutters on the Beach in Santa Monica — not at the condo in Santa Monica. We know from the Secret Service reports that the Vice President has been spending time at Shutters, and we know that when Senator Logan flew to New York on American Airlines a few days ago, Jared Ross was on the flight with her."

President Harp reclined back on the couch with his hands on his head, as he tried to fit the pieces together.

"I see," said Harp. "You're right, maybe it's nothing. But if it's nothing, it all seems like a convenient coincidence. Stay on it. Find out what they're up to. Those guys are too stupid to be dangerous, so I'm not too concerned. But, stay on it."

"Will do," said Donahue, as he got up to leave. On his way to the door, he bent over and picked up the pieces of Lucite, and threw them in the trash. Then he picked up the gold medal, slipped the lanyard over his head, as the medal dangled at his chest. He smiled at the President, who smiled back. Then he left the room.

CHAPTER 17

It was the morning of June 25th, the day he'd be making the 'drop and slip' at JPL. Jared made his best effort to dress like a hockey player. He wore his most faded blue jeans with a tear in each knee. He pulled on his white Kings jersey with Charlie Simmer's name and number eleven across the back (old time hockey). He wore his open-toed Adidas sandals with tube socks, and his CCM ball cap. His hair was long — he was growing it as part of his costume for the trip. He thought about pulling it back into a pony tail, but decided against it. It wouldn't look 'hockey' that way.

It was ten minutes to nine, so he had time for a bowl of cereal. He slept at the Pacific View Suite at Shutters with Janey the night before, then drove home at seven a.m., stopping at the grocery store for cereal, bananas, and milk. Honey Bunches of Oats with almonds was his cereal of choice. And of course, sliced bananas.

At nine o'clock, Jared grabbed his large hockey bag and stick, and headed out the front door to the porch, down the steps, and onto the driveway. Poky was still with Jennifer, although Jared hadn't checked in with her for a few days. He hoped Poky was doing okay.

Hartwell popped out of the front passenger door, and ran to Jared.

"Good morning, Mr Ross. Let me grab your duffle for you, sir."

"Good morning, Hartwell," said Jared. "I got it."

Hartwell popped the back hatch, and together they lifted the bag into the trunk of the big, black SUV. There was no hockey equipment in the bag, although after years of hockey equipment storage, the bag still reeked of it. The bag was filled with hardcover books, roughly the same weight as the forty-five pound Pangea apparatus.

Hartwell walked around to the side of the car, and opened the door for Jared. As he slid into the back seat, he saw Corkoran was already in the car.

"Good morning, Don," said Jared.

"Are you ready?" asked Corkoran.

"I'm a bit nervous, but I'm ready."

The driver backed the SUV out of the driveway, and headed to JPL. Corkoran wasn't much of a conversationalist, so Jared sat silently, staring out the window, and getting more anxious by the minute.

"Remember, straight in and straight out. No monkeying around, got it?"

"I got it," said Jared.

The SUV pulled into the main entrance of JPL, and stopped at security. The driver gave the security guard Jared's name, which was on the security list for the day.

They pulled up to the visitor lot, right in front of the main reception door. Jared got out, went around to the back as the hatch automatically popped open, and he grabbed his bag and his hockey stick. Corkoran didn't want Hartwell to get the bag out for Jared — it might look too suspicious.

Jared headed for the entrance, and checked in at the desk.

"Jared, how've you been?" asked Amy, the receptionist. "I heard you're on leave. You okay?"

"I'm fine, just precautionary stuff. I'm waiting for Judd."

"Yup, he was just here," said Amy. "He just ran to the commissary to grab a coffee. He told me to tell you he'd be right back."

Jared took a seat in a large chair. Within moments, Judd, the security guard and Jared's personal escort, arrived back in the reception area.

"Jared, how the hell are you?" asked Judd with his southern drawl. "How you doing? I heard you're on sick leave."

"I'm okay," said Jared. "They're worried I might have been exposed to a high dose of radiation, so I'm going for tests and laying low for a few weeks. But, I feel fine — I'm playing hockey after this," he said, lifting the hockey bag off his shoulder a couple of inches.

"I didn't even know you played hockey. Want to leave your bag here?"

"No way," said Jared. "There's close to two thousand bucks' worth of equipment in here if you count my skates. Where I go, the bag goes."

They took the elevator down to the sub-basement, and Judd led the way down a long corridor. At the end of the hall was a large black barn-style door. Judd put his key in the lock and turned it. A green light illuminated above the door, and Judd slid the large, heavy door to the right. As soon as the door clicked into place in the open position, lights inside of the storage room began clicking on row by row until the entire room was bathed in bright blue-tinted light. The room was set up in rows, like a public library. However, instead of books on the shelves, there were large items — some were mechanical — like a large movie projector, or what looked like some kind of drone. One long shelf was full of small paintings. On the other side of the room was a shelf full of what appeared to be Astronauts' helmets.

When they arrived at the back of the room, there was a green metal cage about four feet high and six feet wide. The cage was bolted into the cement floor with thick steel screws. The cage had a lock on it. Judd sifted through the keys on his large key ring, found the right one, and opened the lock on the cage. Jared dropped his hockey bag against the wall, and went over to the cage. Jared pulled the door on the cage open and lifted the Pangea duffle out and placed it on the floor next to him.

Jared had conducted this check every six months for the past ten years, and each time, Judd would wander around the room looking at all the interesting artifacts and items on the shelves. Today, however, Judd stood next to Jared watching his every move. How would Jared make the switch if Judd stayed where he was?

Jared began lifting the Pangea pieces out of the duffle, and stacked them on the floor. First, the twelve, one-foot pieces of the copper hoop. The laptop computer was packed into a metal, protective case. The five-inch steel cylinder containing the uranium was packed into its own case, which was very well sealed with foam insulation. Jared began inspecting each piece carefully and methodically. He filled out the status report form, making detailed notes for each item. Judd sat behind Jared on a step stool which was used to reach items on the higher shelves.

"Hey, Judd, any chance you can get me a bottle of water?" asked Jared. "This is going to take a while."

"No problem," said Judd, as he walked across the room, opened the door and exited the room.

Jared raced across the room, and went to the door. There was a shelf to the left of the door, on which sat large rectangular pieces of stacked solar panels. These looked like solar panels which might have been used on space satellites or perhaps the

Hubble Space Telescope. Each panel was long and thin and made of stainless steel. Jared slid one of the panels along the shelf it was sitting on, so that it extended off the end of the shelf, and in front of the door. Jared raced back to the Pangea cage on the other side of the room, and began moving the dozens of hard cover books from his hockey bag into the Pangea duffle.

Just then, Jared heard the door open, followed by a loud crash as the door knocked the solar panel off the shelf and onto the floor.

"Shit!" yelled Judd, as he entered the room with the bottle of water.

Jared came running from the other side of the room.

"You okay?" asked Jared.

"Yeah, I'm okay. The door knocked this panel on the floor. It's pretty well smashed. I think I should call and report it."

"What's the point?" asked Jared. "Just stack it back on the shelf. I'll be done in a few minutes then we can get out of here."

While Judd picked up the pieces from the panel, Jared rushed back to the other side of the room, and began packing the Pangea pieces into his hockey duffle. There were stacks of shelves between Judd and Jared, so there was no way for Judd to see what Jared was up to. Jared zipped up the hockey bag, placed the Pangea duffle filled with books into the cage, and locked it. Then he pulled the hockey bag on wheels over to the door, and helped Judd stack the broken pieces onto the shelf.

"Thanks," said Judd.

"No problem, no one needs to know what happened here."

"Not unless they watch the security tape," said Judd, pointing at the purple glass security cameras mounted on the ceiling along each row of shelves.

Jared hadn't noticed them.

"Well, let's hope they don't," said Jared. "I locked up the cage. Let's get out of here. I have to get to the rink."

Jared followed Judd back down the corridor to the elevator. When they arrived back at the reception area, Jared handed Judd the Status Report file, and he said goodbye to Amy, the receptionist. He headed out of the door to the visitor's parking area, where Hartwell met him at the open hatch of the SUV. They picked up the hockey bag, and placed it in the back. Hartwell opened the back door for Jared, and he slid in next to Corkoran.

"Any problems?" asked Corkoran.

"Piece of cake. I had to improvise a little, but it all worked out. Did you know they have security cameras in the storage room?"

"I assumed they did, why?"

"Well, let's just hope they don't decide to watch them — they'll see some pretty odd stuff," said Jared.

CHAPTER 18

Mark Donahue was sitting in a thick leather swivel chair in the conference room aboard Air Force One. The room had thick oak doors and rich oak paneling on the walls. The beige carpeting had a gold embossed star pattern throughout the airplane. The plane was sitting at Andrews Air Force Base. An aide for the President poked his head into the conference room.

"Director Donahue, the President has just arrived at Andrews," said the Aide. "He will be aboard in a few minutes. You will have ten minutes with him, then you may disembark before we depart."

Mark Donahue sat there reviewing his notes. From what he could tell, his update should not take more than two or three minutes — tops. There were windows along one side of the conference room so Donahue walked over to peek out. He could see the Presidential motorcade pull up alongside Air Force One. The President got out, and walked to the stairway leading up to the aircraft door. Donahue went back to his seat on the other side of the conference table. He fixed his tie knot, pulled his jacket sleeves down, and took a sip from his water bottle. A few moments later, the President walked in.

"Mark, don't stand up," said the President, as Donahue began to stand, but sat right back down.

"Good to see you, Mr President."

"Thanks for coming out here to Andrews. My schedule is crazy the next few days, so I appreciate you meeting me here."

"My pleasure, sir."

"So, what do you have on Senator Logan?" asked the President. "Have your guys been tailing her?"

"They have, sir. Her movements this past week have been unremarkable. No one has been in the condo since we placed the listening devices there. However, we followed up on her friend, the one who co-signed the lease on Silver Lane. It turns out they were in a relationship. But, here's the interesting thing,— Ross is the guy who invented the Pangea Portal."

"Now I'm really lost," said the President. "What's the Pangea Portal?"

"Sir, I know you were briefed on Pangea when you took office, but that was a few years ago. Let me refresh your memory. Pangea is the time travel portal developed by JPL. It was actually invented by Jared Ross."

"Oh yes," said the President. "Pangea. Yes, I recall."

"Pangea has been locked away in storage for the past decade. It hasn't been used or tested since."

The President got up from his seat and walked to the back of the conference room. He pulled out a hidden drawer which was built into the paneling along the wall. He pulled out a bottle of Peach Snapple. He held one up, offering it to Donahue. Donahue shook his head 'no thanks', while holding up his bottle of water.

"What do you make of it?" asked the President. "Coincidence, or do you think they're up to something?"

"If you're asking me if I think Senator Logan and Jared Ross are planning to travel back in time two years to ensure you don't become President, my answer is no. Undoing something like that can have disastrous ripple effects on history. On the other hand, do I think they're up to something? My answer is yes, but I don't have the slightest idea what that might be."

"Okay," said the President. "Get on them, and stick to them like glue. Find out what they're up to. I don't like the sound of this. I'm quite concerned, in fact."

"Yes, sir. We will get to the bottom of it."

Donahue got up to leave, shook the President's hand and headed to the door. The President handed Donahue his unopened bottle of Snapple.

"Take this," said the President. "It's made from the best stuff on earth."

The Daily Lombardi Project meeting was about to begin. The Vice President was on the TV monitor from Washington once again.

"I only have a few minutes today," said the Vice President. "Things are blowing up right and left. Not literally, just the usual fallout from another President Harp announcement. This one relating to a rollback in global warming environmental policies. Anyway, Donny and Jared, how did things go at JPL yesterday?"

"Mission accomplished," said Corkoran. "We have Pangea in our possession, and it's in a safe location. However, we have an urgent matter we must deal with. My team of intelligence sleuths made a sweep of Jared's condo. They found several listening devices — bugs planted throughout the place. These were high grade electronics. The kind our government uses."

"Our guys?" asked the Vice President. "Donny, are you sure?"

"I'm sure it's high grade stuff, but I can't say for certain who planted them. But, do the math. If it's not us, who in the world is planting bugs at Jared's place? You know how paranoid Harp is."

"Right," said the Vice President. "But, I guess in this case, he wasn't just paranoid. So, what do we do?"

"We don't know who knows what, but it seems someone just might be on to us. How? I don't know. So, to be safe, we're sending the team to New York today. I want everyone out there. I have a friend who has a condo in Long Beach — that's out on Long Island."

"Long Beach?" asked the Vice President. "Where is that exactly?"

"It's twenty-five miles east of Prospect Park, on the south shore of Long Island. It's quiet. Remote. No one will look for us there. My friend is in Florida for a few weeks looking for a home down there for the winter months. We have NetJets booked. The reservation isn't under any of our names, so we'll be safe."

"Okay," said the President. "Good luck. Please let me know when you and Pangea arrive safely."

CHAPTER 19

The Executive Director at JPL was George Dundas, an employee of the Federal Government of the United States. Most of George's five thousand employees were focused on the construction and operation of planetary robotic spacecraft that travel over the surface of distant worlds, conducting experiments, gathering samples, and taking photographs.

That's why George was surprised when his guest had questions about something else entirely.

"So, tell me about Pangea," said Mark Donahue.

"Well, it's an amazing time travel tool, but deemed too dangerous by our Government," said George. "It was developed in 2008 by a guy named Jared Ross, a JPL employee. Brilliant kid. Anyway, Pangea is sitting downstairs in storage. It hasn't seen the light of day in more than a decade."

"Is Ross still working here?" asked Donahue.

"He's out on leave. He was apparently exposed to some radiation a few weeks ago, so we sent him for R&T — rest and testing."

"What does he do here now?" asked Donahue. "I mean, when he's not on leave."

"I'm not certain, to tell you the truth. I know he was working in our Artificial Gravity unit. But, I'm not sure what he's doing right now. What I do know is he's responsible for our semi-annual Pangea status reports."

"What's that?" asked Donahue.

"Every six months, Ross conducts a survey of the Pangea apparatus. He doesn't test the equipment, he just ensures that everything is accounted for and in order."

"When was his last survey conducted?" asked Donahue, holding his breath.

"I saw the report this morning," said Dundas, checking through various files on his desk. "Ah, here it is. Um, looks like he conducted the most recent survey just yesterday."

"Can I see the storage facility where Pangea is located?" said Donahue, rising to his feet. "Right now!"

Donahue held his cell phone to his ear.

"Mr Donahue, go for the President," said the Aide.

"Mr President, it's Donahue here. Thank you for taking my call."

The President was sitting in a hot tub in a hotel room in Virginia. He had a cigar in his mouth, a Martini in his hand, and a woman was sitting between his legs. The woman was not the First Lady. She was very attractive and very young — at least thirty years his junior.

"Go ahead, Mark," said the President. "I can hear you."

"I spent the day at JPL, Mr President. Jared Ross is on some kind of bogus sick leave, I don't know who arranged it, but I will find out. Anyway, for the past ten years, Jared's been responsible for conducting a bi-annual status survey of the Pangea apparatus, just to make sure everything is in order. He conducted the most recent survey two days ago. I went down to check on Pangea myself. It's gone. He took it."

"How do you know he took it?" asked the President.

"We have the whole thing on tape — from the security cameras in the storage room. He manufactured an accident in the room which distracted the guard who was assigned to watch him. Then he transferred the apparatus into a sports bag, and wheeled it out of there."

"We have to find him! He stole government property. That makes him a fugitive. Put him on top of the FBI's Most Wanted List!"

"We're after him, sir. We will find him and Pangea. I just wanted you to know where things stood."

"Well, you ruined my night," said the President, in a sullen tone. "I had a very nice evening planned. Now I'm not in the mood, Mr Donahue."

"My apologies, sir. I didn't intend to…"

The President interrupted, "Just find him!"

The President extinguished his cigar in his Martini glass. He pushed the woman, forward with his forearm, as he struggled to his feet. The President was wearing his boxer shorts which were filled with water from the tub. His boxers drooped down as he stood there for a moment in the hot tub. Finally, he grabbed a towel, stepped out of the hot tub, put his feet into his slippers, and headed for the bathroom. He slammed the door loudly behind him. The woman, who was completely nude, got to her feet and wrapped herself in a towel. She walked to the bed, grabbed her clothes, and headed for the door. A Presidential Aide was standing outside the door.

"What do I do now?" asked the woman.

"Go to your room," said the Aide. "We'll call you if we need you."

CHAPTER 20

The apartment was located in The Avalon Condominiums on West Broadway, overlooking the boardwalk which sat right on the beach. The apartment had three bedrooms — one for Snyder, one for Corkoran, and one for Jared and Janey to share.

Corkoran connected the monitor in the living room to the secure video conferencing software. The Daily Lombardi Meeting would be conducted from the sectional couch in the living room of the Avalon Condominium. The Vice President joined via video conference from Washington.

"Just five days to Jared's travel date," said the Vice President. "And, not a minute too soon. I was in a security briefing this morning, and I can now confirm that the FBI is aware that Pangea is missing. We all need to take every precaution. Be careful. Stay under the radar. Be careful who you talk to, and how you talk to them."

"We don't talk to anybody but each other," said Janey. "We only leave the apartment as a group, and only to go shopping and to go for a periodic walk on the beach or boardwalk. We're hobbits."

"Good, keep it that way, please," said the Vice President. "Snyder, let's go through the items Jared will be bringing with him. The items he'll use in an attempt to convince Washington that he is who he claims to be."

Snyder placed an authentic period linen knapsack on the table. It was the bag Jared would be traveling with. Snyder took an item from the bag.

"This is the iPhone you'll be taking with you. The phone will be charged to a hundred percent, and we'll be sending you with twenty-four PowerStation battery pack chargers. Each battery pack is good for two full charges. That means you will probably have enough juice for a month and a half. You'll be there for no more than a week, you won't be receiving emails or calls so you will be in very good shape.

"We loaded a variety of photos and videos which you will share with Washington. You'll have this letter he wrote to General Israel Putnam in 1779. Some of the photos and videos will be overwhelming for him to view. We loaded them in a specific order — if possible, you should try to stick to it."

"Got it," said Jared. "What about clothing?"

Snyder showed him his uniform.

"You will just have this one outfit. You'll wear it each day. You'll have three pairs of underwear. I suggest you wear each pair for two days, then switch. Remember, you will have an odor. You won't be clean in the way you're clean today. Yes, you will take a bath — not every day, likely. You will notice that others will have body odor as well. That's just part of life in the 1700's. There is no indoor plumbing. Water is carried in buckets into the homes. It's a lot of work. Water is heated on a stove for bathing. You will be using outhouses to relieve yourself. Bedpans at night. Don't worry if you get dirty. Everyone wore dirty clothing. You won't be there long enough for it to really become a problem."

"I'm looking forward to coming back already," said Jared.

"Don't be," said Snyder. "You have an opportunity to see things and people no one else on earth will ever have an opportunity to see. Try to enjoy it."

"Easy for you to say. Think of me when you take a crap at

night in your nice warm bathroom, and I'm in the smelly outhouse."

"We'll be sending you with some rations," said Snyder. "This stuff will be packaged. It's important no one sees any of it. Keep everything hidden, especially the iPhone and batteries. Bury your garbage, including the used PowerStation battery packs when you're done with them. Bury or burn everything when you're finished with stuff. But most of all, bury Pangea someplace safe or you may never come back here."

"Got it," said Jared. "What about the letter to Washington from Gates?"

Snyder pulled a small thin wooden box from the lined knapsack, and placed it on the table. He opened the box and withdrew a letter, sealed with a replica of Horatio Gates' official seal.

"I guess you could say this is your lifeline," said Snyder. "This is your ticket to Number 1 Broadway, the house in which Washington will be headquartered. If confronted by a Continental Army officer, show him the letter, and tell him your story. When you get to the Brooklyn Ferry, show this letter. When you get to the Kennedy Mansion on Broadway, show them the letter and explain that you must have a private audience with General Washington. Remember, it's 'General' Washington, not 'President' Washington."

"Oh, crap!" said Jared. "I could totally see myself effing that up!"

"Don't," said Snyder.

He pulled a small red velvet bag from the knapsack. He handed it to Jared.

"As we talked about, here is your compass. It will be a big help to you. Yes, you will have a compass on your iPhone, but you'll have no internet connection, so it will be useless. It will take a while for you to adjust to the lack of technology. Your mind is used to having technology all around. It will take a while to get used to it. No electricity, no plumbing, no cars. It will be an eye opening experience."

"Where will I stay?" asked Jared.

"Good question. We hope that Washington will invite you to stay at the Kennedy Mansion. Washington's top lieutenants will be staying with him at headquarters. If not, on your way out of the house, ask someone if they could recommend a good room to rent nearby. They will likely know of some good options. We will pack various denominations of currency for your trip."

"I bet a dollar went a long way in the 1700's," said Jared.

"Were there even dollars back then?" asked Janey.

"Yes, there were," said Snyder. "But, they looked a lot different."

Jared sat and thought about that for a moment.

"Jared, one more thing," said Snyder. "Your name will be John. John Ross."

"Okay, we're done for the day," said the Vice President. "I think we're in good shape. We'll review everything tomorrow, and then start laying out the timetable for the trip. Get some sleep everyone. You'll need it. Especially you, John."

Everyone laughed except Jared.

Jared and Janey had gone for a swim in the ocean. The air was warm, but the ocean was still pretty cool, at least by Pacific Ocean standards. It was nice for them to get away from it all for a little while. Not that what they were working on wasn't exciting and interesting, but it caused a fair amount of stress and anxiety. Especially now that they FBI was on to them.

When they arrived back at the condo, Snyder and Corkoran were sitting on the couch. Snyder called them over and told them to sit down.

"Can we at least take a shower and change into some dry clothes first?" asked Janey.

"No," said Snyder. "We need to talk to you right now. It's important."

Janey and Jared removed their towels from around their waists, laid them on the sectional couch, and sat on them.

"Okay, what's up?" asked Janey.

"Don just got off with the Vice President. Don, tell them what you told me."

"When the Vice President got back to his office after a lunch meeting this afternoon," said Corkoran, "his assistant, Cynthia, told him someone had been in his office playing around on his desktop computer. They had told Cynthia not to mention it to the Vice President, but they had underestimated her loyalty to him. Twenty-six years is a long time."

"So, what did they find?" asked Jared.

"There's no way to know," said Corkoran. "But, the Vice President is concerned they may have tapped into the secure video conference software. He's been making his calls for the Daily Lombardi Project meeting on his desktop. If they got into that program, they might be able to figure out what we're up to and where we are?"

"What do we do?" asked Janey.

"We've managed to stay one step ahead of those guys so far," said Corkoran. "We need to keep it that way. Jared, you're traveling tomorrow."

"Tomorrow?" asked Janey. "Are we ready?"

"Yes, we'll have to be," said Corkoran. "Jared and I will leave here at three thirty a.m. in my rental car. Janey and Snyder will follow in Hartwell's SUV at five thirty a.m. We'll set up the hoop, and we'll be ready for the trip as soon as you arrive."

Corkoran went to his bedroom and pulled the Pangea duffle bag out from under his bed (was that really the most secure hiding spot?). Jared decided that he'd sleep in his uniform. He thought it would help to get used to the feel of it, plus he could wrinkle it up a little bit. But most importantly, he'd really like Snyder's help getting it all on — the outfit was complicated.

Snyder double checked all of the supplies in Jared's backpack. He laid out the weapons and ammunition.

"Try to get some shut eye, Jared," said Corkoran. "You have a very big day tomorrow."

"What about you?" asked Jared.

"I'm staying up. I'm the lookout. No way I way I could sleep anyway."

CHAPTER 21

Monday, July 2nd — Travel Day

It was Monday, July 2nd, and it was officially travel day. It was a full week earlier than the originally planned date of July 9th, which was now the last possible return date. Jared popped up in bed, and looked at the clock. It was 3.12 a.m. Close enough, he thought.

He kissed Janey softly on the cheek, gently got out of bed, and made his way into the living room. Just then, the door opened and Corkoran came though.

"Well, everything is packed in the car," said Corkoran. "Did you sleep at all?"

Jared pulled a bottle of orange juice from the fridge, and took a long swig.

"A couple of hours, I think. I feel good. How about you?"

"Not a wink," said Corkoran. "I feel good, too. You ready for this?"

"I hope so."

Corkoran and Jared made their way down to the parking area. No shower for Jared — his messy hair was a nice authentic touch. The sun was just rising — the forecast called for a clear and sunny day with temperatures in the low eighties. They got into the car, and headed out of the parking lot. As they traveled, Jared tried to take it all in. At the moment, he was in a world that he was familiar with. He felt nervous pangs swirling in his belly.

He wasn't worried about his safety. He knew the technology well, and he knew it worked flawlessly. Yes, there was that little issue of burying the apparatus so that no one would find it, but even that was pretty straightforward. However, Jared wanted to soak it all in — he wanted to remember exactly what the world looked like, felt like, and smelled like in 2018 so that he could compare it to what he saw once he arrived in 1776. All of the high rise buildings along Broadway in Long Beach, the repulsive electric power plant, which sat on the inlet beside the bridge connecting the barrier beach to the mainland. The strip malls along Long Beach Road, the gas stations, houses, the cars. It all looked so normal and natural to a person living in 2018, but they'd all be gone once he reached 1776. Would the world of 1776 look anything like a place that might exist in 2018? Obviously, it wouldn't look like New York City. But, might it look like someplace that currently exists, for instance, in upstate New York? Perhaps in the Adirondacks? Or would it look completely foreign, like nothing he'd ever seen before?

The Belt Parkway, which hugged the coast in Queens and then Brooklyn, led to Ocean Parkway. They remained on Ocean Parkway until it became the Prospect Expressway, then took Prospect Park West around Bartel-Pritchard Square, and continued north to Grand Army Plaza. They turned right onto Eastern Parkway, where the Brooklyn Public Library Building met Mount Prospect Park. Corkoran saw a car pulling out from a space on the North Service Road of Eastern Parkway, so he made a quick U-turn, and parallel parked in the spot.

They were directly across the street from Mount Prospect Park, so they grabbed their stuff from the trunk, and made their way to the same stairway they ascended a few weeks earlier. The leaves had filled in on the trees, which swayed gently in the morning breeze. The park was green and lush. They walked to the large clearing, which they identified during their last trip, as the ideal location for the portal. They placed their equipment down, and Jared immediately began assembling the hoop.

Meanwhile, Corkoran began setting out Jared's supplies — his rifle, bayonet, ammunition, and his bags with his supplies.

Back in Long Beach, Janey and Snyder were dressed, and made their way down to the SUV. As they exited the building, Hartwell popped his door open, greeted Janey and Snyder, and opened the back door for them.

"Good morning!" said Hartwell with enthusiasm.

"Good to see you again," said Snyder. "We're heading to Prospect Park in Brooklyn. If you see a Dunkin Donuts or Starbucks along the way, we'd love to stop."

Hartwell nodded. He got back into the passenger seat, and the driver backed out. As they reached the light at the intersection of Broadway and Long Beach Road, the driver made an announcement.

"I think we're being followed," said the driver. "Don't look back. There's a dark blue unmarked sedan trying to squeeze into the turning lane right behind us. He was sitting in a spot on Broadway, and followed us as soon as I turned out of the parking lot."

The SUV turned onto Long Beach Road, and went over the bridge into Island Park, which was located on the mainland. Hartwell saw a Dunkin Donuts ahead.

"Let's turn in there," said Hartwell, pointing.

The blue sedan went on past the Dunkin Donuts. The SUV headed for the drive thru window, and they ordered their drinks. As they turned out of the Dunkin Donuts back onto Long Beach Road, they saw the blue sedan parked along the curb about one hundred yards up.

"This is it," said Hartwell. "If that car pulls out when we pass it, we'll know they're following us."

Sure enough, the sedan pulled away from the curb behind them.

"They're not trying too hard to fool us, are they?" said Janey. "If they're attempting to stay under the radar, they're failing pretty badly."

"I'm calling Corkoran," said Snyder. "Jared needs to go now! Right now! We can't lead these guys to the Prospect Park."

"But, I want to be there," said Janey. "I want to say goodbye to Jared before he goes."

"No way," said Snyder. "We can't risk it. He's got to go."

The SUV travelled north towards the Southern State Parkway, but instead of taking the parkway west towards Brooklyn, they took it the opposite direction towards eastern Long Island.

Snyder called Corkoran on his cell phone.

"Don, it's Snyder. We're being followed."

"Are you sure?" asked Corkoran.

"Positive. He's on us like glue. We're not coming to Prospect Park. We took the Southern State east, so we'll just keep leading him until you call me back and tell me Jared's gone."

"And back," said Corkoran. "Remember, it will be instantaneous for us. I'll let Jared know, and we'll get him going right now."

"Good luck," said Snyder.

The hoop was assembled and upright. It stood twelve feet in the air. He attached the laptop to the control input, and slid the cylinder into the slot on the side of the bottom hoop. Jared began logging into the computer to input the power formula for the

114

target date and time.

A young man in a jogging outfit stopped by the site where Jared and Corkoran were working on the hoop. He was wearing a black jogging suit, a headband, and had an iPhone clipped to his belt with ear buds on. He approached Jared.

"What are you guys up to?" asked the jogger. "And what's with the weird uniform?"

Jared and Corkoran were on high alert after the report from Snyder and Janey. Jared thought about saying nothing, but the jogger seemed harmless.

"This is a Continental Army uniform," said Jared, pulling up the collar on his jacket. "We're filming a commercial for Sam Adams Beer. It's the Fourth of July in a few days."

"Cool, can I stay to watch you guys shoot the commercial?" asked the jogger.

That was not an option. Jared had to come up with something.

"Sure, no problem, but we won't be shooting for hours," said Jared. "The production crew will get here around noon. If you want to go home and shower, I'll save a spot for you."

"That would be great, thanks," said the jogger, as he walked off.

"Good thinking," said Corkoran. "Let's not take any chances of someone else showing up. Let's do this now."

The hoop was ready to go, and the laptop was set. Jared pressed the start program, and the artificial gravity field was generated. Jared rechecked the arrival date and time to make sure it was set for six a.m. on July 2nd, 1776. Corkoran was checking the supplies one last time. He hung the musket on Jared's shoulder, and the knapsack on the opposite shoulder.

"The haversack is in your knapsack. It contains all the most important things — cell phone, battery packs, compass. Here's the letter from Gates." Corkoran opened Jared's waistcoat and slipped the letter into his inside breast pocket. "Don't lose this."

Jared stood there for a second, and looked around at the opening in the trees atop Mount Prospect. He stood straight, arching his back a bit, making his best attempt at displaying good posture. He tried to look and feel like a soldier. "I think I'm ready," he said. Corkoran took a few steps towards Jared and extended his hand. Jared reached out and shook it." "I'm nervous," said Jared. "I'm trembling."

"You're excited," said Corkoran. "You're about to embark on a trip of a lifetime. You are the luckiest man on earth."

"If you say so," said Jared with a smile. Jared checked for the letter in the breast pocket of his waistcoat. It was still there right where he left it. "Okay, let's do this."

"Remember, shave every day. Your blade is in the satchel in the back of your knapsack. And don't forget, your name is John Ross."

"See you in a few days," said Jared.

"We'll see you in a split second," said Corkoran.

Jared saluted, then turned and took a step towards the hoop. He took a deep breath, held it, and then he stepped through.

"God speed," said Corkoran, under his breath, as Jared lifted his right foot to step through the hoop. Then Corkoran reached for his cell phone to dial Snyder.

Corkoran could have sworn he saw a bright flash of light, and then suddenly…

CHAPTER 22

It was quiet. It was so peaceful and quiet. The constant sound of traffic, of car engines, rubber tires on pavement, air conditioners running — it was all gone. Yes, this was Brooklyn, but it wasn't like any version of Brooklyn Jared had ever seen or heard before. It looked, sounded, and felt more like Montana. It was also dark. Daylight savings time didn't exist in 1776, so it was the equivalent of 4.51 a.m. Jared could see the sunlight on the horizon to the east, as it rose above the Atlantic Ocean. Jared reached for the satchel, which was packed inside his backpack, and he retrieved a small flashlight — the same flashlight he would hopefully be showing George Washington within the next few days. He turned on the flashlight and pointed it towards a stand of trees facing west. He saw a small wooded area just thirty yards away. He took out his compass and made sure to make a note of the exact direction. He walked towards the group of trees, and found a Dogwood tree. The tree had a relatively thin trunk, just fourteen inches around. Jared pulled out a long strip of white fabric which Snyder had packed into his bag for this purpose, and he tied it around the trunk of the Dogwood tree. For anyone who has had trouble locating his or her car in an airport parking lot after returning from a long trip, this might make sense. When Jared returns to this spot with General Washington in a few days, the white fabric strip will help ensure that he finds the right tree.

Jared returned to the Pangea hoop, and began dismantling it. He turned the laptop off, and packed it securely into the duffle.

Then he placed the twelve pieces of the hoop into the duffle, making sure not to damage anything. Finally, he pulled the cylinder from its compartment in the bottom piece of the hoop, and placed it in its case next to the three extra cylinders — one of which he'll use for the return trip. He zipped the duffle closed, and carried it over to the trees.

Jared pulled the small hand shovel from the knapsack, and began digging a hole at the base of the tree. The earth wasn't too rocky, but it was densely packed, so it was a slow process. When he reached a depth of two feet, he began widening the hole so that it could fit the three foot wide duffle. Jared gently placed the duffle into the hole, laid a towel over it, and covered it with dirt. He worked the dirt for a few minutes, making sure it was flat, and that it appeared natural. It was unlikely people would be roaming in this area of Mount Prospect over the next few days, but Jared could not risk someone finding the duffle, otherwise, he'd likely spend the rest of his life in the 1700's.

In the thirty minutes that it took him to bury the duffle, the sun had come up. He could now see his surroundings in detail. There it was, Manhattan Island off to the west. It was quite hilly and green, with several steeples and low lying buildings visible at the southern tip. Nearer to him was the western end of the village of Brooklyn. It too was quite hilly, the result of the terminal moraine left by the receding Wisconsin glacier. From atop Mount Prospect, a hill about two hundred feet high, he could see several houses, open fields for farming, and the winding path of the Flatbush Road.

Jared made his way down the hill towards the Flatbush Road. The stone stairway that the Lombardi Team had used to ascend and descend the hill a few weeks earlier was of course gone, as was the Brooklyn Public Library. When he reached the Flatbush

Road, Jared was surprised to see that the road was not yet paved. It was a hard-packed earthen road, with hoof marks and wagon wheel tracks scattered throughout. The road ahead was quite hilly, and it meandered around hills, farms and kettle holes. The kettle holes were relatively small, shallow, sediment-filled bodies of water formed by the retreating glacier. The kettle holes were everywhere across the landscape, and when combined with the rolling grassy hills, it reminded Jared of County Kerry in Ireland — a place he visited in his youth.

Jared turned left onto the Flatbush Road, and began his trek west towards Manhattan, just as he had a few weeks earlier with Janey and Snyder. The road was much narrower in 1776 — no more than ten yards across. It appeared to Jared that two horse drawn wagons could just pass without hitting one another, but perhaps not.

It was a warm morning with a temperature in the mid-seventies. The sky was blue, with a few stratus clouds above. Jared attempted to determine if the air somehow felt different, with no pollution from auto exhaust, factories, or cigarettes. Yes, the air seemed different — crisper and cleaner. Perhaps it was all in his mind. However, it was a beautiful morning, and the breeze was blowing through the trees which lined the road. Up ahead, Jared saw a man outside a small gray house, as he led a Jersey cow across the front lawn. The man turned and led the cow to the barn, which sat along the right side of the house. As Jared approached, the man waved. Jared waved back.

"Who are you with?" asked the man.

"I beg your pardon," said Jared.

"Are you Militia?" asked the man.

"My apologies, sir. It's early and I am not quite awake as of yet."

"No apology necessary, son."

"I am John Ross, with Mott's Militia of the Connecticut Colony. I am a Corporal, and serve under General Gates at Fort Ticonderoga. I am traveling to the Island of Manhattan to personally deliver a letter to General Washington on behalf of General Horatio Gates."

"Well, you have a nice morning for a walk, Corporal," said the man. "You just follow the Flatbush Road to the Ferry Road."

"Thank you, sir. Good day."

Jared tipped his hat to the man, and walked on. Jared's heart was beating quickly, as he worried about his ability to converse in a manner suitable for the period. He hoped that any mistakes he might make would be chalked up to a regional Connecticut dialect. He meant to ask Snyder before he left if dialects from various regions in America at that time, were significantly different from one another? If he were to accidentally slip in some common words or terms from 2018 from time to time, might it go unnoticed? However, Jared forgot to ask Snyder that question, so he just kept his fingers crossed that his speech wouldn't raise too much suspicion. As Jared thought back to his interaction with the man, everything seemed to go fine. The man didn't seem to suspect that Jared was a time traveler from the future.

Jared walked off the road and crossed a field to a small outcropping of spruce trees. He sat in the tall grass, and removed a glass bottle of water from his knapsack. He took a long sip of water. The sun was warm — not hot but the entire experience had made him uncomfortable and a bit jittery. He took a few minutes to rest, he placed the water bottle back in his bag and returned to the road.

As the Flatbush Road turned and worked its way around a

kettle hole, it rose to the top of a small hill. At the top, Jared stopped and looked out towards Manhattan Island. He was much closer now than he was when he first glanced out toward the west from his perch at the top of Mount Prospect. Then he looked out at the Brooklyn side of the East River, and saw the Brookland Ferry Landing. He estimated that it was about a half-mile away, perhaps a twenty minute walk.

The Flatbush Road bent around to the left, and became the Brookland Ferry Road. The narrow road, wide enough for a single horse cart, was surrounded on both sides by small houses and buildings as it ran downhill to the river. At the river bank, there were two small wooden docks, in front of which, stood a small grey dock house. A sign, painted in black on an old, weathered board, hung from a thin rope on the front door. The sign read, "Blow Horn for Ferry Service".

A horn hung from a rope on the door. Jared squeezed the horn, and within seconds, a thin gray haired man barreled through the door of the dock house, tripping on the step down to the street, and almost falling over.

"Good morning, sir," said Jared. "I am interested in ferry service to Manhattan Island."

The ferryman looked at Jared, up and down.

"You Militia?" asked the ferryman.

"I am John Ross, with Mott's Militia of the Connecticut Colony. I am serving under General Gates at Fort Ticonderoga. I am traveling to the Island of Manhattan to deliver a letter to General Washington on behalf of General Gates."

"You come down from Fort Ticonderoga? What are you doing on Long Island?"

"I was advised by General Gates that General Washington might be on the Long Island, inspecting the progress of construction of Fort Putnam and Fort Greene, and on the line of entrenchments connecting them with Fort Sterling and Fort Box. However, I was informed last evening that General Washington had returned to his headquarters on Manhattan Island."

This was the story that Snyder had fed Jared as a response to this very question. A soldier traveling south from Fort Ticonderoga would cross at the King's Bridge in the Bronx, to Manhattan. So, Jared needed a story to explain why he ended up in Brooklyn, despite the fact that General Washington was headquartered on Manhattan Island. The story worked.

"What kind of currency are you carrying?" asked the ferryman.

"I have Continentals," said Jared, pulling a stack of bills from his inside jacket pocket.

"That's a lot of paper you're carrying, soldier, but it'll only be one-third dollar for the trip to Manhattan Island. If you want me to serenade you on the crossing, the fee goes up," said the ferryman with a smile."

Jared handed the ferry man his one-third bill, and they walked to the smaller dock. The dock on the left hand side was for individuals making the crossing, while the dock on the right hand side was for a larger ferry, used to take animals and supply carts across the river.

The ferry was a type of row boat, the likes of which Jared had never seen before. It sat low in the water, with a flat deck, and a seat for the oarsman. Jared stepped onto the boat and took a seat on one of three long benches which spanned the boat from side to side. The ferryman took his place at the oars, and shoved off. The river was calm, with barely a ripple on the surface. The river was flowing ever so slowly, so the ferryman had no trouble rowing cross-current. Jared had to resist the temptation to remove his iPhone from his knapsack and snap a few photos of the village at the tip of lower Manhattan, as it came closer into view. What an amazing sight — Jared's mouth was hanging wide open. He saw the dock on the Manhattan side of the river, which sat at the foot of Wall Street. He could see the spire of the first Trinity Church, which was built at the western end of Wall Street. He saw the wall, for which Wall Street was named, with its gates and guards. And at the southern tip of the island, he saw Fort Amsterdam, which sat on a low hill. Jared tried his best to take a mental photo of this awesome scene.

When they arrived at the shore on the Manhattan side, the ferryman tossed a line to a man standing on the dock. He pulled the boat up tight to the dock, and wrapped the line around an iron stanchion. The man reached down towards Jared.

"Can I give you a hand, soldier?" asked the man.

"Thanks," said Jared, as he stepped up onto the dock.

"Who're you with?" asked the man.

The ferryman interrupted, "He's with Mott's Militia in Connecticut. He has instructions to deliver a letter to General Washington directly."

"Is that so?" asked the man on the dock. "Do you need help finding the General's Headquarters?"

"Thank you, sir" said Jared. "I am aware that the General is headquartered at Number 1 Broadway, but I am not certain how to find the address."

"It's quite simple, lad. Just follow Wall Street until it ends at Trinity Church, turn left and follow Broadway till it ends. Number 1 will be on the right side of Broadway. You can't miss it — it is surrounded by guards day and night."

"Thank you again, sir."

Jared crossed Pearl Street, which, at that time, ran along the

East River. He walked across Wall Street, heading west towards Trinity Church. Midway down Wall Street, he saw Federal Hall on the right hand side, the original building, in which in 1792 — on the second floor balcony — George Washington would be inaugurated as the first President of the United States. Again, Jared had to fight the urge to grab his iPhone to take a picture.

Jared turned left at Broadway, and followed it south. A few blocks later, he could see Bowling Green, with its familiar black iron fence surrounding it. And beyond Bowling Green he saw Fort Amsterdam, looming high above the harbor. Just a couple of weeks ago, Jared stood on this exact spot, in front of the Alexander Hamilton Customs House. It was so hard to comprehend that this was the same spot — it couldn't have looked any more different. Jared guessed it was approximately eleven a.m., and there were people in the streets. Men were selling fresh fruit in front of Bowling Green, and a mother was watching her two little children playing in the Park. Jared took a minute to remember his lines, then crossed the street to Number 1 Broadway.

Jared walked up to the front door on Broadway, and approached a Sentry standing on the front steps.

"Good day, officer," said Jared.

The officer stared at Jared, but didn't say a word.

"My name is John Ross, I am a member of Mott's Militia of the Connecticut Colony. I am serving under General Gates at Fort Ticonderoga. I have been sent by General Gates to hand deliver this letter to General Washington."

Jared took the letter out from his breast pocket, and he showed it to the officer. The officer reached out and took it from Jared. He held it up to the sun as he inspected the seal. He handed the letter back to Jared, and without uttering a word, the officer turned, reached for the door handle to the mansion, and opened the door. Then, with a wave of his hand, the officer motioned for Jared to enter.

Jared walked into the main hallway, where a small table was set up. The table was colorful and intricately carved. Upon the table were a quill pen in its holder, a short stack of parchment paper, and a candle. There was a young man sitting in a chair behind the table. The young man looked to be approximately twenty years old, and he wore a colorful uniform.

Jared approached the young man at the table, holding the letter out.

"Yes," said Jared nervously, "I have been sent by General Gates to hand deliver this letter to General Washington."

"And, your name, sir?'

"My name is John Ross. I am a member of Mott's Militia of the Connecticut Colony. I am serving with my unit under the command of General Gates at Fort Ticonderoga."

The young man took the letter, inspected it and placed it on the table.

"I regret to inform you," said the young man, "that General Washington is on the Long Island presently. I will see to it that he receives this letter as soon as he returns tomorrow."

How ironic thought Jared. Washington was actually in Brooklyn, just as that made up story from Snyder suggested he might be.

"I beg your pardon, sir, but my orders from General Gates were to hand deliver the letter to General Washington myself. If I must wait for the General's return, then I shall."

The young man handed the letter back to Jared.

"Very well. I expect General Washington to return by midday tomorrow."

Jared turned, and was about to exit the mansion. He suddenly turned again, and faced the young man.

"Sir, I was wondering if perhaps you could recommend a room to rent nearby?" asked Jared.

"Mrs Miller's on Beaver Street would be your best option."

"Thank you," said Jared. "Could you help me find Beaver Street?"

"It's on the east side of the Bowling Green."

Jared thanked the young man, and exited the mansion. He walked around the south end of Bowling Green, and found Beaver Street. A sign at the door of 23 Beaver Street said "Miller's Inn", so Jared entered. It did not resemble a hotel or even a bed and breakfast. It simply looked like a home.

"Hello?" said Jared loudly.

A woman came running to the entryway. He assumed it was Mrs Miller.

"Oh, hello," said the woman, as she attempted to catch her breath. "Can I help you?"

"Yes, I'm looking for a room to rent for the night."

"Well, you've come to the right place, young man. We have the nicest rooms in town. Will you be staying just one night, or perhaps longer?"

"I'm not entirely certain," said Jared. "Perhaps I can pay you for one night, and if I need to extend my stay, I will inform you."

"That would be fine. What currency will you be paying with?"

"I can pay you with Continentals."

"Then, that will be three Continentals for the one evening."

Jared paid Mrs Miller from the stack of Continentals in his vest pocket. Then she yelled for her daughter.

"My daughter Becky will show you to your room."

From around the corner came Becky, a young woman with auburn hair piled high in a bun atop her head, piercing blue eyes, and a plain light blue dress. Jared was instantly taken by her natural beauty.

"Becky, I'd like you to meet..."

"My name is Ross, John Ross."

There was no chance anyone alive in 1776 had seen a James Bond film, so Jared elected to play the role of a debonair, suave spy.

"The blue room," said Mrs Miller.

Becky nodded, and said, "Right this way, Mr Ross."

Becky led Jared around the parlor to a stairway next to the kitchen. The stairway was narrow and dark, but he could see that Becky had a very thin waist, and long legs. Her auburn hair was wavy and braided, and reached the middle of her back. When they reached the landing at the top of the stairs, she turned, and led him down a hall.

This is the blue room," said Becky, as she opened the door at the end of the hall. It's our nicest room. I trust you will find it comfortable. Lunch is served daily in the kitchen at noon — now, and breakfast is served at seven a.m. Will you be joining us for lunch?"

"Yes, I will get myself settled, and I'll be down momentarily," said Jared.

Jared sat on the bed, and took a moment to reflect on everything that occurred so far during the day. Had it sunk in that he was really in 1776 Manhattan? No, it hadn't. However, he took comfort in the fact that he'd interacted and spoken to several people, and so far, there were no issues. He hadn't made a mistake, and no one seemed to question whether or not he belonged. The plan had gone perfectly well — from burying the Pangea apparatus, to the trek to the ferry, the ferry crossing, and gaining entrance to Washington's headquarters using the Gates letter. It had all worked. He even had a place to stay for the night, would have meals served to him, and he could spend the remainder of the day flirting harmlessly with the beautiful Becky Miller.

When he made his way downstairs and to the kitchen, a long oak table was set for three people: Mrs Miller, Becky Miller and Jared. Jared took his seat.

Mrs Miller went to the counter, and returned with a bowl of bean porridge and brown bread, and placed it in front of Jared. She also placed a mug of beer in front of him on the table.

"So, where are you from?" asked Mrs Miller.

"I'm from Fairfield, Connecticut. However, most recently, I've been at Fort Ticonderoga with General Gates. I was sent to Manhattan to deliver a personal letter from Gates to General Washington."

"How exciting," said Becky. "I've never stepped foot off this island in my eighteen years. I'd love to travel some."

"I knew I detected an accent," said Mrs Miller. "I couldn't place it."

Jared took a taste of the Bean Porridge, which was fairly bland. The brown bread was fabulous, however, and after finishing in two bites, he asked for another piece of bread.

"So," asked Becky, "what do you think of our city?"

"I think the city is marvelous," replied Jared. "After we defeat the British and win our independence, I believe the city will grow to be the largest and most important city — not only in the colonies — but throughout the world."

Mrs Miller and Becky smiled, thinking Jared must be

slightly crazy. How could this city ever compete with the likes of London, Paris or Rome?

After lunch, Jared retired to his room. He hesitated removing any part of his uniform, as he lacked the confidence that he'd be able to dress correctly without Snyder's help. He laid down on the bed fully clothed, and closed his eyes.

CHAPTER 23

Tuesday, July 3rd

Jared awoke to the sound of someone knocking on the door.

"Hello, Mr Ross, it's Becky. Would you like to join us for breakfast?"

It took a few moments for Jared to emerge from his groggy state.

"Yes, thank you, Becky. I will be down in a moment."

Jared headed down to the kitchen for breakfast. Mrs Miller and Becky were sitting in the same seats as they had been for lunch the day before, so Jared took his same seat as well. Mrs Miller went to the counter and retrieved a plate of hoecakes and a bowl of porridge. She placed them in front of Jared, along with a mug of cider.

"What are your plans today, Mr Ross?" asked Mrs Miller, as she sat back down at the table.

"My plan is to return to Number 1 Broadway in hopes of getting an audience with General Washington. I was told he is expected to return around midday."

"And until then?" asked Becky.

"I had hoped to see the seaport. I've heard it is quite a lovely place. Becky, as I am unfamiliar with the environs, I would be honored and appreciative if you would join me."

Before she could open her mouth to respond, Mrs Miller chimed in.

"She would be happy to," said Mrs Miller. "She could purchase some fresh fish for dinner this evening while she's at it."

"Wonderful," said Jared. "It looks like a splendid morning for a walk."

After breakfast, Becky went up to her room to change into something appropriate for a public stroll, while Jared waited for her in the parlor. When Jared saw her, he was speechless. Becky was absolutely radiant in her long yellow gown and white linen jacket. Becky's long hair was covered by a coif. While Jared missed seeing her long auburn hair, the cap accentuated her beautiful features and perfect skin tone.

He smiled as he extended his arm, and she took it as they stepped out onto Beaver Street. They walked east until they reached Pearl Street.

"So tell me a little about yourself," said Jared.

"I'm not sure there's much to tell, actually. I was born in the house on Beaver Street. I work for my mother at the inn. As I mentioned, I've never stepped foot off the island of Manhattan."

"Do you have a man in your life?" asked Jared.

"A man in my life?" asked Becky.

"A boyfriend?"

"No, there's no man in my life. And, I'm afraid, there never has been."

They turned right onto Broad Street and followed it towards the river.

"I find that difficult to believe," said Jared. "A woman as attractive as you are must have many suitors."

Becky blushed then smiled.

"Thank you, Mr Ross, but I simply have not had an opportunity to meet a man, as I stay home all day long. I was schooled at home by my mother. Why do you think she was so excited by the prospect of my joining you on this walk? She is constantly suggesting that I get out and meet people, but it's not something I'm comfortable with. I prefer to stay at home."

"A homebody," said Jared.

"A homebody?"

"Yes, it's a phrase that's commonly used where I'm from," said Jared. "It means, someone who prefers to stay at home, rather than go out."

Becky thought for a moment as they crossed Stone Street.

"I know you said you're from Connecticut, Mr Ross, but I don't think I've ever met a person who seems as different as you do — in so many small, but peculiar ways."

"Should I feel honored or offended by that?" asked Jared.

"Honored. Yes, it was a compliment. In New York, everyone seems so similar. But you… you are quite different, and I find it refreshing."

They reached Pearl Street, and while it wasn't a bustling seaport, there was some activity along the street. They walked to a store front advertising fresh fish. There was a line of people waiting to get into the shop, so they waited in line on the sidewalk.

"May I ask you, Becky, about your father?"

"I never knew my father. He was French. He was a man my mother knew a long time ago. They were not married, and when my mother became pregnant with me, he disappeared. My mother lived with her parents and her brother in the house on Beaver Street. Both of her parents died of Yellow Fever when I was seven years old. Her brother, Samuel, is an officer, currently serving with General Greene in Brooklyn."

"I'm sorry," said Jared.

132

"Oh, don't be, Mr Ross. My mother and I are both quite happy."

"Please call me ‚John," said Jared.

"Yes, I will," said Becky. "But you have to promise to tell me the truth, someday, about who you really are and about where you are really from."

"If you don't mind me saying so," said Jared, "I find you quite different and refreshing as well."

"And why is that?" asked Becky.

"Where I'm from, the people I know like to complain a lot. They have very high expectations with respect to what they feel their lives should be like. When they don't get what they want, they get angry and sometimes they even get mean. But you are nothing like that. You seem quite happy and content with what you have. You are an optimist. A 'glass half full' type of person."

"I would ask what that means," said Becky, "but I'm sure it's just another unique phrase commonly used by the people where you're from."

"Yes it is," said Jared. "It proves my point. There are so many negative people where I'm from, they needed to come up with a phrase that identifies whether a person tends to be a negative or positive type."

Becky looked into Jared's eyes.

"I don't mind telling you, John, that I find you fascinating."

"Good," said Jared.

After purchasing some fresh Tuna at the shop on Pearl Street, Jared and Becky returned to the inn on Beaver Street. Jared retired to his room for a little rest, and he spent time reviewing his plans and his lines for his meeting with Washington. He checked to see that his cell phone was fully charged. From the location of the sun in the sky, Jared estimated that it was approximately one p.m. He decided to wait another thirty minutes, and then head back to Number 1 Broadway.

As Jared made his way downstairs and out the door onto Beaver Street, Becky called after him.

"I hope your meeting with General Washington goes well!"

"Thanks," said Jared, as he tipped his hat.

Jared walked up Beaver Street to Bowling Green, then around the park, to Number 1 Broadway. There was a different guard on duty at the front porch. Jared approached.

"Officer, my name is John Ross, I am a member of Mott's Militia of the Connecticut Colony. I am serving under General Gates at Fort Ticonderoga. I have been sent by General Gates to hand deliver a letter to General Washington."

"May I see the letter?" asked the officer.

Jared removed the letter from his breast pocket, and held it up.

"I am under explicit instructions from General Gates that I must hand this letter directly to General Washington. No one else may open it, and no one else may deliver it. Those were my instructions."

"My instructions," said the officer, "are to protect General Washington from those who have no business seeking an audience with him. I must first know the reason for your meeting before I can allow you to pass."

"I'm afraid I shared all the details that I'm aware of with you. Only General Gates knows the contents of the letter. I am simply not privy to that information."

"Then I'm afraid I must ask you to leave, and return with a letter from General Gates outlining his instructions to you. We must have confirmation from Gates himself, that he has asked you to deliver this letter."

"But, sir," said Jared, "it would take me more than a full week to trek to Fort Ticonderoga. The contents of this letter are timely, of that I am certain. The two weeks it will take for me to return with a letter from General Gates will be too long. Our cause will suffer. Please, officer, there was a young man at the desk inside. When I arrived yesterday, he informed me that the General was in Brooklyn, and he requested that I return today. I know the young man understood the gravity of our situation, and he welcomed my visit. I ask you to please confer with him."

"Very well," said the officer, as he turned and entered the mansion. After a few minutes, the officer returned to the porch.

"You may enter," said the officer. "My apologies for any inconvenience, private."

"Not at all," said Jared. "And please, my rank is that of corporal."

"Again, my apologies," said the Officer.

Jared entered the mansion, and approached the young man at the desk.

"Good afternoon, Corporal Ross. General Washington is meeting with his military advisors at the moment. Please take a seat in the library, and the General will be with you momentarily."

"Thank you," said Jared, as he followed an African American woman down the hall to the Library.

The library was beautifully furnished, with ornate but comfy couches set out in a square around a low table. This was the home of Archibald Kennedy, of the Royal Navy. Jared assumed the large portraits which covered all four walls of the library, were members of Kennedy's family. After approximately ten minutes, the African American woman returned and asked Jared to follow her. The woman approached a closed double door at the end of the hallway, knocked, and opened the doors.

"General Washington, may I introduce John Ross of Mott's Militia of the Connecticut Colony, here to see you on behalf of General Horatio Gates."

Jared entered the room, stopped, and bowed his head. George Washington, the man, in the flesh, was sitting behind a desk. Another man, in uniform, was sitting beside the desk in a chair, his legs crossed at the knee. Washington looked at Jared with a curious look on his face.

"Am I to understand that you were sent to deliver a letter to me from General Gates?" asked Washington in a stern voice.

Jared took a few steps toward Washington and spoke, "Yes, General Washington, that is correct."

Jared removed the letter from his breast pocket.

"Bring it to me," said Washington. "Quickly."

Jared took a few more steps toward the desk.

"Excuse me, General Washington, but General Gates requested that I ensure no one else be present when I pass the letter to you. That was his request."

Washington looked over to the man sitting in the chair.

"General Greene, if you would excuse us."

Nathanael Greene stood up from his chair, nodded at Washington, walked to the double door, and exited the room.

"Please sit down," said Washington, directing Jared to the chair Greene had been using.

Jared walked to the chair and sat down. Up close, he saw Washington as a man — not as a painting. His skin was clear, but he had small wrinkles around his eyes and on each side of his mouth. His hair was light brown, and apparently, only appeared white when he powdered it. Washington did not wear a wig.

"General Washington, I must confess something to you. This

letter is not from General Gates. That was a story that was conjured up to allow me to gain access to you."

"Conjured up by whom?" asked Washington.

"Please read the letter, General, and I will explain."

Washington cracked the seal and opened the letter. On official White House letterhead, with the seal of the Vice President of the United Sates, was a typed letter. It read as follows:

Dear General Washington,

I am writing this letter to you from my office in the West Wing of the White House. It is the year 2018, two hundred and forty-two years since America declared its independence from England.

Over the course of those two hundred and forty-two years, many advances have been made in science, including man's ability to travel through time. The man who handed you this letter, Jared Ross, did so at my request. Like many Americans alive today, he is concerned about the grave state of our beloved country and its future. He will provide you with more details, and he will show you many things that will prove to you that he is who he says he is.

I want to thank you, on behalf of the American people, for giving Mr Ross an opportunity to discuss our situation with you.

Sincerely,

David R. Bashoff

Vice President of the United States of America

Washington folded the letter and handed it back to Jared. Washington sat there speechless, unsure how to react. Jared attempted to say something in an effort to end the silence, but Washington raised his hand and uttered a 'shush' sound.

Washington sat in silence for a few more minutes, then he looked at Jared.

"I am speechless," said Washington. "If this is some kind of joke, I can't imagine, for the life of me, what the point of it is. If it's true, and I can't imagine how it could possibly be, then I am puzzled as to why you are here."

"First, General Washington, let me assure you that it is indeed true. My name is Jared Ross, and I am a scientist at the Jet Propulsion Laboratory. Ten years ago, by accident, I invented a time travel portal. The United States government decided it was too dangerous to use. They were concerned that the technology might fall into the wrong hands. Due to some terrible things that have occurred recently in the United States due to poor leadership and shortsighted decisions, the state of our country has fallen into a dangerous position. I have come here to consult with you, and to ask you a favor."

"A favor?" asked Washington.

"If you don't mind, I'd prefer to get to that a little later."

"As you wish."

"The time travel portal," Jared continued, "is constructed of a copper hoop about twelve feet high. We placed the hoop at a location on Long Island, which in 2018, is a large public park. Without going into too much scientific detail, we power up the gravity force to a predetermined level, and then step through the hoop to the year we want to travel to. I did that yesterday morning. When I return to 2018 in a few days, I will return to the precise moment when I left. No time will have passed at that location."

"It sounds remarkable, Mr Ross, but I'm not sure I follow, nor am I certain I believe or understand any of it," said Washington.

"I understand, and we expected that would be the case. People living in 2018 have seen so many advances in technology, many of which I will share with you. But even the people of the twenty-first century would have a difficult time believing that man has invented a way to travel through time."

"So, what is next?" asked Washington.

"With your approval, I would like to show you things that I believe will convince you that what I have told you is true. We don't have to go through everything today. I believe some of the things I will show you will be somewhat overwhelming. I will start slowly, and we can build our way up."

"I will agree to that, as long as we can stop the process if I feel it is warranted."

"Yes, absolutely, General," said Jared. "Also, I will not divulge any details about the war with England. I will not discuss any successes or failures of your strategy, and you may not ask me for details. We do not know a lot about time travel, and scientists in 2018 are concerned about the effects of making any changes to history. Small changes could lead to big changes, and any change could have a disastrous effect on the future. You may, however, ask me any questions about the future that do not relate to the war or its outcome."

"Yes, I agree."

Jared reached into his satchel and retrieved another letter. This one was in a manila envelope. Jared opened the letter and handed it to Washington.

"This is a letter you wrote to John Hancock on June 11th, 1783. The letter discusses your vision for the young United States. My being here, General, confirms the existence of the United States of America as an independent power. I will not, however, discuss with you how or when that occurred."

"I understand," said Washington, as he took the letter from Jared, and began reading. The writing was in his own hand, which he immediately recognized. A tear formed in the corner of Washington's right eye as he read the letter.

(The letter begins as follows)

Sir,

The great object for which I had the honor to hold an appointment in the Service of my Country being accomplished, I am now preparing to resign it into the hands of Congress, and to return to that domestic retirement, which, it is well known I left with the greatest reluctance; a retirement for which I have never ceased to sigh through a long and painful absence, and in which (remote from the noise and trouble of the World) I meditate to pass the remainder of life in a state of undisturbed repose. But before I carry this resolution into effect, I think it a duty incumbent on me to make this my last official communication; to congratulate you on the glorious events which Heaven has been pleased to produce in our favor, to offer my sentiments respecting some important subjects which appear to me to be intimately connected with the tranquility of the United States, to take my leave of your excellency as a public character, and to give my final blessing to that country in whose service I have spent the prime of my life, for whose sake I have consumed so many anxious days and watchful nights, and whose happiness being extremely dear to me, will always constitute no inconsiderable part of my own.

"It must be very strange for you to read this," acknowledged Jared.

"Yes, indeed it is. I recognize the writing style as my own, and I recognize my penmanship, but I do not recognize my thoughts."

"General Washington, I know I shared a lot with you today. If you would like to stop here, and resume this conversation, perhaps tomorrow, I would be delighted to return in the morning, assuming it suits you."

Washington took a deep breath, but continued reading the letter.

"This is indeed remarkable," said Washington. "Assuming this is not a forgery, this is remarkable. Yes, why don't we break here for today, and resume our discussion at ten a.m. tomorrow morning?"

"I agree, that sounds like a good idea," said Jared, and he stood up. "I have some remarkable technology to share with you tomorrow, which I believe you will find fascinating."

"I look forward to it," said Washington. "Mr Ross, I would be honored if you would stay with us here at my headquarters."

"I appreciate your invitation, General Washington, but I am currently staying with Mrs Miller at her inn on Beaver Street. I am quite fond of Mrs Miller and her daughter, and would like to remain their guest for the duration of my journey."

"I understand," said Washington. "Then, would you please do me the honor of joining me for dinner tonight? You may bring a guest."

"I'd be delighted," said Jared.

"And, Mr Ross, I think it would be prudent if we agreed that the point of your visit was to deliver the letter from General Gates, and that I am now discussing details of a strategy I want you to deliver to Gates when you return to Fort Ticonderoga."

"Yes, General Washington, I am in complete agreement."

Jared half walked, half ran around Bowling Green to Beaver Street. When he arrived at the inn, he burst through the door, and found Becky sitting in the parlor. "How was your meeting, John?"

"It was amazing," said Jared. "General Washington was a terrific host. But, we weren't able to discuss everything on my agenda, so I will be returning to Number 1 Broadway tomorrow morning to continue our conversation."

"Will you be staying with us again tonight?" she asked.

"Yes, tonight and perhaps tomorrow night as well." Becky couldn't hide her happiness. "Becky, would you do me the honor of joining me for dinner tonight at General Washington's headquarters?"

"Dinner with General Washington?" asked Becky. "I would love to, except I don't think I have an appropriate dress for such an occasion."

"Is there a dressmaker nearby?" asked Jared. "It would be my pleasure to buy you a dress to wear tonight."

"Mrs Conway on Broad Street is the best dressmaker in the city, but on such late notice, I'm not sure…"

Jared took the stack of Continentals from his pocket, and flipped through until he found a fifty dollar bill. "Here," said Jared as he handed Becky the fifty dollar bill. "Find the best dress in the shop, and explain to Mrs Conway that you've been asked to dine with General Washington. If she requires more money, please call me"

"Call you?" asked Becky.

"Call for me, I'll come and pay her whatever she deems appropriate, considering the late notice."

"Can you mind the inn?" asked Becky. "I'd like to bring

mother with me to Mrs Conway's."

Becky wore a stunning jacket and petticoat, with elbow-length sleeves. It featured a copper colored fabric, with vertical stripes of white and gold, and thin horizontal stripes of white. She wore silk brocade shoes with straps for shoe buckles.

What Jared noticed first was the dress's extremely thin, tapered waist, which accentuated the female form. However, what made Jared feel really great was the look in Becky's eyes, which radiated with joy and excitement.

"You look absolutely stunning," said Jared, when he saw her in the parlor. He took her hand and kissed it.

Becky's smile beamed even wider. She had never dressed in an outfit like that before in her life.

"Thank you, John," said Becky. "The evening has not yet begun, and this is already the happiest day of my life."

Jared smiled ear to ear. How could he not feel wonderful about giving Becky the best day of her life? She was so sweet, and she appreciated the small things in life. She didn't have large expectations, the way Janey did. How could he not love... wait! He told himself to slow down.

"Shall we go?" asked Jared, and he extended his arm to her.

Everyone was already situated in the dining room at the Kennedy Mansion when Jared and Becky arrived. Both of them. General Washington and Major General Nathanael Greene. They were seated at the table, across from one another at the respective heads. Had Martha Washington been present, she would have insisted that they meet their guests in the parlor, and after some time, they would move to the dining room. However, the two Generals were more matter of fact, so when it was time to eat, it was time to eat.

"Miss Miller," said Washington, "Mr Ross tells me you are an innkeeper."

"Yes, General Washington," said Becky. "My mother and I operate the inn at 26 Beaver Street."

"Mr Ross speaks very highly of your inn," said Washington. "He chose to remain there, instead of taking me up on my offer to stay with us here at the Kennedy Mansion. Having met you, Miss Miller, I can now see why. Major General Greene and I cannot compete with your charms."

Becky smiled and blushed.

"Mr Ross," said Washington, "please share your impressions of New York with us."

"I think it's a very impressive city," said Jared. "I'm told it has the deepest harbor of any harbor on the continent. The people of this city have an extremely optimistic outlook, and they seem to be driven to succeed — primarily — their desire to make money."

"If you were to imagine this city in the future, years after we succeed in gaining our independence, what do see?" asked Washington.

"I truly believe this city will be a leader throughout the world — from a financial and cultural perspective. A city is nothing more than a reflection of the people who inhabit it. The people of this city are special."

"Well said," said Greene.

The group finished their meal, then they retired to the parlor for an after dinner drink and for some more conversation. The discussion centered on the looming battle with the British, and the impact it would likely have on daily life in the city. Suddenly, the gravity of the situation hit Jared, as he realized, for the first time, that the Miller's might have to vacate the city and leave the inn on Beaver Street to the British. On the walk back to Beaver Street, Jared noticed that Becky was quieter than she normally was.

"Is everything okay?" asked Jared.

"Everything is wonderful," said Becky, I just don't want this evening to ever end."

That's when he felt it. That exciting, happy, crazy, amazing, scary, terrifying feeling of falling in love.

CHAPTER 24

Jared did not sleep well. He was concerned about his feelings for Becky, and what that could mean. On one hand, he was happy and excited. On the other hand, he knew the relationship had no possible future. That meant it would end sooner than later. While he was concerned about missing Becky when he left, he was more concerned about hurting her.

Jared took the short walk from Beaver Street to Number 1 Broadway just before ten a.m., and before he knew it, he was back in his seat across the desk from General Washington. "I hope you enjoyed dinner last night," said Washington.

"I did, sir, very much. Becky had a wonderful time as well."

"She is quite attractive," said Washington. "You two certainly seem to have made a connection."

"Yes, she is really terrific," said Jared. "I'm concerned we may have connected too well, perhaps."

"You feel that way because you'll be heading back to 2018, I presume," said Washington, with a smirk.

Jared felt Washington was mocking him. It seemed Washington wasn't yet convinced that Jared was who he claimed to be. Jared didn't expect that the letter, alone, would convince Washington of the validity of his time travel claim. However, he had hoped he'd made some progress. Perhaps not. It was time to introduce the "big guns". Jared pulled his iPhone from his satchel and powered it on. "This is called a cell phone. An iPhone. It's a device that allows people to speak with one another. In 2018, virtually every person in America has one. Even children. The cell phone became popular around twenty-five years ago. Before that, you could only talk to people using a phone that was connected to a wire."

When the phone powered on, Washington could see the screensaver — a photo of Jared's brother Erik riding a huge wave on his surfboard. Jared handed the phone to Washington.

"That's marvelous," said Washington, holding the phone, turning it over, and looking at the photo. "Is that a tiny painting or a sketch?"

"No, it's a photograph," said Jared. "Here, I will take one of you."

Washington handed the phone back to Jared, and he snapped his photo. He handed the phone back to Washington.

"That's extraordinary," said Washington. "How does it work?"

"I'm not exactly sure," said Jared. "It captures the light. For many years, people had to use a camera which used film. You'd have to take time to get your film developed. Now, everyone just uses their phone, and we get instant photos. It's digital. Here, I'll take a video of you."

Jared pointed his iPhone, in video mode, at Washington.

"Say something, sir."

"What does one say to an iPhone?" asked Washington.

Jared stood up, walked around the desk to Washington, and played the video back. *"What does one say to an iPhone?"*

Washington was startled. "Does my voice actually sound that way?"

Jared decided to demonstrate a few of the other iPhone functions.

"This is a calculator. Five times five equals twenty-five."

"Why would I need that thing to determine what five times five equals? I learned that as a school child."

"Okay, how about 3,455 times 112?" asked Jared. "It's 386,960," he said holding the screen up for Washington to see.

There was a knock on the door, and one of Washington's aides entered the office.

"General Washington," said the aide, "General Putnam requests your presence at Fort Amsterdam immediately. He says it's urgent."

"Very well," said Washington, dismissing the aide with a flip of his hand. Then Washington turned to Jared. "I'm afraid I must cut our session short today. Can you return tomorrow morning at ten a.m.?"

"Yes, of course," said Jared. "You have a war to fight — that takes first priority. However, before you leave, can I show you one more thing?"

"Quickly" said Washington.

Jared tapped the photo button on his phone, then scrolled down and tapped a photo. He held it up for Washington to see.

"Do you know what this is?" asked Jared. "It's a photo of the earth from space."

Washington saw the bright blue and green marble with wispy white clouds surrounding it. Washington was mesmerized.

"That's astounding," he said.

"Tomorrow, I will show you how that photo was taken."

Jared walked around Bowling Green, and stopped in front of Fort Amsterdam. From where he was standing, he could see the northern wall of the fort, and New York Harbor beyond it. Jared took the iPhone from his vest pocket, looked around to make sure no one was watching him, and he snapped a selfie. Then he stuffed the camera back into his pocket, and headed to Beaver Street.

When he entered the inn, Mrs Miller mentioned that Becky was in the yard. Jared walked past the kitchen, through the pantry and out the back door of the inn, and into the small but well-manicured courtyard. Becky was sitting on a chair reading a book. She looked up and smiled when she saw Jared.

"Back so soon?" asked Becky.

"General Washington had to attend to some important business, so he cut our session short today. I'll be returning at ten a.m. tomorrow morning."

"How much longer will you be staying in the city?" asked Becky.

"I don't know for certain," said Jared. "But, if I were to guess, I'd say two or three more days."

"Do you think we'll see one another again after you leave?"

Jared had to think for a moment before he answered. He wanted to try to answer as truthfully as he could.

"I don't know how I could ever see you again, Becky. It's complicated, and I'm not sure I could realistically return. But, I don't know how I could possibly go through the rest of my life without seeing you. So, the truthful answer is that I just don't know."

Jared walked towards the chair Becky was sitting in, and sat down next to her on a row of brick steps. He picked a daisy from a plant which grew in a flower bed next to the row of bricks on which he was sitting. He reached over, pushed her hair back, and slid the flower onto Becky's right ear. Jared looked at Becky and smiled, as she met his gaze. Jared leaned in and kissed Becky gently on her lips. Becky closed her eyes and returned the kiss. Jared sat up and looked at the tiny, faint freckles on her cheeks.

He tried to memorize every bit of her face. Becky's eyes remained closed, as if she were trying to savor the moment.

"Keep your eyes closed, please, just for a moment. I'll tell you when to open them."

Jared took the cell phone from his pocket, pointed it at Becky, and snapped a picture. The courtyard blocked the direct rays from the sun, so it was just dark enough to set off the automatic flash on the phone. Jared slid the phone back into his pocket, and gave Becky the 'okay' to open her eyes. However, what Jared didn't know was that Becky had peeked. She saw the strange metallic, rectangular object in his hand, and the bright light that flashed like a bolt of lightning. Of course, Becky didn't know what the metallic object was, why he pointed it at her, or what the flash of light was. It made her a bit nervous and uncomfortable, and it added to the mystery surrounding Jared. But, she didn't acknowledge that she had seen any of it.

Becky Miller, July 1776

CHAPTER 25

"I'd like to see the photograph of the earth again, if I may?" asked Washington. "I simply couldn't get the image out of my mind since you showed it to me yesterday." Jared tapped the image on his phone, and handed it to Washington. "Astonishing!" said Washington, a smile on his face. "You indicated you'd explain how this image was crafted,"

"Yes, I will," said Jared, taking the iPhone back from Washington. It was dark in the office as it was pouring outside, and the sky was dark gray. "But, first I have a few other things to show you." Jared scrolled through his photo library until he found a photo of a large airplane. "This is a Boeing 747," said Jared, as he handed the phone back to Washington. "Until recently, it was the largest commercial aircraft in the world, able to carry nearly four hundred passengers across oceans and continents." Jared took the phone and flipped to a photo showing the interior of the 747, with its rows of seats.

"It looks luxurious. I assume only exceedingly wealthy members of society have ever experienced travel by air?"

"No, not at all. Most Americans fly fairly often." Jared then flipped to a video showing a 747 lumbering down a runway. The large jumbo jet made a graceful leap into the air. He handed the phone to Washington, and the look on his face told the story.

"How could something so large fly off the ground?" asked Washington.

"Well," said Jared, "I'm not an expert in the field of aviation or aeronautics, but it has something to do with the shape of the wing. The shape causes air to flow faster over the top of the wing, resulting in less pressure pushing down. Slower air flowing under the wing causes more air pressure underneath, causing great air pressure pushing up. Or, something like that. The 747 has four very powerful engines pushing it forward. The engine pulls in air, it mixes with fuel and it combusts, and then is shot out the back of the engine, pushing the airplane forward. Does that make sense?"

"No, but it hardly matters," said Washington. "Can a vessel that large return to the ground without inflicting too much damage?" Jared flipped to the next video and hit play. He handed the phone back to Washington as a typically flawless landing of a 747 played on the screen. "Magnificent!" said Washington. "What a glorious sight."

"There are thousands of take-offs and landings every day. It's an incredibly safe way to travel. And, even though I've flown hundreds of times in my life, it never really gets old. It's a thrill — most of the time." Jared flipped through the videos until he found the one he was looking for. It showed a Saturn Five moon rocket on a launch pad at Cape Canaveral in Florida.

"This is a rocket. It works in a similar manner to that of a jet engine, but creates many times the amount of thrust and it doesn't rely on the intake of air — it operates by the combustion of its contents."

Jared pressed play, and there was the familiar countdown. Then, the rocket came to life, as the engines roared and smoke came billowing out from beneath the launch pad. Then the umbilical structure detached from the rocket, and fell back onto the service structure, the vertical tower which sat next to the rocket. Finally, the rocket began its slow rise off the launch pad, cleared the tower, and began its familiar roll. Then the rocket began to accelerate, and the television cameras had trouble tracking it smoothly. The rocket continued to rise, and in a blast of controlled fire, the first stage separated and dropped back down to earth.

"Did that vessel explode?" asked Washington.

"No," said Jared, "the rocket used several stages. As one stage consumed all its fuel, it dropped off and landed in the ocean. But, there have been many explosions over the years during the development process of the Manned Space program. Some were quite serious."

Jared took the phone back, and scrolled down to find another video. He pressed play, and handed the phone back to Washington. On the screen appeared a grainy black and white video. It showed the lunar lander flying across the lunar surface as it descended. The accompanying audio was that of the flight control director, as he spewed out various computer readings in a monotone voice. The features of the moon appeared unrecognizable, liked flattened putty. As the LM descended to a few hundred feet above the moon's surface, Washington could make out the shapes of craters and large boulders. Then the LM slowed, and appeared to touch down on the surface of the moon. "Tranquility base here, the Eagle has landed."

"That was Astronaut Neil Armstrong speaking," said Jared. "In the year 1969, he and Buzz Aldrin were the first two humans — Americans — to land on the moon."

"I'm speechless," said Washington. "Humans live on the moon?"

"No, sir. Humans have visited the moon several times, but no one lives there. The environment is quite harsh. No atmosphere, limited gravity. It would be very difficult to live there on a permanent basis."

"Have other countries landed men on the moon?" asked Washington.

"No, actually, only Americans have gone to the moon."

"Remarkable."

Jared pressed the 'home' button on his phone, and the picture closed.

"So what do you think, General? Do you believe that I've traveled here from the future?"

Washington thought for a moment before answering.

"For the life of me, I can't explain the things you've shown me over the past few days. Nor can I explain that device that plays the static image and moving images. As difficult as it is for me to comprehend, I must admit — you being a time traveler seems to me to be as logical as any explanation."

"Thank you, General Washington. Thank you for taking the time to sit with me while I shared these things with you."

"So, what now, John Jared? This process must be leading to something. A statement, a question. What is it you want to say?"

"Yes, General, I have a question I'd like to ask you. However, it's quite complicated. It will take some time to lay out the details. It is important that you understand the context. If it is all right with you, I'd prefer to do that at a later date — perhaps tomorrow?"

"I have to take a ride to the northern end of Manhattan tomorrow to review the terrain of that part of the island. Why don't you join me? I'll be leaving at seven thirty a.m."

Jared and Becky took the short stroll from Beaver Street to the corner of Broad and Pearl Streets. They stood in front of a yellow brick building, which was originally built by Stephen DeLancey as his home. DeLancey's heirs sold the building to Samuel Fraunces in 1762, who converted the home into a popular tavern which he called the Queen's Head.

The air was warm and humid, and the streets were filled with people going about their business. As they walked, Becky tripped and nearly fell to the ground. Jared reached over and caught Becky, but the damage was done. The heel on Becky's shoe had broken, and she was now unable to walk normally.

"Oh, my," said Becky, "I'm afraid I've ruined the evening."

"Not at all," said Jared, as he swooped her up into his arms. Becky let out a laugh, as she looked into Jared's eyes.

"Jared, this is completely improper," she said, pulling her dress hem down to make sure she was well covered."

"Nonsense, the tavern is right here. Let's have dinner and some ale, and we'll worry about your shoe later."

Becky took a deep breath, smiled, and laid her head on Jared's shoulder.

Jared carried Becky up the steps to the entrance to the tap room. The place was loud, with a crowd of men standing around the main bar, and many others sitting at tables. This was a typical scene at the Queen's Head on a Friday during the early evening. When the men in the taproom saw Jared enter with Becky in his arms, the place grew silent. Everything stopped, and everyone stared. Jared stood there for a moment — frozen. Then a man, with a long gray beard and a mug of ale in his hand, stood and took a step towards Jared and Becky.

"She don't look too heavy," said the man, "but if your arms are tired, I'll take her off your hands."

The place broke into laughter. Jared laughed as well, and then he turned and carried Becky down a narrow hallway to the dining room. The room was small, with a fireplace and eight small tables. He pulled out a chair, and gently set Becky down onto it. Then he sat down himself. A waiter walked over, and slapped four mugs of ale down on the table.

"Looks like you'll be needin' these," said the waiter. Then he walked away.

"How did your conversation with Washington go today?" asked Becky.

"It went well. I believe my duties here may be coming to an end. That's what I'd like to talk to you about today."

Becky looked down at the table, and placed her hands in her lap.

"Yes, I suspected that might be the case," she said.

"Becky, I have really developed feelings for you in the short time I've been here. However, things are really complicated."

"You have shared so little about yourself," said Becky. "Is there anything you can share with me to help me understand?"

"I know, and yes, I intend to. But, you need to understand — I promise to be one hundred percent truthful with you, but what I share with you will seem outrageous."

"I don't care," said Becky. "If you are telling the truth, I will accept whatever you tell me."

Jared reached into his breast pocket and withdrew his iPhone. When he turned it on, the phone made a familiar tone sound, and it lit up. The screen saver photo was that of Becky with her eyes closed — the photo he had taken of her with the daisy in the courtyard a few days earlier. Becky was in shock as she looked at the photo.

"This is what's called a photograph. I took it a few days ago when we were in the courtyard. This is called an iPhone. It does many things. People in the year 2000 use it to speak to one another — sometimes at very great distances."

"Are you from the future?" asked Becky.

"I am. I traveled here through a portal that I designed."

"That explains a lot," said Becky. "Are you here to tell General Washington something? Something important? Something, perhaps, that might influence the outcome of the war with England?"

"Actually, I'm here to see if I can take Washington back with me to the year 2018."

Becky sat there for a moment, trying to digest everything she'd heard. Jared sat there silently, wondering if Becky was thinking about the prospect of traveling with him to 2018 as well. Would she want to do that? Would she be open to leaving the world she knew and traveling to the foreign world of 2018? Would she leave her mother alone to run the inn?

"I peeked," said Becky. "When you painted that picture of me on that thing, I just couldn't control my curiosity and I peeked. I saw a flash of light."

"It's called a flash bulb," said Jared. "It comes on automatically when there's not enough natural light."

Jared turned the phone to video mode.

"Say something."

"Can I come with you to 2018?" asked Becky.

Jared directed the phone towards Becky, and pressed the 'play' button.

The video played back: *"Can I come with you to 2018?"* Becky jolted a bit as she watched.

"Is that what my voice sounds like?" asked Becky.

"Yes, it does. Becky, you really need to think about whether that's really a good idea. I do too. You are a product of the 1700's. This is the world you know. You are comfortable here. You need to think about whether you can really be comfortable in a world that will feel so foreign to you. It's crowded, and loud. The streets outside this tavern, in 2018, are filled with cars and buses and there are subways running beneath the ground. The buildings surrounding this tavern are huge, hundreds of feet tall."

"I don't know what any of those things are. Are you comfortable here? You are a product of your time, and now you're here. Are you comfortable?"

"No, actually I'm not comfortable. Except when I'm with you."

He reached out and held her hand.

"Everything is so different," continued Jared. "The way people speak is different. The things you do, how you do it, how things look. It's all so different. And, these are simpler times. I believe going from 2018 to 1776 is far easier than the other way around."

"Are you saying you don't want to be with me?" asked Becky, as she wiped a tear from her cheek.

"No, that's not what I'm saying. Of course I want to be with you. You are the most amazing woman I've ever met in my life. When I go to sleep at night, I am thinking of you, and when I wake up, I'm still thinking of you. But, I'm trying to be realistic."

Jared took a handkerchief from his pocket, and handed it to Becky. The tears came rolling quicker now, and she wiped the tears away.

"Well, I don't want to go with you, John, if you don't want me. I think it's best if I went home now, and I think you should consider finding somewhere else to stay tonight."

"But, your shoe. Let me carry you home."

"No, I'll manage on my own."

Becky removed both of her shoes, got up from her seat and walked out of the dining room. Jared sat there in shock. He immediately felt a huge hole in his heart. He was certain he was looking at the situation the right way. He was, after all, looking out for Becky's best interests. The idea of taking her away from her mother, and dropping her into a foreign world was difficult for him to come to terms with. But, the pain in his heart was real, and the hole in his heart was very large. He decided to sleep on it and see how he felt in the morning.

Jared walked over to Number 1 Broadway, and requested a bed at the mansion for the night. He was assigned a small room on the second floor, which was far more lavish and comfortable than his room at the inn on Beaver Street. Washington sent a man to retrieve his personal belongings from the inn, and Jared did a quick inventory check to ensure that everything was accounted for.

Jared got into bed. As he lay there, unable to sleep, he couldn't stop thinking about Becky. He tried to remind himself that his mission was to retrieve Washington — his task was to save America, not to fall in love with a woman from 1776. He tried to remain focused, and he was determined to get Washington's approval to travel to 2018 with him the following day. The sooner he departed, he believed, the quicker he could get past his feelings for Becky. But, he felt terrible. He was angry at himself for letting things progress as far as they had. He knew the situation, and the hopeless reality that he could never have a long term relationship with her. But, she was innocent, a woman who let her feelings go, unaware that the man beside her was a time traveler. What if she were heartbroken, so much so, that she never got over him? Jared did not want to accept that possibility — it just hurt too much.

CHAPTER 26

Jared slept fitfully, awaking several times throughout the night. Each time he awoke with Becky on his mind. He wished that he had handled things differently with Becky. He hadn't intended on becoming emotionally involved with Becky, it had just happened. As was often the case, his emotions got away from him. If he had thought about it, he would have concluded that getting emotionally involved with a women who lived more than two hundred years in the past, was a bad idea. But, he wasn't thinking. His friendship with Becky began innocently, but then blossomed into a romantic relationship without him even noticing. He wondered if he should have been more upfront about his situation from the beginning. But, could he have been? Could he have shared with Becky, before he had gotten to know her, that he was a time traveler? Perhaps things turned out the only way they could have. It was an impossible situation, one for which, there really was no blueprint. Jared was plowing new ground, so it' was only reasonable to expect that he'd make some mistakes along the way.

In just the four short days that he'd been in 1776, Jared had become quite skilled at estimating the time of day based on the position of the sun. He didn't have an alarm clock in his room at the mansion, so he peeked out the window. It was light outside, so he knew it was approximately six thirty a.m. He fixed his hair in the mirror, put his jacket on, and headed downstairs for a bite to eat. At seven thirty a.m., he headed to the foyer.

The general emerged from his office. "Seven-thirty, right on time, Mr Ross," said Washington. "Well, I suppose we should get going."

Washington and Jared were on their horses. Washington's was a white stallion, while Jared rode a grey mare. They headed north on Broadway until they reached Trinity Church. Then they turned west towards the Western Gate which passed through the wall, so that they could continue their journey north. It was a warm and humid morning. Jared assumed it was around eighty degrees already, and the sun was still low in the sky. Just north of Wall Street, Broadway became the Bloomingdale Road. This narrow path mainly hugged the coastline along the Hudson River, but it meandered a bit around a few low lying hills. Jared was surprised to see how hilly the terrain was. These hills were to be cut down in the coming years, and the earth would be used to fill in the surrounding ponds and marsh lands. It was difficult to determine exactly how far north they had traveled, but Jared estimated they had reached midtown, approximately where the Jacob Javits Center would be located. It is the neighborhood known in 2018 as Hell's Kitchen. "General," said Jared, pointing east, "that's where the Empire State Building stands in my day."

"How tall?" asked Washington.

"One hundred and two stories. Nearly a quarter of a mile up."

"A lot of stairs to climb."

"True, but I prefer to take the elevator," said Jared with a smirk. Washington was about to ask what an elevator was, but he let it go. They stopped at the edge of a small pond, dismounted, and let their horses take a drink of water. It was downright muggy, and Jared could smell his own body odor in the air. He had not changed his clothes in four days. They continued their journey north, and soon he saw the top of a fort emerging from the trees ahead. When they pulled alongside the fort, Jared saw an awesome and commanding view of the Hudson River below.

"Welcome to Fort Washington," said the General. "This is the highest point on the island. And that, across the river, is Fort Lee. From this position, we can target any British ship that attempts to pass north up the Hudson."

Washington and Jared dismounted their horses, and tied their shanks to a nearby tree. They walked towards the river, and found some shade on a large schist slab protruding from the hill under some birch trees. They sat and gazed across the wide river, and watched the construction work being completed on Fort Lee. "Beautiful country," said Washington.

"It is," said Jared. "In my time, there is a bridge here, right in this spot, which spans the river. It carries your name — the George Washington Bridge. It's beautiful and breathtaking. It starts right there, at Jeffrey's Hook, and crosses to what is called Fort Lee, New Jersey."

"A span across the North River?" asked Washington incredulously.

"It's called a suspension bridge. Towers are erected on each side of the river. Huge cables are strung over the towers on each side, across the river. Then a roadway is hung by smaller cables. There's an even longer span across the Narrows."

"A bridge across the Narrows?" said Washington. "How remarkable. I would really like to see how something like that could be accomplished."

"You can, sir" said Jared. "In fact, that is the point of my visit with you."

"You want to show me the engineering feats of the future?"

"Well, not exactly, General. I am here to deliver a message

on behalf of the current Vice President of the United States, David Bashoff, and Senator Janey Logan. You see, America is currently in a perilous state. A dangerous and potentially critical state."

"I see," said Washington, a look of concern on his face. "Please tell me more."

"For years, the two major political parties, the Democrats and Republicans, have grown ever more vicious towards one another. The parties are supposed to represent the attitudes and wishes of their constituents. There are some real fundamental differences in the attitudes of Democrats, who tend to be liberal in their outlook, and Republicans, who are generally conservative. This is the case from both a fiscal perspective, as well as on social issues. For years, this has led to a healthy debate, but now, it has become very personal and quite vicious. The parties do not work together. In fact, they do everything they can to ensure that the party in power will fail. There are special interests, and those interests have taken priority over the interests of the average, hard-working American. Where America used to welcome immigrants seeking freedom and opportunity, the topic has created anger and resentment among many Americans. For generations, the very basis of what America has stood for — the freedom of religion, equal rights for all people, and other social rights, have come under attack. There are two America's and it is tearing the country apart at the seams. Our current President, Harp, is doing everything in his power to drive a wedge between Americans, and he is thriving on the chaos he has created. He has no interest, whatsoever, of uniting the people. He has nearly three more years remaining on his term, and there is a real danger that America, as we know it, won't survive before we have a chance to vote him out."

"But, there must be a process. Laws. A method of dealing with such a situation. Does the Constitution not address such a situation, and how it is dealt with?"

"If laws were broken, then yes, there would be a process to impeach the President. But, he hasn't broken any laws. He has poisoned the minds of many Americans, those who are frustrated with their own situation. He has divided the people, and has destroyed everything that America and Americans stand for. America has long been the most powerful country in the world, and it has always attempted to do good — not just in America, but around the world. We have looked out for our allies, and for people and nations who couldn't fend for themselves. We have taken care of our own people with social programs. We have worked hard to elevate minorities — African Americans, women, Hispanics. America is now a country where the rich and powerful do well, but the average American suffers."

"That is precisely what we are fighting against today," said Washington.

"Exactly, sir. Which is why I am here. We need your help. We need your perspective. We need you to remind all Americans about who we are, where we came from, and what we fought for."

"And how shall I do that?"

"I want you to accompany me to 2018. You can travel with me through the portal. It is completely safe. There is no possibility of any danger. You will spend some time in 2018, and when you return here to 1776, no time will have actually passed. You will arrive back at the precise moment that you left."

"And what will you have me do while I'm in 2018?" asked Washington.

"The plan is to have you address a joint session of congress. We would like you to share your vision for what America stands for. We would like you to share what you and your men are doing right now. The commitment and the selflessness you are all demonstrating. The hope for a new nation and all the things it will stand for."

"And, you believe that will make a difference?"

"Yes, we do. Absolutely. Keep in mind, no one in 2018 knows that we have the technology to travel through time. When Americans see you, they will be shocked and awed. Plus, you won't only be speaking in front of Congress. Virtually every American will be watching at home on their television sets — you will have an audience of three hundred and fifty million Americans — not to mention the millions or perhaps billions who will be watching around the world."

"Around the world?" asked Washington. "They can do that?"

"Oh, yes. It's called satellite technology."

"I would like to help," said Washington. "How could any man, when presented with such a fantastic opportunity, say no? The opportunity to see how the world will look two hundred and forty years from now is incredibly tempting. However, I have the burden of preparing for this war."

"As I said, you will lose no time. When we depart 1776, the clock stops ticking here. When you return, it will be the exact same second as when you left. You will lose no time. No one will know you left. You will have all the time you need to prepare for your next battle."

"And, when do you propose we leave?" asked Washington.

"Today," said Jared.

CHAPTER 27

Jared and Washington rode back down the Bloomingdale Road until they reached Broadway, then through the gates at Wall Street and down to Number 1 Broadway. Jared went to his room and collected his belongings. He made sure all his equipment was securely packed into his satchel. Jared thought about walking over to Beaver Street to say goodbye to Becky. He wanted to. He wanted to see her very much. But, it didn't seem like the right thing to do — it seemed like the selfish thing to do. Why add to the pain? She wanted to return with Jared to 2018, but he was trying to do the right thing on her behalf — whether she understood or not. It would have been easier — less painful — to bring her along and hope that his instincts were wrong. But, that certainly would have been the selfish thing to do. Jared knew, simply by spending four days in 1776, that a leap in time of two hundred plus years was extremely difficult to make. 1776 seemed like a foreign land to him — 2018 would have seemed as alien a world to her as living on Mars.

Washington told his staff he was heading to Brooklyn to check on the construction of Fort Putnam, Fort Box and Fort Greene. They mounted their horses, and headed off towards the Ferry at the foot of Wall Street. Jared tried hard to take a mental photograph of the city. He wanted to remember it all — not just the sights, but the smell and the sound of it. They followed Pearl Street north until they reached Wall Street. There, the ferry man leapt from the wooden crate he was sitting on, and saluted

General Washington.

"A ferry to Brooklyn?" asked the ferryman.

"Yes, please," responded Washington. "For the Corporal and I — and our horses."

"Right away, General."

A large flat-decked ferry was brought up to the dock. This ferry was three times as large as the one that brought Jared across from Brooklyn four days earlier. Two men rowed this ferry. Washington and Jared dismounted their horses, and they led them onto the ferry deck. The ferryman refused to accept the fare from them, and he waved as the ferry shoved off.

Once on the Brooklyn side, the men mounted their horses, and made their way up the Brookland Ferry Road toward the Flatbush Road. As they rode east, Jared realized that the landscape did not seem familiar to him at all. He had been nervous and preoccupied with the task at hand on his way to Manhattan — how he'd pay for the ferry, avoiding unnecessary questions from the locals, the challenge of getting an audience with Washington, and the reality of meeting the man himself. Now that he was in the company of Washington, with nothing to fear, he was determined to take in the entire scene. The small wooden homes that lined the Flatbush Road, the hills and kettles that dotted the landscape, and the farms that went on into the distance for miles. As they ascended a hill along the road, Jared could see the Atlantic Ocean and the barrier beaches to the south, and Long Island as it stretched out for a hundred miles to the east.

A bit of panic set in as Jared realized he couldn't precisely tell where he was. He felt he should be in the vicinity of Mount Prospect, but he wasn't entirely sure. It was just four days ago, but he couldn't decipher the landscape. There were no street signs. There was a painted sign hanging on a tree here or there, but no orderly system of identifying streets or thoroughfares. In 2018, it was pretty clear where Prospect Park was located. If you traveled southeast along Flatbush Avenue from Manhattan, you eventually run right into the Park. You couldn't miss it. But, in 1776, Prospect Park didn't yet exist, and the terrain looked exactly like the rest of the area. He knew it was approximately three miles, or about an hour's walk, but now he was on horseback.

"How far do you think we've traveled on the Flatbush Road?" asked Jared.

"I'd say approximately two and a half miles" said Washington.

"Then we're approaching the spot," said Jared. "It will be up ahead on the right."

Jared thought he recognized the spot where he descended the hill a few days ago, so he led Washington up. But, he quickly realized he had been wrong.

"What are you searching for?" asked Washington.

"There's a hill — Mount Prospect…"

"Mount Prospect, you say?" asked Washington. "I know precisely where that is. It is the highest point on the island."

Washington led Jared to Mount Prospect, about a quarter mile further up the Flatbush Road. They ascended the hill, and when they reached the top, Jared saw the clearing and the tree with the white fabric tied around it. Jared went straight for the tree, and pulled the small hand shovel from his bag. He began to dig. The earth was soft so he made quick progress. When he hit the duffle, he found the strap and pulled the bag out of the ground. He decided he would get the equipment set up, and save the construction of the hoop for last. If someone came across them, they'd have a difficult time explaining what the hoop was.

Jared pulled the laptop from its case and switched it on. But, it didn't turn on.

"Shit!" exclaimed Jared. "The battery is dead! Why didn't I think about that? I never thought about that!"

"Is everything all right?" asked Washington.

"The previous journey's I had taken into the past were just few a few minutes or two. A half hour at most. I never thought about the laptop battery dying, but of course it would never retain its charge over four days."

"So, what can we do?" asked Washington.

"I'll have to charge it with one of my back-up battery packs, but it will take a while. Maybe an hour."

Jared connected the battery pack, and the laptop began to charge. The two men took a seat on the ground under the shade from the Dogwood tree with the white fabric on it. Washington pulled two apples from his satchel, and tossed one to Jared.

"So, tell me, what do you think of 1776?" asked Washington.

"It has been fascinating. I had learned so much about this time period in school. All kids do. It's the most significant period in the history of America. There were no photos, obviously, so my image of everything was based on paintings and sketches. When you learn about history in textbooks, it all seems so flat. But, when you're here, and you see the people and the city, it is a completely different experience."

"And, the people? What do you think of the people?"

"What amazes me is that the people here are so much like the people I know at home," said Jared. "You'll see that as well when we get to 2018. I thought I would feel like such an outsider, but I feel like I fit in pretty well."

"You seemed to hit it off pretty well with the young lady, Becky."

"She is a special person, General. We got very close in a very short period of time, but there is really no opportunity for us to go any further. We're two people separated by 240 years. Talk about a long distance relationship!"

"Could she perhaps join you in 2018?" asked Washington.

Jared checked the laptop, and it had charged to seven percent. Not enough power yet.

"She wanted to," said Jared. "But, I think it would have been a mistake. Sure, that would have been great for me. But, think about her — ripped from her reality and everyone she knows — including her mother. What kind of life would that have been for her? I couldn't do it to her. It would have been too selfish on my part."

"That's too bad," said Washington.

"I know," said Jared. "I feel so…"

Washington interrupted.

"I mean, it's too bad that you don't understand matters of the heart."

"I beg your pardon?" said Jared, surprised.

"I too, once attempted to protect someone I loved from pain," said Washington. "When I met my wife, Martha, she was twenty-seven years old and recently widowed. She had four children. We had grown close, and the next obvious step would have been a proposal and marriage. But, how could I ask this woman to marry me? She had recently dealt with the death of her husband, which she had told me, was extremely painful. Here I was, recently retired from my Virginia Regiment commission, but knowing full well, a lifelong military man such as myself, would not stay away for long. And now here I am, today, the Commanding General of the Continental Army. I am a traitor in the eyes of England, and I will be tried and hanged for treason should we lose this war — which, as of this day, seems quite likely. How could I put the woman I love in this position — to potentially lose another husband?"

"I completely understand your position," said Jared.

"But, I was wrong," said Washington. "She said to me, '*It's not your place, George, to tell me what is good for me. That's my decision to make. I will gladly trade the possibility of heartache, for the possibility of true love.*' And so, we were married. While she does, indeed, worry about my wellbeing, she reminds me every day that she made the right decision."

Jared sat silently for a moment and pondered all Washington had said. Jared may be the first and only man on earth to have received advice about his love life from George Washington.

"I appreciate your words," said Jared. "You may be right, but I'm afraid it may be too late to do anything about it now. Anyway, the laptop is charged to fifty percent. That's more than enough for the trip, so we'd better set up the hoop."

Jared began removing the twelve arched pieces from the duffle, and placed them on the ground. The pieces could be assembled in any order, as long as the power arch, with the laptop connector and slot for the uranium cylinder, was placed at the bottom. When all pieces were in place, Jared connected the cord from the laptop, and he gently slid the cylinder into its slot. Jared wasn't sure why he was so gentle with the cylinder. He was certain it was safe, encased in its lead jacket. But, it contained uranium, so his natural instinct was to treat it very delicately. Washington and Jared lifted the hoop upright, standing it on its large base. Washington tapped Jared on the shoulder, and put his index finger to his lips. Just then, Jared heard it — a sound from the forest of trees to the north. Washington and Jared stood motionless, hoping whoever (or whatever) was responsible for the sound, would turn and go in another direction. No such luck. A man emerged from the forest with a musket in his hands. He walked up to the hoop, his musket aimed at Washington and Jared. "What the bloody hell is this?" exclaimed the man. He looked at Washington and immediately recognized him. "General Washington" said the man, standing at attention and saluting. "My apologies, General."

Washington walked towards the man. "What is your business here, sir?" asked Washington.

"General, I live in the gray house on the Flatbush Road, the one beside the grist mill. There were reports, sir, from a neighbor, of a black bear roaming this hill last night. I came to see if I could locate and kill the bear, sir."

"I see," said Washington. "Do you have loyalist leanings?"

"No sir! I am a patriot. My son, Jacob, fought with the Colonial Troops at Bunker Hill."

"Very well," said Washington.

"What in God's holy name is that thing?" asked the man, pointing to the hoop.

"Your name?" asked Washington.

"Pardon?" asked the man, who was visibly shaken.

"Your name, sir. What might I call you?"

"Patrick McFadden. I go by Paddy."

"Mr McFadden, this is a new weapon, developed in France. It is on loan to us. It is the latest in modern warfare."

"I've never seen anything like it, General. And, what of those flickering candles?" said McFadden, pointing at the lights on the laptop computer.

"Ammunition," said Jared, in a French accent.

"I see," said McFadden, still nervous and ready to leave.

"Mr McFadden," said Washington. "I respectfully ask that

you leave us now, so that we may continue testing our new weapon. Please descend the hill immediately, and please, do not discuss what you saw here today with anyone."

"Of course, sir, you have my word. I will not discuss this with anyone."

When the man was out of sight, Jared opened the program and entered the target date and time. He pressed the enter key, and the hoop began to spin. As the engine revved, the motor let out a high pitched sound. "Are you ready, General?"

"I am."

Jared took Washington's hand. "On the count of three, step with me through the hoop. One, two... three."

CHAPTER 28

…And then suddenly, two men emerged on the other side of the hoop.

For Don Corkoran, it was instantaneous. One second, he was watching Jared step through the hoop, and then shockingly, he saw Jared and another man stepping back through the hoop on the other side.

"*Instantaneous,*" thought Corkoran. He had forgotten. It was absolutely instantaneous on his side. Four and a half days had passed since Jared had left 2018, but no time had passed for Corkoran. "You're back?" asked Corkoran.

"Four days," said Jared. "General Washington, meet Don Corkoran, intelligence expert for Project Lombardi." Corkoran shook Washington's hand, while he stared, in amazement, into the face of the legendary man. Meanwhile, Jared was moving quickly, unplugging the laptop and breaking down the hoop. "Don, a little help here," said Jared. The two men worked quickly as they returned the Pangea apparatus to the duffle. Washington, meanwhile, took in his surroundings. The park appeared manicured as compared to the natural setting of Mount Prospect of the 1700's. He could see the rooftops of buildings over the trees that lined the roads and avenues.

They crossed the open space and descended the granite stairway adjacent to the Brooklyn Public Library to Eastern Parkway. That's when Washington saw a car for the first time. He stopped and watched as several cars passed in both directions.

"Astounding," said Washington. "What makes them go?"

"It's called an internal combustion engine," said Jared. "It's powered by gasoline, which is made from oil. I can show you a demonstration of the engine on the computer when we get to the hotel."

They crossed Eastern Parkway to the North Service Road, where Corkoran's car was parallel parked. Jared opened the back door for Washington, as Corkoran slid into the driver's seat. They wanted Washington in the back seat, protected from view by the darkened windows.

They headed east on Eastern Parkway one block, and made a U-turn at Washington Avenue. Jared turned around to Washington and pointed at the street sign.

"Check out the street sign," said Jared. "That was named after you, General."

"Named after me?" said Washington.

"Oh yes, it's one of probably fifty thousand streets, buildings, bridges, schools, colleges and monuments that have been named after you."

They headed the opposite direction on Eastern Parkway until they reached Grand Army Plaza, swung around the circle, and took Flatbush Avenue north toward Manhattan. Washington was mesmerized by the sights outside his window. He sat silently, taking it all in.

"This is the road we travelled on horseback about an hour ago," said Jared. "It looks pretty different now."

"It certainly does. Where are all the fields?"

"Paved over," said Corkoran.

"That's a large structure," said Washington, as they passed the Barclay Center, home of the NBA's Brooklyn Nets and NHL's New York Islanders.

"That's a sports arena," said Jared. "Sports are a very big deal these days. They play basketball and ice hockey there, and twenty-thousand people come to watch."

Of course, Washington had no idea what those sports were, and couldn't imagine the spectacle which took place inside the building when the Islanders or Nets were playing.

Corkoran pulled out his phone, and dialed Snyder's number.

On Long Island, Snyder and Janey were still being followed by the blue sedan. The driver of the SUV they were in, had headed east on the Southern State Parkway towards Montauk, then took the Meadowbrook Parkway north, got onto the Northern State Parkway heading west back towards New York City, then took the Cross Island Parkway South. He was now approaching the Southern State Parkway east again. The result was a big circle — or, more correctly, a large rectangle — about twenty miles around the entire circuit. The blue sedan had been right behind them the whole way. Janey and Snyder were baffled by the presence of the blue sedan. Who were these people, and why were they following them? What was their goal? It seemed that they were just trying to keep their eyes on them. They had made no attempt to stop the SUV. They just seemed to want to know where the occupants of the SUV were going.

Snyder's cell phone buzzed.

"Hello, Charles Snyder here."

"Snyder, it's Corkoran. How's everything going?"

"We're driving in circles on the highways of Long Island. Boring as hell, but the blue sedan is still following us. We don't want to lead them to Prospect Park. We're not sure what to do. I'm assuming Jared is gone."

"Yup, gone and back."

"Back?" said Snyder. "Holy crap that's right — instantaneous! Is Washington here?"

"Yes, here's here, sitting in the back seat of my car right now. We're heading to the hotel. You should head to the city and meet us there now."

"But, what about the blue sedan?" asked Snyder.

"He can follow you to the hotel, but he can't follow you up to the room. I don't see it being a problem."

Corkoran suddenly heard a loud bang, then heard the cell phone drop from Snyder's hand mid-sentence.

"You okay?" asked Corkoran. There was no answer.

The blue sedan had rear-ended the car Snyder was riding in as they circled around the exit ramp getting back onto the Southern State Parkway West. The SUV had been hit on the left rear side, so that they skidded slightly to the right, but not far enough to hit the concrete barricade.

"The blue sedan just rear-ended us," said Snyder. "We're okay, just a bit shaken. "He's still back there. Not sure what he's trying to accomplish, but our car is still drivable."

"I think he's just trying to scare you," said Corkoran. He may be angry that you're leading him in circles. Don't stop. Drive straight to Manhattan now. We'll meet you at the hotel."

As Corkoran, Jared and Washington approached the ramp at the Manhattan Bridge, Washington shuddered. As they crossed the span, Washington looked to his right and saw the Williamsburg Bridge, and looked to his left and saw the Brooklyn Bridge.

"Three bridges?" asked Washington incredulously.

"There's a need for it. Eight million people live in the city of New York."

They headed north on FDR Drive, and turned west on 48th

Street. When they reached Park Avenue, they turned right and pulled up in front of the Waldorf Astoria. Jared and Washington headed inside, while Corkoran waited for the valet to take the car.

As they passed through the lobby, Washington received several strange looks from people who noticed his strange attire. If anyone had asked, Jared was prepared to say that they were shooting a commercial for next week's 4th of July celebration.

"This is an elevator," said Jared quietly, as they waited at the elevator bank.

Washington was surprised by the sensation of rising in the elevator, and he felt a slight discomfort in his stomach. Once at the suite, Jared used his card key to enter.

"The door is locked," said Jared. "This magnetic key opens the door."

It suddenly occurred to Jared just how many technological innovations he used in his life on a daily basis. Not all innovations were revolutionary, however, everything was new and interesting to Washington. Jared enjoyed watching Washington marvel at things that seemed common place. Jared took the time to explain as many things to Washington as he could.

"May I try that?" asked Washington.

Jared handed the card key to Washington. He placed the key in the slot and slowly removed it. The green light did not illuminate, nor did the door open.

"This is a magnetic strip," said Jared. "You have to line it up with this dot on the lock. And, you have to pull the card out a little quicker. You'll get the hang of it."

Jared also realized there were so many details we take for granted, like using a card key to open a door. It's not difficult to do it correctly, but it does take a bit of practice.

Once inside, they saw the large suite, which was impeccably decorated in a "modern" traditional style. The suite featured three bedrooms, two bathrooms, and a large living area with a long dinner/conference table.

Washington walked to the window in the living area, and peeked out. From their perch on the forty-second floor, Washington could see many of Manhattan's famous landmarks. The corner suite faced Park Avenue on one side, and faced north on the other side. Looking left, he saw the hundred and two storey Empire State building, looking straight ahead, he saw the seventy storey 30 Rockefeller Plaza, and looking north, he could see a portion of Central Park, with its sharp perimeter edges and interior greenery.

There was a knock on the door. Corkoran entered the room and looked around the suite.

"This should do," he said. "Anyone hungry for lunch? Let's order something."

Corkoran flipped on the TV, and sat down on the couch. Washington sat down as well, and Jared handed him the room service menu. Washington flipped through the menu options.

"I can't make sense of this," said Washington.

"Do you like pizza?" asked Corkoran.

"I'm sorry, but I don't know what pizza is," said Washington.

"You'll love it," said Corkoran. "Everyone loves pizza, and New York pizza is the best in the world. Let's get a couple of pies — Snyder and Janey will be here soon."

The television was tuned to CNN. The scene on the TV showed a huge gathering of people in Pittsburgh, Pennsylvania. The CNN commentator was reporting from the site of the rally.

"...*people here are angry. These are good, hard-working Americans. Their lives were changed for the better eight years*

179

ago when Affordable Health Care was the law of the land. Now, with the Harp Administration's all-out effort to repeal those laws, these people are looking at a bleak future. From Pittsburgh, Pennsylvania, I'm Janet Rigazzio, reporting for CNN."

"This is what I was talking about, General," said Jared. "President Harp is making a concerted effort to rewind all the social progress this nation has made over the past one hundred years. The cost of quality healthcare in this country is astronomical. People simply can't afford it. As a result, many people have stopped going to the doctor when they need to, and the results have been disastrous. It eliminates the benefits of early detection for many diseases. People suffer immeasurably, often times, when modern medicine has the ability to cure people."

"You think my presence here can help undo the bad that this man is doing?'

"Yes, we do," said Jared. "You are the wake-up call the people of this nation needs right now. We, as a people, have forgotten that this is a nation of the people, by the people, and for the people. The job of our leaders in government is to represent us. People have the power to enact change."

CHAPTER 29

"The situation room?" asked Vice President Bashoff.

"I think privacy would be best, wouldn't you agree, David?" asked President Harp.

The situation room is a five thousand square foot conference room located in the basement of the West Wing of the White House. The room has heavy oak paneling, a long oak conference table, and thick leather chairs. Harp and Bashoff sat across from one another at one end of the table.

"So, what are you up to, David?" asked Harp.

""I'm not up to anything."

"So, what are we talking about?" asked Harp.

"I wanted to fill you in on something that has come to my attention," said Bashoff. "I believe it's something you really want to know about."

"If you're talking about the break-in at JPL, I already know about it. Donahue is on it. We have surveillance video from inside the storage room. You had better not be involved, David. That's Federal property."

"Slow down, let me explain," said Bashoff. "Of course I'm not involved. First, it wasn't a break-in. It was a routine inspection, and during the course of the inspection, something was removed from the room."

"Call it what you will. The surveillance video clearly shows a very well-coordinated heist."

"Ron, I wasn't involved," said Bashoff, angrily. "About a

month and a half ago, I was contacted through a mutual acquaintance …"

"Senator Logan?" guessed Harp.

"Yes, Janey. She said the kid who invented the Pangea portal had a plan. He's a bright kid, obviously. He's a good American — he loves this country. Yes, he's angry and frustrated, just like the rest of the good people…"

"Oh, give me a break, David," said Harp. "There you go again with your whining and belly-aching. You watch too much cable news. America is fine. The good people voted for us based on our platform and the promises we made. We are delivering on our promises to the people who voted for us. This is the America they want. The America they want for their kids."

"Come on, Ron. I really don't want to get into that now. There's no point. You know how I feel."

"Yes I do."

"The country is in a state of mayhem. You know that. You see that. You must. Every day there's another huge protest, another complaint, another incident. This country is divided and it's literally tearing apart."

"I don't see it that way at all," said Harp. "I see this as a period of correction. The pendulum had swung, under the previous administration, so far to the left, it needed to swing back. Yes, there will always be people who are unhappy. Conservatives were unhappy for eight years. Now, Liberals are unhappy. That's the way it goes. It's the way it has always been."

"I don't agree," said Bashoff. "Things are so bad right now — it's not just a philosophical issue. People are suffering. Minorities are being abused. Immigrants are being deported. The poor are dying without access to healthcare. This is not a correction, it's a disgrace. It's shameful."

Harp threw up his hands as if to say, 'You're full of it'.

"So what's the connection to the JPL break-in?" asked Harp.

"There was no conspiracy. I told you. The kid devised the plan on his own. It's pretty far out there, to tell you the truth. I told him I wouldn't get involved."

"But, you were aware of it, and you did nothing. A Federal crime was committed — you are involved!"

"You can't prove that, Ron, and the kid has my back."

"Okay, okay. What's his plan, for God's sake?"

"He did it!" said Bashoff

"He did what?" asked Harp, obviously confused.

"Think about it. This kid invented a time portal. He goes to JPL to retrieve it. He had a plan. He wanted to help put a bandage on this broken nation that he loves. He wants to help the country unite and heal."

"I'm losing my patience, David. What did the kid do?"

"Some conditions first," said Bashoff.

"No way. I won't agree to conditions."

"Have it your way," said Bashoff. "But, that's a big mistake. You're going to be blindsided — beginning tomorrow."

"Are we on opposite teams?" asked Harp.

"Yes we are. Don't act so surprised. You know I'm not onboard with your agenda. I haven't been since we won the election. I was blindsided by you, just like the rest of the American people were. I will not do anything to hurt this country, but if over the next few days, as this thing plays out, I have an opportunity to extricate myself from the insanity of this administration, I'm gone. You can count on that."

Now Harp was concerned. He was convinced Bashoff was not bluffing. Whatever it was, it must be big.

"What are your terms?" asked Harp.

183

"You will not seek to prosecute. Not the kid, not me, nor anyone else you feel — correctly or incorrectly — was involved in the plan. Also, we'll need you to approve Secret Service support."

"The Secret Service?" asked Harp. "Why?"

"You'll understand if you agree to the terms," said Bashoff.

Bashoff slid a piece of paper across the table, and handed Harp his pen to sign. He knew this document wasn't worth the paper it was printed on, but it was symbolic. Harp signed, and slid the document back across the table. Harp leaned forward in his chair and stared at Bashoff with an unamused look on his face, as if to say, 'Okay, talk'.

"George Washington is in New York City, right now, as we speak."

"Fuck!" said Harp.

"Tomorrow, Tuesday, we're having a press conference in New York to let the American people know that, through the miracle of science, George Washington is here. We will share a basic overview of Pangea, while protecting all pertinent details. On Thursday, Washington will address Congress, and the event will be televised across the country and around the world. It will likely be the most watched television event in history."

"No one will believe it. No one will believe it's actually Washington. It's a conspiracy theorist's dream."

"We got that covered," said Bashoff. "I can't tell you how, but we will be able to demonstrate, beyond any doubt, that it is George Washington."

"But, you can't do this. He was brought here illegally..."

"That may be, but he's here. The ball is rolling now, and it can't be stopped. Not by me, not by you." The President took a water glass, and threw it at the oak paneled wall across the table, missing Bashoff's head by a mere few inches. The glass splintered into a thousand tiny pieces. His face was red, and his upper lip was quivering. Harp felt like a caged animal. Harp was a man who was used to getting his way. Since he was elected President, he very rarely heard the word 'no'. Everyone said yes to him, except, of course, certain members of Congress who were sitting on the other side of the aisle.

"And, what are you hoping to accomplish?" asked Harp.

"You mean, what does the kid hope to accomplish? He hopes Washington, who was a mere few weeks away from engaging the British in the Battle of Long Island when he came here, will be able to share his vision for America — the vision that the founding fathers wanted for this nation, and what they felt it should stand for. He wants them to recognize the vast difference between that ideal, and the nation we have become under your administration. He wants them to yearn for that vison of America, where every man or woman can succeed, regardless of race, creed or religion. He wants them to understand that America has, and still can, stand for goodness and compassion for our neighbors."

"You make me sick, David. The man I knew, the politician you were, was not this bleeding heart liberal. You got to where you are, by being cold hearted and ruthless — same as any successful politician. Now you're a two-faced, weak traitor. A traitor to your party, a traitor to me. Go fuck yourself, David. The plan is a joke."

"We'll see", said Bashoff. "Now pick up the phone and call the Secret Service. We need to protect General Washington at all costs."

CHAPTER 30

Jared jumped off the couch in the Waldorf Suite to answer the door. Waiting in the hall with wide smiles from ear to ear were Snyder and Janey.

"Is he really here?" asked Snyder.

"He is," said Jared. "He's in the bedroom trying on clothes. Corkoran's here too."

Corkoran heard his name called, so he walked into the main living area of the suite.

"Washington is in the house," said Corkoran, pointing at the bedroom door.

Jared knocked on the door of the bedroom Washington was in.

"General Washington?" said Jared.

"Please, come in," said Washington.

The Lombardi Team had arranged to have clothes delivered to the suite, so that Washington could change and be comfortable. The plan was to have him wear twenty-first century appropriate clothing during his stay, so that he wouldn't stand out as much in public. His eighteenth century garb would be reserved for official public events only.

Jared opened the door and was immediately in shock. Washington was standing in the middle of the room, completely naked. His 1776 clothes were in a pile on the floor, and stacks of 2018 clothes, wrapped in clear plastic, were on the bed.

"My apologies for the dreadful sight I must be, but I'm not

familiar with the proper way to wear these garments."

Jared slipped into the room, and closed the door behind him, leaving Snyder and Janey in the hall outside. Jared helped Washington into his underwear, tan khaki pants, and light blue polo shirt. He wore comfortable black loafers on his feet. If not for his long powdered hair, you'd have easily mistaken Washington for your best friend's grandfather. Washington walked to the full length mirror on the wall next to the bathroom door, and he looked at himself. He turned sideways, then turned around and peered over his shoulder at his reflection. Then he faced the mirror again.

"Amazing!" he exclaimed. "I hardly recognize myself."

"Are you comfortable, does everything fit right?' asked Jared.

"Fine. The shoes are particularly comfortable. But, I must say, going outside in public wearing these garments does not sit well."

"You look wonderful," said Jared. "Come with me, please. There are a couple of people I'd like you to meet. They are very, very excited to meet you."

Washington and Jared walked out into the main living area. Janey and Snyder did a double take at first, not expecting to see Washington in casual khaki's and a polo shirt. Then, realizing it was him, they rushed up to him to say hello.

Snyder shook his hand.

"General Washington, I am honored to meet you, sir. My name is Charles Snyder, and I am a Professor of History at Princeton University."

"The honor is all mine," said Washington. "Are you referring to the College of New Jersey, located near the township of Stony Brook in the New Jersey colony, Mr Snyder?"

"Yes, that is correct. The University was renamed Princeton University in 1896." A tear of emotion rolled down Snyder's cheek. Next, Janey reached out to shake Washington's hand.

"General Washington, my name is Senator Jane Logan. I represent the great state of Connecticut."

"A female Senator from Connecticut?" said Washington. "I am pleasantly surprised to know that women participate in the process of government in America."

"Indeed they do," said Snyder. "We almost elected a woman President in the last election. It was quite close, but unfortunately for this country, that effort fell short. Had the other side won the election, we likely would have avoided the need to bring you here.""

"I see," said Washington. "Jared shared the details of the current state of affairs in America with me. Do you agree with his assessment that the country is in a dire position?"

"I do," said Snyder. "The current administration seems to be doing everything in its power to divide the people. There are inherent differences in attitudes among conservatives and liberals. For years, the two ideological sides were able to co-exist, and could even find common ground. But, no longer. This administration is pitting one side against the other. It's a dangerous situation. People are suffering — the country is not operating properly. People are really angry and they are divided — and it's getting worse by the day. The government isn't working, it's broken. We are not serving the people as we were elected to do. I'm afraid things will continue to spiral downward, and might lead to a civil war."

"That certainly is disturbing," said Washington. "Do you agree with Jared, as well, that my presence here could improve the situation?"

"I do," said Snyder. "I think the people of this country have lost perspective. Politics should not be about winning or losing. It's become a sporting event for many people. Our side versus your side. We win, you lose. We beat you. That's not what America should be about. It's about creating a system under which everyone is treated fairly and given an equal opportunity to succeed. I have no idea why President Harp and his administration want to divide the people of this country. What is his end goal? I have no idea. But, I do think you will be able to remind people what America is meant to stand for."

"I am happy and willing to do my part," said Washington.

There was a knock on the door, so Corkoran went to answer it. There were two large men standing in the hallway wearing navy suits.

"Secret Service, I presume," said Corkoran.

"I'm Agent Franco," said the taller and thinner, dark haired man. "This is Agent Erdmann," he said, pointing to the shorter, squatter blonde haired man.

"Pleased to meet you both," said Corkoran. "We're ready to head out — I'll let everyone know you're here."

Washington, Snyder, Jared and the two Secret Service Agents headed to the elevator, down to the lobby, and out the main entrance onto Park Avenue. A large, black customized Mercedes Sprinter van was parked right out front, and when the driver saw the group coming, he jumped out and opened the passenger doors.

"I'd enjoy a walk if that is possible," said Washington.

Corkoran looked back at agent Franco who shook his head 'no'.

"I'm afraid it's just too far, General," said Corkoran. "We'll be late for the meeting. We can take a walk later today or tomorrow so that you can see the city."

The Sprinter wove its way through city traffic, and pulled up in front of the Morgan Library, located on 36th Street between Park and Madison. The building was built to house the private library of J.P. Morgan in 1906. The library was designed by Charles McKim, of the famed architectural firm of McKim, Mead and White, and cost $1.2 million to build.

The library is open to the public, but it closed early on this day due to an appointment with a very, very special guest. They entered through the rotunda, where they were met by a small man, who pulled a large case on wheels behind him. He appeared to be about seventy years old. He had thinning gray hair which he combed over his head from ear to ear, and thick black glasses. He wore a black suit and a burgundy bow tie.

"My name is Malcom Moore. I'm Deputy Curator with the Morgan Library. Please follow me."

The group followed the small man to the right, and into Mr Morgan's Library. The Library is by far the largest and grandest of the rooms in the main building. The walls reach a height of thirty feet, and are lined floor to ceiling with triple tiers of bookcases made of bronze and inlaid walnut. Two staircases, concealed behind bookcases at the corners of the room, provide access to the balconies above. A pair of casement windows, incorporating fragments of stained glass, provide natural light from the north. The mantelpiece on the east wall of the Library is carved of Istrian marble in the Renaissance style.

Once in the library, the small man pulled his large black case to the center of the room where he set it upright, and opened it.

"Good afternoon," said another man, as he entered the library from the rotunda. "My name is Jonathan Lee. I am a forensic science specialist with Columbia University."

"Nice to meet you, I'm Charles Snyder. We spoke on the phone. Please, let me introduce you to Jared Ross, Don Corkoran, and this is General Washington."

Snyder didn't bother introducing the Secret Service Agents who stood at the entryway to the Library.

"Ah, yes," said Jonathan Lee, as he looked at Washington's face — first his forehead, then his nose, then the right cheek, and finally the left cheek.

Malcom Moore removed the object from the large black case, and placed it on a podium in the middle of the room. Jonathan Lee removed a package of metal instruments from a leather case, and laid them out on the podium. He asked Washington to sit on a stool, which was positioned next to the podium. Then he went to an HD camera, which was set up on a pedestal, and turned it on. He faced the camera and began to speak.

"My name is Jonathan Lee. I am a forensic specialist with Columbia University in New York City. Today is Monday, July 9th, 2018." He looked at his watch. "It is 3.41 p.m., and I am here to examine General George Washington. I have been asked to confirm his identity by comparing the specifics of his facial features, to those of a life mask which was produced in 1785 by the French sculptor Jean-Antoine Houdon, when he visited George Washington at his Mount Vernon residence. The mask he produced, known as the Morgan life mask, is here today at the Morgan Library in New York City."

Lee proceeded to use a variety of instruments to take precise measurements of Washington's face, and then marked notations on a form which sat on the podium. Length of the nose, width, distance from eye to eye, brow ridge to nose tip. Nose tip to chin.

Nostril to nostril.

All the while, Washington sat there stern faced, and didn't say a word. Malcom Moore showed up with a tray of bottled water, he asked Washington if he'd like some, and the General just waved him off. There were more than one hundred and fifty measurements. Then Lee took the same measurements from the life mask.

When Lee was finished, he looked up at Snyder and said, "I never like to say a hundred percent, but in this case, I'm willing to say it."

Then Lee turned off the video camera.

CHAPTER 31

A Media Alert was blasted out to thousands of media outlets, announcing a press conference at Federal Hall in lower Manhattan. The press conference was set for ten a.m., and credentials were offered on a first come, first served basis. A pool feed was set up, so that media outlets who were interested in distributing a live video feed from the event, could pull it down from a satellite. The Media Alert was extremely vague, mentioning that "an event of historic proportions" would be announced. The announcement was printed on letterhead from the Vice President of the United States of America. There was a frenzy of interest as news outlets began speculating on the nature of the announcement. Plans were made, from news outlets around the world, to converge immediately on New York City in order to have their personnel present live on site in lower Manhattan. Those who couldn't attend in person, made arrangements to tap into the satellite feed which was being made available.

The original Federal Hall was built in 1700 as New York's City Hall. It later served as the first capitol building of the United States of America under the Constitution, as well as the site of George Washington's inauguration as the first President of the United States. It was also where the United States Bill of Rights was introduced in the First Congress. The building was demolished in 1812.

The current building is known as Federal Hall National

Memorial. It opened in 1842 as the United States Custom House, on the site of the old Federal Hall, and later served as a sub-Treasury building. It is now operated by the National Park Service as a national memorial commemorating the historic events that occurred on the site.

At precisely ten a.m., Vice President Bashoff entered the rotunda from behind a curtain, and he stepped to the podium. There were approximately two hundred media personnel in seats arranged from one side of the rotunda to the other, in front of the podium. Behind the last row of seats, approximately two hundred more cameramen were manning their cameras on tripods, some set on makeshift, temporary platforms in order to get an unobstructed view of the Vice President.

In the audience were Jared, Snyder, Corkoran and Janey. Washington was back at the Waldorf with his Secret Service watch dogs.

Bashoff began:

"Thank you to everyone for coming. What I'm going to share with you today is both stunning and exciting. As I stand here at this podium, I, myself, still cannot believe the details of what I'm about to share with you.

"About ten years ago, a very bright engineer at JPL in California accidentally stumbled upon a technology, which allows humans to travel back in time. He was, at the time, working on producing an artificial gravity generator, when he discovered that his apparatus actually provided humans with the ability to time travel. He presented his discovery first to his superiors at JPL, who then presented the technology to senior members of the United States government. After reviewing the technology, government officials determined that the potential for disastrous results and outcomes, were we to use the

194

technology, was just too great a risk. Therefore, the portal apparatus and the technology were packed away in storage, and for the most part, it has been forgotten for the past ten years.

"This brilliant and industrious young man, who is with us here today, obviously did not forget about it. He was disappointed, of course, that his discovery had never been shared with the general public, or used in some way to advance our understanding of science and history. But, he accepted it — our understanding of the impact of time travel on history is an unknown, and the human race could not take a chance testing and perhaps impacting history as we know it, in terrible and risky ways.

"This young man is a proud American, and he, like so many others across this nation, has grown worried and frustrated about the current state of the United States and our future. He is worried that the issues that divide us so vehemently, will break the nation apart. This man decided to take matters into his own hands. Without the knowledge of anyone in the U.S. government, he assembled the time travel portal that he had invented ten years earlier, and he successfully travelled back in time to the year 1776. Once there, he approached General George Washington, spent days convincing him of his identity, and convinced the General that the United States of America, was in dire trouble. General Washington agreed to travel with this young man back to 2018."

A buzz of chatter engulfed the room. Everything they had just heard was so surreal. It was too much for them comprehend — this crazy story must be a hoax. But, why then, was Vice President Bashoff up there behind the podium telling the world this insane story? No one knew what to make of it.

"Please, please," said Bashoff. *"I know how this all sounds. But, I am here to tell you it is the truth. In a moment, I will introduce a forensic scientist who will tell you how he confirmed the identity of General Washington.*

"On Thursday, General Washington will address the American people from the U.S. Capitol in Washington, DC, with the hopes that he can help restore confidence to the American people as we navigate this difficult time in our nation's history. He will remind the people of the United States of the principles under which this nation was founded. And hopefully, he will be able to convince all of us that our best and brightest days are still ahead of us. His address will be televised in primetime, to households across America, and throughout the world. At this time, I would like to introduce Jonathan Lee, a forensic scientist from Columbia University here in New York City."

Lee stepped to the podium, and proceeded to explain his methodology for confirming Washington's identity. He explained the origin of the Morgan Life Mask of George Washington. He then stepped aside, and played the video from his examination from the day before at the Morgan Library. This was the first time members of the audience saw Washington, albeit on video tape, and a loud gasp echoed across the room.

"In my line of work, I am used to a certain number of inconsistencies in my examinations," said Lee. *"But, during this examination, there were none. Let me say that again, I took more than one hundred and fifty measurements, and there were no inconsistencies. Therefore, I must conclude, with absolute certainty, that the man that I examined at the Morgan Library*

yesterday was indeed the same man from whom the life mask was produced. And that man, is General George Washington."

The crowd gasped again. Lee stepped down from the podium, and returned to his seat in the first row. Vice President Bashoff returned to the podium.

"For those of us who knew about the existence of the time travel portal, and mankind's ability to travel through time, these recent events are still very difficult to comprehend and accept. However, we know, beyond any doubt, that it is indeed true. There will be skeptics, there always are. There will be conspiracy theorists. But, I am here to tell you that George Washington is here in New York City, in the year 2018. I can tell you that he is fascinated by what seems to him to be an alien world. However, he is excited to address the American people, and to do whatever he can, to get the country back on the right track.

"Please make time in your schedule to tune in on Thursday night to watch his address to the nation. As of today, I can tell you that all local stations and national news networks will carry the address. I wouldn't be surprised if, between now and Thursday evening, all television outlets — up and down the dial — elect to carry the address live. It will be an evening of truly historic proportions, and I'm certain you will find it interesting and hopefully uplifting. Thank you."

Bashoff stepped away from the podium, and disappeared behind the curtain. The room was stunned. Reporters in the back of the room turned to their cameras and began discussing what they'd just heard. It was science fiction! The Vice President may have well just informed everyone that aliens from outer space just landed on Earth and intended to blow it up. How could any intelligent person on this Earth believe the crazy story they were just told?

Back at the Waldorf, George Washington turned off the television set. He sat and thought about what he had just watched. It began to settle into his mind that he had a big task in front of him, and he started to worry whether he would be up to the task.

In Washington, DC, President Harp turned off the television in the Oval Office. He turned to Mark Donahue, Deputy Director of the FBI, who was sitting on the other side of the desk, and who had watched the address with the President.

"Mark, you need to find out what Washington is going to say."

"But, how?" asked Donahue.

"They must be writing a speech for him to deliver," said the President. "Find the speech. It could be dangerous. I don't want to be blindsided on this."

CHAPTER 32

Janey and Jared stood, and began walking to the back exit of Federal Hall.

"I can't believe we have gotten this far!" said Janey, a huge smile on her face.

Jared didn't respond. He just kept walking.

"Are you okay?" asked Janey. "You haven't said more than five words to me since you got back."

"I'm fine," he said. "I just have a lot on my mind."

"Want to get a bottle of Champagne, get a room, and celebrate?" she asked, grabbing for Jared's hand.

Jared pulled his hand away.

"Janey, we need to talk. Let's grab a cup of coffee."

They headed west on Wall Street towards Trinity Church, and turned right onto Broadway. Jared was distracted, thinking about and remembering what this intersection looked like in 1776. Of course, it was the first Trinity Church which stood on this spot. And, he and Washington had to pass through a gate in the wall in order to pass north. Jared and Janey walked north one block to Pine Street, and found a Starbucks on the corner. They ordered their coffees, and took a seat at the window overlooking Broadway. "So, what's going on?" asked Janey.

"I've had some time to think while I was away. Remember, for me it was four full days."

"And, what?"

"And, I just don't feel right about us," said Jared."

"What are you talking about, it's been great," said Janey.

"No it hasn't. Getting back together was exciting, and I got caught up in it. When you called that night, it felt amazing."

"Right, it was amazing."

"It was exciting" said Jared. "The idea of you coming back to me. I really thought I wanted that. And, the idea of getting involved in this project with you was exciting. For years, after you left me, I felt that my life had no purpose. Then suddenly, all this. You. The Lombardi Project."

"Jared, this can be our future. You and me. Working together. Doing good for America." Jared took a sip of his coffee, which in truth, he didn't really like at all. He stood up, walked to a nearby trash can and dumped his still-full coffee cup out.

"What was that?" asked Janey.

"I don't like coffee. I'm done pretending I'm things that I'm not. Janey, we are not right for each other."

"Bullshit," said Janey. "We're perfect for each other."

"No, we're not. I know that now. We never were."

"And, how do you suddenly know this?" asked Janey.

"I met someone. Not that way, it's not what you're thinking. She's a friend, but she taught me a lot about who I am, and what type of woman I want in my life."

"And, what is your friend's name?"

"Becky" said Jared. "Her name is Becky."

Janey sat for a second while she thought. "By any chance, is Becky from 1776?" she asked. Jared felt a bit embarrassed. The way Janey asked the question made Jared feel uncomfortable.

"Yes, she is. So what?"

"Jared, you're way too wrapped up in this. You live in 2018. Becky lives — she lived in 1776. She's dead. Move on. I'm right here."

She was right, of course. As he sat there, in that Starbucks, Becky had been dead for more than two hundred years. As people often do in 2018, Jared multi tasked and glanced at his iPhone. "Oh shit" said Jared.

"What?" asked Janey.

"Harp is addressing the nation from the Oval Office tonight."

"Five, four, three, two one…"

"My fellow Americans," said President Harp, *"I am speaking to you from the White House tonight because I feel compelled to address the press conference which Vice President Bashoff participated in earlier this morning. I have been in office as your President for two years now. As President, I am informed about, and am kept up to speed on, any and all national security matters. I can assure you, beyond any doubt, that the time travel portal, of which Vice President Bashoff spoke, does not now, nor has it ever existed. If it had existed, I would have been made aware of its existence. The far-fetched story of which he spoke — was just that, a far-fetched story. As I sit here tonight speaking to you, I do not know if the Vice President is part of an effort to fool the American people, or if he is a victim who, himself, has been fooled. In either case, please accept my assurance that America is not in possession of a time travel portal, nor is George Washington, a man who lived two hundred and forty years ago, in New York City today. It is simply an extravagant hoax, perpetrated by someone, or perhaps some group, for unknown reasons. I commit to all of you tonight, to keep everyone in this great nation apprised of all details as this story plays out. God bless you all, and God bless the United States of America."*

President Harp ascended the stairs at the White House, heading to his bedroom. He thought about his speech, the one that he just gave, and he knew it was all a desperate lie. He'd been in this game a long time, and he knew things were beginning to unravel. He was now lying in order to cover up other lies. He knew there'd be many who might go on the record confirming that Pangea did in fact exist, and that the President was indeed briefed on the project, and that he knew the status of Pangea. Things were beginning to go very poorly for the Harp administration, and he knew it.

When he entered his bedroom, the First Lady, Angelica Harp, was lying in bed reading a magazine. She put the magazine down and addressed her husband.

"That was awful," said the First Lady. "You looked like a desperate man."

Harp sat down on the end of the bed, and began removing his shoes and socks.

"Well, honey, that's because I am a desperate man."

"How did you let this happen, Ronald? I told you when you asked me to marry you that I wanted to be the First Lady. You assured me that I would be."

"And, you are!" said Harp, raising his voice as he stood to remove his shirt and slacks.

"But, we are the laughing stock of Washington," she said, sobbing. "People are laughing at us behind our backs. In front of our backs, too. We're a disgrace. You're a disgrace, Ronald. How did you let this happen?"

Harp was standing in nothing but his boxers.

"I don't know," said Harp, suddenly deep in thought. "It just spiraled out of control. Things were going great at first. All those people, the ones who hated the status quo, the ones who hated political correctness. They loved my style and they loved what I stood for. I was brash and arrogant, and I said what was on my mind. I said all of the things that were on everyone's minds. But, I was wrong. Everyone didn't feel that way. It was just a small subset of people, a fringe element. Yes, they were vocal, and they came out to vote. But, they were a fringe group. It went too far, I didn't see it at the time, but I see it now."

"Now we're a joke, Ronald. You're going to be impeached. They are saying so on the news channels. They hate you."

Harp walked to his side of the bed, and lifted the cover.

"Get out!" said Angelica. "I can't even look at you. You've ruined my life!"

"I've ruined your life?" said Harp. "You are First Lady of the United States of America! You are living in the White House. You think you would have been better off if you were still living in the Czech Republic?"

"I beg your pardon? I was already living here when you met me. I was a successful model, and I had a great career. I was dating athletes who make more money than you do."

"Yes, but I'm the President."

"You *were* the President. It's over, Ronald. And you're an old, flabby loser. Get out of my room!"

"This is my room, Angelica. And, I'm not flabby. I work out every morning. Trust me, I look damned good for my age!"

"Well, I can't stand you."

"Angelica, I know we've had our issues. All married couples do. But, I really need your support now."

"Forget it," said Angelica. "You can't fix this, Ronny. It's too late. You're going to be impeached, and when that happens, I want a divorce."

Harp put his slippers on, grabbed a pillow from the bed, and walked to the door. He looked back at the bed as Angelica rolled over, and pulled the cover securely over her body. Then he stepped out into the hall, and pulled the door closed behind him.

CHAPTER 33

The Mercedes Sprinter was waiting at the curb outside the Waldorf at seven o'clock on Wednesday morning. Agent Franco sat in the passenger seat, Washington, Snyder, and Agent Erdmann in the middle row, and Corkoran and Jared in the back row. The van headed up the West Side Highway to the George Washington Bridge into New Jersey, then up the Palisades Parkway until they reached West Point.

They arrived at campus along Thayer Road, stayed right onto Cullum Road, and passed under Mahan Hall. They emerged in the heart of the campus, where they had a magnificent view of the Hudson River, Duck Island, and the athletic fields on their left.

"This is The United States Military Academy at West Point," said Snyder. "This place factors significantly in the Revolutionary War, so we're not going to spend too much time here. We just wanted you to see this magnificent spot while you were here."

"I'm very well aware of the strategic value of this location," said Washington. "My men and I have had several conversations regarding this location. It is, in my opinion, perhaps the most important strategic position in America."

They drove around campus, saw several monuments, and then headed back out along Thayer Road. They continued north for approximately twenty-five minutes until they reached Stewart Air National Guard Base in Newburgh, New York. The Sprinter pulled along a Boeing C-32, a modified Boeing 757 which is often used as the Vice President's transport. The aircraft was parked adjacent to the Marine Corp hangar, across a runway from the main passenger terminal.

As they pulled close, they could see Vice President Bashoff standing and waving from the top step of the air stairs which led up to the boarding door. The C-32 was smaller than the President's 747 (which operates as Air Force One). However, it is no less impressive, its sparkling baby blue and white paint scheme with United States of America painted across its fuselage and American flag on its tail.

Washington had rolled his window down, and was gawking at the airplane.

"It's magnificent!" said Washington. "It's a wonder that something so large could fly through the air."

The vehicle stopped, and everyone stepped out of the van. Washington walked straight up to the front landing gear, and placed his hands on one of the two tires. Then he walked to the engine on the right wing, and peered into it. At six foot, three and one half inches tall, his shoulders reached above the bottom of the engine frame. Then he looked up at the wings.

"Why do the wings point up at the tips?" asked Washington.

"They're called winglets," said Captain Murphy, pilot of the C-32. "Pleased to meet you, General Washington, my name is Captain Reginald Murphy, and I'll be flying the aircraft today. Winglets help reduce drag and increase efficiency."

"Pleased to meet you," said Washington. "Do you have military experience?"

"I do, indeed, sir. I flew combat missions during the Gulf War."

"Would that be the Gulf of Mexico, Captain?" asked

Washington.

"No, the Persian Gulf," said Murphy.

"This way to the stairs," said Jared, "the Vice President is eager to meet you."

The group ascended the stairs to the boarding door. Washington was engrossed in the airplane — its shape, its height, its color.

"It appears so elegant in its shape," said Washington. "Is it designed that way for aesthetic purposes, or does it serve a functional purpose?"

"Its shape is functional," said Captain Murphy. "Airplanes are designed these days using wind tunnel and computer simulation technology. Everything is done to ensure the least possible amount of drag on the aircraft as it passes through the air."

As they reached the top of the air stairs, Vice President Bashoff extended his hand and introduced himself.

"General Washington, I am so thrilled to meet you, I am Vice President David Bashoff."

"The pleasure is mine," said Washington.

"I want to thank you, on behalf of the American people, for agreeing to help us through this difficult time in American history."

Washington glanced away, saw Captain Murphy enter the aircraft, and turn left into the cockpit. Washington slid past Bashoff, and followed the pilot.

"Take a seat," said Murphy, pointing to the co-pilot's seat. "Captain Sobal, my co-pilot, is inside filing some paperwork. Let me show you around."

"It's so tight in here," said Washington. "And, so many knobs and buttons. How do you keep track of it all?"

"It's not as complicated as it looks, General. "We pilots don't like to admit it too often, but flying is rather easy. The hardest part is coming to terms with the level of responsibility. Commercial airline pilots have hundreds of lives in their hands. Today, I will have the responsibility of protecting the lives of the Vice President of the United States, and America's Revolutionary War General. That's a lot of responsibility."

"Indeed it is," said Washington, a man who knew what great responsibility felt like.

Washington walked out of the cockpit, and strolled the aisles of Air Force Two. The passenger cabin was divided into four sections: the forward area had a communications center, galley and ten business-class seats (plus a lavatory). The second section was a fully enclosed stateroom for the use of the Vice President (including a changing area, private lavatory, separate entertainment system, two first-class swivel seats and a convertible divan that seats three and folds out into a bed). The third section contains the conference and staff facility with eight business-class seats, and the rear section of the cabin contains general seating with thirty-two business-class seats, galley, two lavatories and closets.

Washington was peering into the stateroom, and was marveling at the luxurious appointments. The Vice President walked up beside him.

"You are the primary traveler on today's trip," said Bashoff. "So the stateroom is all yours. The divan folds out into a bed should you need to rest."

"Thank you, Mr Vice President," said Washington. "I will be looking out the window during this trip — I don't want to miss a second of it."

Captain Murphy's voice came on the PA system.

"Please take a seat and secure your belt buckles. We will be taxiing toward the runway, and will be airborne momentarily."

Washington took a seat in the rear section of the aircraft, in one of the business-class seats. He sat by himself, and put his forehead on the window as he peered out. As the aircraft began to taxi, Washington could feel his heart begin to pound. Once in position, the engines powered up, and the aircraft began to accelerate down the runway. Washington had never traveled so fast in his life, and the sensation was like nothing he had ever experienced. As the aircraft began its roll, and it lifted off the tarmac, Washington began to giggle, a sound even he was unfamiliar with.

The ground fell further and further away, as the aircraft banked and headed south. As they headed due south, he could see the Hudson River below them, and West Point was just up ahead, coming into view. Within a few minutes, Washington was able to see the bridge which carried his name, and the island of Manhattan. Down at the tip of the island, he saw the Freedom Tower, the Battery, and the bridges across to Brooklyn. In just a few days, he'd be back in 1776, and he'd be strategizing how to protect New York from the approaching British. He saw Staten Island, where the British were gathering, the wide Harbor, and the Verrazano Bridge which spanned the Narrows. What an incredible perspective. It all looked so small from up above, while down on the ground, the idea of defending it all seemed overwhelming.

Suddenly, the aircraft bounced in some mild turbulence as it passed through a few white fluffy cumulus clouds. Again, Washington let out a giggle, as for the first time in his life, he was able to look down on a cloud.

"That was just a little turbulence," said Captain Murphy over the PA. "Turbulence is normal, and not at all dangerous, so just sit back and enjoy the flight."

The aircraft was out over the Atlantic. The ocean looked so blue, and the small whitecaps were beautiful. The sun reflected off the surface of the ocean, creating a brightness from which Washington had to shade his eyes. He could see tiny cargo ships cutting their paths in all directions.

In less than an hour, the aircraft descended into the Washington, DC area, as it approached Andrews Air Force Base near Alexandria, Virginia. He saw the buildings, and the lakes, rivers, fields, and the endless array of highways. To Washington, the landing was spectacular, although, not as exciting as the take-off.

Once on the ground, the aircraft came to a stop, and the boarding door opened. The air stairs were rolled into place, and they all descended down to the tarmac, where another large, black SUV was parked awaiting their arrival.

The SUV exited Andrews AFB, and followed Interstate 495 across the Potomac River to the George Washington Memorial Parkway south. As the Parkway wound along the Potomac, Washington recognized generally where he was. None of this was here during his lifetime — the highway, parking areas, the houses and rooftops which popped up above the tree tops. But, it somehow felt familiar.

"Are we far from Mount Vernon?" asked Washington.

"We're about six miles away," said the driver.

After driving for approximately forty-five minutes, they entered the grounds and followed signs for the parking area. A three-wheeled security vehicle met them, and waved for them to follow. They took a sharp left off the main road, and followed the security vehicle around the back of the Ford Orientation Center.

Now, Washington was home. They turned right, and circled the gardens which looked very much as he remembered them. At the top of the Bowling Green, he had a full view of the small white gates, and the estate which was framed by the trees on either side.

"This is remarkable," said Washington, who was now visibly emotional. "It looks very familiar, although, the vegetation has grown substantially."

"Would you like to walk?" asked Snyder.

"Yes, I would."

They all got out of the SUV, and they followed behind as Washington slowly made his way through the Bowling Green. He stopped periodically just to look around. Sometimes he'd walk up to a tree and pull a leaf from it. Sometimes he'd smell the leaf.

As they approached the main house, Washington saw approximately forty people standing outside the building to the right of the front door, the building which served as the kitchen.

"We temporarily closed the tour so that you can spend personal time on your own inside," said Snyder.

From where they stood, Washington could see beyond the North and South Colonnades, to the banks on the south side of the Potomac River.

"It's remarkable," said Washington. "The view has not changed at all. It looks exactly as I remember it."

"It didn't happen by accident," said Snyder. "For more than fifty years, an organization called the Ladies of Mount Vernon, have been working to preserve the view across the Potomac. At one point, someone wanted to build oil tanks on that side. Then they wanted to build a water refinery over there. This organization, the Ladies of Mount Vernon, with help of donations from regular American citizens, purchased the land and fought any effort to change the landscape and the view across the river."

Washington was speechless. In a world as fast-paced and busy as this one, he wondered how anyone living in this century could possibly have the time or interest in something so seemingly trivial as preserving a view from his home across the Potomac River. Why would they care?

"You are loved and revered, General Washington," said Snyder, "as much today as you were in your time. That will never change. Now, go inside. Take your time, stay as long as you'd like. We'll be out here if you need us."

Washington meandered towards the front door, stopping to look at the storehouse building and the South Colonnade, before finally arriving at the front door.

He entered through the Central Passage, the main entryway into the home. The elegant space, which runs the width of the house, provides magnificent views of the Potomac and the Maryland shoreline to the east, and of the pastoral bowling green, fields, and woods beyond to the west.

Washington stopped to inspect the native black walnut staircase, which he added when he enlarged the house in 1758 and 1759.

In the central hall, he saw a key mounted in a case, hanging on the wall. It was the Key to the Bastille, given to him by the Marquis de Lafayette in 1790, after the destruction of the infamous prison in Paris. Washington didn't recognize it, of course, but thought to himself, '*That will likely make sense to me at some point in the future.*'

Washington continued his tour of the house, visiting the bed chambers, his study, the small dining room, and the little parlor on the first floor. Upstairs, he saw the Yellow Bedchamber, the bedchamber belonging to his daughter Nelly, and of course, the bedchamber which he shared with his wife Martha. He got emotional, and a tear slid down his cheek as he thought of Martha. Although he knew he would see her again upon his return to 1776, he couldn't get the thought out of his head — as he stood there in their home — she was lying outside in a tomb on the grounds of the estate. So too, were his remains, also buried in the tomb — one of the great perplexities of time travel. If he were to go outside to the tomb and dig up his own remains, would they be there? Could his bones — the same bones which occupied the interior of his body — be in two places at once?

Washington walked back down to the first floor, and stepped out onto the piazza. The two-story piazza is the Mansion's most distinctive architectural feature, extending the full length of the back of the house. As he stood there and gazed across the river, he felt, for an instant, that he was back in 1776. Was he? Could he be? What is time, and how does one travel through time? Is time a physical thing, or is it a mental state? Could his mind travel through time, and was his body just a mental reflection of what his mind saw and remembered? Perhaps that answered the question about how his bones could be in two places at once. Perhaps they weren't. Perhaps his bones were in the ground, but his mind was alive and operating here in 2018. These were questions Washington couldn't answer.

When Washington emerged from the house, he saw the group sitting on the grass out front.

"What a remarkable experience," said Washington. "Thank you for bringing me here."

"So, does it look like you remember it?" asked Snyder.

"In a way it does," said Washington, "but it is different in many ways as well. May I ask you a question? It may sound more than slightly odd, but it occurred to me as I walked through the home."

"Of course, you may ask us anything," said Snyder.

Washington bent down slowly, and sat on the lawn with the group. He sat with his legs curled underneath him, as if posing for a painting. Jared handed Washington a peeled orange, and Washington proceeded to pull it apart and eat it.

"If I were to go out to the tomb and dig up my bones," asked Washington, "could they possibly be in two places at once? Out there," he said pointing, "and in my body?"

"That's a great question," said Jared. "We don't know, and we really don't want to try it out right here, right now. Similarly, we often think about this riddle: how could I travel to 1776 and meet my great, great grandfather, when my own mother and father have yet to be born? The answer is, we don't know. Physicists believe there may be parallel universes. They call it the Multiverse.

"Since the days of Einstein, who was the greatest physicist the world has ever known, scientists have been attempting to solve the unified theory — or the theory of everything. The term was coined by Einstein, who attempted to unify the general theory of relativity with electromagnetism. Currently, Gravity has yet to be successfully included in a theory of everything. The solution to this problem is the existence of parallel universes. So, it's not like physicists have discovered parallel universes, but some believe they exist, because it solves a problem they believe should have an answer."

Back on Air Force Two, Jared stared out the window as the pilot prepared to taxi towards the runway. "Mind if I join you?" asked Snyder as he sat down next to Jared.

"Not at all."

"Why are we going back to New York if we're going to be in DC tomorrow?" asked Snyder.

"Agents Franco and Erdmann said the powers that be at the Secret Service are comfortable with the situation at the Waldorf. They feel it's secure and want Washington there tonight."

"Makes sense, I guess," said Snyder. "Where is Washington?"

"He retired to the bedroom" said Jared, "probably sleeping by now."

"Must have been a long day for him."

Jared debated whether he wanted to start this conversation, or whether he'd just prefer to get some shut eye on the way back to New York. But, he decided to go for it. "I think there's an ethical question associated with time travel," said Jared. "It's not just a question of the potential danger associated with changing the historical landscape and its impact on future events. I think there's an equally important ethical question which must be considered."

"What are you talking about?"

"Look at Washington."

"Yes, and…?"

"The man who was as excited as an eight year old this morning during his first airplane flight, is now asleep in bed."

"He's tired, that's to be expected," said Snyder.

"I think it's more than that," said Jared. "The man toured the house he lived in more than two hundred years ago, the home he lived in with his wife, his family. But, they weren't there today — they were dead. He was dead, too. As he said, his bones were buried out on the lawn. That's more than a human brain can handle. It's too much. What we did… what we did is cruel and unusual."

"I don't agree," said Snyder. "The human brain is capable of making sense of the situation. He knows the difference between 2018 and 1776. He knows he'll be returning to his time, and his wife and family and his friends will be there, and he'll have this incredible experience to remember for the rest of his life."

"I think you're wrong," said Jared. "The human mind can't easily make sense of it. I know, from my own experience."

"Fill me in. What happened, Jared?"

"When I first arrived in 1776, I felt a loneliness like I never knew before. I didn't think much of it because I was so wrapped up in the mission. However, it's very strange to know — to feel that there isn't a single person on earth that knows you. No family, no friends. No one you can count on in times of need. It's so lonely, and you feel so hollow. During the summer between junior and senior year of college, I travelled by myself through Europe. I was there for a month. I made a few friends along the way, but I was alone most of the time. I loved it — it was such a cool experience. But, I knew my family and friends were a few hours away in America, and that I'd see them again soon. When I was in 1776, it was very different. I didn't know a single soul on earth. No one knew me. I didn't dwell on it — like I said, I was focused on the mission. If I didn't have the mission, I think I would have totally collapsed. I think that might be what Washington is feeling right now."

"That's terrible," said Snyder.

"There's more. When I was there, I developed an emotional and romantic relationship with a woman."

"What? But, you were only there for four days. How is that even possible?"

"That's what I'm talking about," said Jared. "I was so lonely, I needed to find companionship. I must have come on so strongly with that poor girl. My emotions were running in hyper-drive."

"Did it get physical?" asked Snyder.

"Somewhat, but mostly emotional — that part was a much bigger issue. She wanted to come back here with me."

"What did you say?" asked Snyder.

"I told her she couldn't. That she shouldn't. I told her I cared too much about her to take her away from her mother and everything that she knew there. I understood the pain she'd feel, and I just couldn't allow her to do it. She hated me for it. I'm pretty sure she still hates me."

"But, why, Jared? She would have had you. Had you brought her back here, she would have had you."

Jared just sat there, confused. Was Snyder right? Would she have been happy with him here in 2018? It's true that they had strong feelings for one another, but he was just one person. Could one person — Jared — make her existence in a foreign land and in a foreign time a happy one? And then it hit him. Yes, she would have been happy. He knew this because Jared knew he'd be happy in 1776, as long as he had Becky in his life. Of course it would be the same for her, the other way around. Why had it taken so long for Jared to understand this? Why?

Upon his return to Washington, Vice President Bashoff received a call from President Harp.

"David," said Harp, "how's the old man doing?"

"He had an eventful day. He visited West Point and Mount Vernon. It was really quite amazing. Ron, I want to thank you for approving Secret Service coverage."

"My pleasure, David. The man is, after all, the father of our country."

"So that stuff… you believe he is Washington?"

"Of course," said Harp. "I know about Pangea."

"So what was…"

Harp interrupted.

"David, do me a favor and drop the address tonight. I get it. I hear what everyone is saying. Perhaps I've pushed too far. Maybe I got caught up in the moment, and I pushed too far. I can relax the rhetoric. I'll pull it back."

"It's too late, Ron."

"You'll address me as Mr President, David" said Harp angrily. "Don't forget who you're talking to. I'm your boss!"

"It's too late, sir. The people you appeal to, *your people*, have no interest in relaxing the rhetoric regardless of what you do. You instilled anger and hate in those people. You made them feel like it was okay to spew hatred, racist and elitist attitudes. You can't just turn that off. And, if you turn it off, trust me, they'll start hating you too. They'll look for new leadership in people who will carry their message of hate and intolerability. And, they're out there, believe me. There's always someone out there seeking power, people who will do and say anything in order to gain power. You started something you can't stop, but we can."

"You're crazy! You think a ghost from 1776 can change twenty-first century America?" asked the President.

"I'm sorry, but you're the crazy one, Ronald."

Harp's face contorted in anger. He stood up, and for the second time in three days, he grabbed a glass from a table in front of him, and threw it against a wall and it smashed. Bashoff heard it all through the phone, and he smiled.

"Better get control of that anger," said Bashoff, "it's not very becoming behavior for the President of the United States."

And then Bashoff hung up.

CHAPTER 34

Jared and Snyder stayed at the Waldorf Suite on Wednesday night, partly because they were tired and didn't want to travel, and partly because they were a little worried about Washington and the downturn in his mood. Jared had no idea where Janey was, but he really didn't care much.

The three men sat at the dining/meeting table in the main room of the suite eating breakfast from room service. Jared and Snyder each ate an omelet, while Washington ate pancakes and toast.

"Do you have a speech prepared for tonight, General?" asked Snyder. "Did you write it down on paper, or will you speak from memory?"

"Oh, I've written quite a bit down. I will select some of my words in the moment as well."

"Please let us know if we can help," said Jared. "What would you like to do today? It is a beautiful sunny day, and we won't be leaving for Washington, DC until three o'clock this afternoon. Is there anything you'd like to see or do?"

"Are there any buildings in Manhattan that date from the 1700's?" asked Washington.

"Due to a series of fires that burnt structures in the old city, there aren't many," said Snyder. "But, I know you're familiar with Fraunces Tavern. Perhaps you know it as the Queen's Head. We can have lunch there before we head to Washington."

It felt strange to Snyder to say the words 'Washington, DC'

to General Washington, knowing that the city was named after him.

The three men were driven down to Fraunces in the Sprinter. Corkoran called ahead and had the restaurant and museum closed for lunch for the day. The Tavern was damaged over the years by several fires, and was almost demolished in 1900. The building was saved due to the efforts of an organization known as the Daughters of the American Revolution. In 1907, under the supervision of early historic preservation architect, William Mersereau, an extensive reconstruction was completed. Though it required a fair amount of guesswork, an effort was made to restore the Tavern to its original look and style. According to Washington and Jared, both of whom were familiar with the 1776 version of the building, the architect and builders did a fine job.

The men went up to the second floor to the Long Room, and took seats at a very long and narrow table. This room was part of the Fraunces Tavern Museum, but it was made available for lunch for them on this day. The Long Room was the site of General Washington's famous farewell to his officers at the end of the Revolution.

Snyder excused himself, and headed to the men's room. On his way, Snyder stopped to look at a framed document which hung on the wall. Colonel Benjamin Tallmadge, Washington's Chief of Intelligence, was in attendance during Washington's farewell at Fraunces. Several decades later, in 1830, Tallmadge wrote his account from the events of that day. His original document, now framed and hanging on the wall near the men's room at Fraunces, was the actual document Snyder was now reading:

The time now drew near when General Washington intended to leave this part of the country for his beloved retreat at Mt. Vernon. On Tuesday the 4th of December it was made known to the officers then in New York that General Washington intended to commence his journey on that day. At twelve o'clock the officers repaired to Fraunces Tavern in Pearl Street where General Washington had appointed to meet them and to take his final leave of them. We had been assembled but a few moments when his Excellency entered the room. His emotions were too strong to be concealed which seemed to be reciprocated by every officer present. After partaking of a slight refreshment in almost breathless silence the General filled his glass with wine and turning to the officers said, "With a heart full of love and gratitude I now take leave of you. I most devoutly wish that your latter days may be as prosperous and happy as your former ones have been glorious and honorable." After the officers had taken a glass of wine General Washington said, "Please join me in a toast to John Jared Ross, a man who could not be with us today, but provided invaluable counsel and insight to me, without which, I am certain we would not have enjoyed this sweet victory. Now, I cannot come to each of you but shall feel obliged if each of you will come and take me by the hand." General Knox being nearest to him turned to the Commander-in-chief who, suffused in tears, was incapable of utterance but grasped his hand when they embraced each other in silence. In the same affectionate manner every officer in the room marched up and parted with his general in chief. Such a scene of sorrow and weeping I had never before witnessed and fondly hope I may never be called to witness again.

Snyder was in shock as he read these words.

*"Please join me in a toast to **John Jared Ross**, a man who could not be with us today, but provided invaluable counsel and insight to me, without which, I am certain, we would not have enjoyed this sweet victory."*

He read it again. Then, he scribbled a note on a scrap of paper, ran back to their table in the Long Room, and slipped it to Jared.

The note read: "Go read the framed document hanging on the wall directly across from the men's bathroom. Run... don't walk!"

Aboard Air Force Two (although it didn't carry that air traffic control sign since the Vice President was not aboard), Jared and Snyder sat next to one another.

"What are the chances that the John Jared Ross in that letter is not me?" asked Jared.

"I have no idea, but if it is you, we have a big problem."

"I just don't get it," said Jared. "Could a conversation I had today with Washington have had an impact on history — two hundred and forty years ago? How is that possible?"

"I think it has something to do with the space-time-continuum," said Snyder. "Think about it, from Washington's perspective, I mean the man we know, the man on this airplane sitting a few rows back — he hasn't fought the war yet. At least not all of it. When he goes back there, he'll have the knowledge that he's gained on this trip. Things we've said to him will be in his head, the things he saw and did will be with him as well. He won't suddenly forget everything when he goes back. You didn't forget all your experiences in 1776 when you returned to 2018, even though you technically weren't born yet when you were there. He will fight the war, and he will say farewell to his officers at Fraunces Tavern. He will make his speech, and he will have known you and he will have remembered the things you two discussed. Yes, it appears he will mention your name."

"But, it's so confusing," said Jared. "Hasn't the Revolutionary War already been fought, and didn't he fight that war before he ever met me? How could he have met me before I was born? Is he fighting the war for a second time now?"

"I don't know, but I don't think so," said Snyder. "I think the events of today and of the past are irrevocably intertwined. There's no 1776 without the influence from 2018, and no 2018 without the influence from 1776. I did a little research on Google during the drive to Stewart National Guard Base. Here's what scientists today believe."

Snyder held his iPhone up for Jared to read:

Physicists now routinely consider our world to be embedded in a four-dimensional Space-Time continuum, and all events, places, moments in history, actions and so on are described in terms of their location in Space-Time.

"What does that mean?" asked Jared.

"I don't know exactly, but it seems to me that space and time are intertwined, they can't be separated. You can't necessarily say something happened in the past, or that something will happen in the future. They might be the same thing."

"That makes no sense to me. I guess my brain just isn't big enough to understand that thinking."

"That's understandable," said Snyder. "The brightest scientists in the world don't understand either. Just another reason to put the Pangea portal back in mothballs. That thing could do some real damage."

"I say we send Washington back to 1776 and just blow it up."

"But, there is another issue," said Snyder. "It appears from the account of his farewell speech at Fraunces, that you said or showed something to General Washington — something significant — and in his opinion, it helped him win the war. Any idea what that thing might have been?"

"No, no idea," said Jared. "I've been operating under the assumption, as we discussed way back at the beginning, that anything we share could have a negative impact on the outcome of the war. So, I've kept my mouth completely shut."

"Well, we better figure it out," said Snyder. "If you don't share that thing with him, whatever it is, there may be no United States of America in a few weeks."

"Thanks, Charles. No pressure there."

CHAPTER 35

At approximately ten minutes to eight, the large black SUV stopped on Constitution Avenue, alongside the U.S. Capitol. Washington, Jared and Snyder stepped out, followed by Agents Franco and Erdmann. As they walked to the main entrance facing the mall and the Washington Monument, Washington marveled at the white neoclassical building and its massive dome. They walked up the main staircase and into the rotunda.

As Washington gazed up at the ceiling, he saw The Apotheosis of Washington, a fresco painted by Italian artist Constantino Brumidi, which depicts Washington sitting exalted amongst the heavens. What an odd sensation it must have been for the man to see himself depicted as a deity.

The men went up to the second floor, and into the House Chamber on the south side of the Capitol Building. Vice President Bashoff met them there, and shook Washington's hand vigorously.

"Thank you again, General Washington," said Bashoff. "Your presence here is very much appreciated."

As Washington entered the Chamber, dressed in full Revolutionary War uniform, the four hundred and fifty senators, Congressmen, and guests broke into spontaneous applause. Everyone stood as Washington made his way down the center aisle to the podium. The Vice President had considered speaking first to introduce Washington. However, he decided that Washington needed no introduction, and the people inside the

Chamber, as well as the millions viewing on television, were not at all interested in what Bashoff had to say. Washington was the star of the show.

Washington walked to the platform and stood there while the audience continued to cheer. The emotion was genuine. Everyone felt the significance of the moment, as George Washington, General, hero, President and larger than life figure, stood in the U.S. House of Representatives Chamber in the year 2018. The figures wouldn't be released for another twelve hours or so, but Nielsen ratings would confirm that the address was the highest rated and most watched television program in the history of the United States.

For ten full minutes, the applause continued. Finally, everyone began to settle down, and they took their seats.

Washington began:

"I am humbled by the reception I have received here tonight. I thank you for your hospitality. Since I arrived here at this place, the United States of America, in your year 2018, I have been welcomed with open arms. Although I don't know or understand the details of everything that has transpired since 1776, I know that the American people love and value their freedom. The spirit that led to our Declaration of Independence is still evident today in all of you.

"I have been asked to share our vision for America as set out by myself and my contemporaries. I regret that my talent with the spoken word, is not as strong as that with the written word. However, I will try my best to convey to all of you, the situation we are dealing with at home.

"The world in which I live, is a world governed by few. Men who derive their power from birth. These men, some good, some

evil, care not about the people they govern, but only of themselves and their families. They institute laws which are intended only to help their own cause and ensure their own wellbeing. My contemporaries and I envision a different kind of Union, one in which the people of the Union have the power to determine their own destiny. Our Declaration to the King of England states that it is our belief, that all men are created equal, that every man has certain unalienable rights, and that among these are life, liberty and the pursuit of happiness.

"This peremptory attitude has, to state it mildly, angered the King. He thinks us bumptious, indeed. But to the men and women of the colonies, they are willing to die for this cause. And many already have. I often ask myself why? Why do these men, these farmers and tradesmen, men of simple means, leave their homes and their families to fight for this cause? These men know that they, themselves, will likely not benefit from the fight, even in victory. Why do they risk their lives? They do it because there is a common thread which runs through all the American people. We are a people who have already left our homes in Europe to seek a new and better life for our families and ourselves. That is who we are. That is who we will always be. We cannot wash that fact away. It is inside of all of us. We came from somewhere else, and we — all of us — strive for something better. We are all connected in that way. We are a good people, and we see a better way of life for ourselves and our neighbors.

"Today, the men and women of America have lost sight of our common bond. Of our vision. There are forces in your midst today that are attempting to drive a wedge between you and your neighbor. Don't let them do it. Don't allow them to succeed. They are interested in personal gain, just like the Kings of Europe. Look inside yourselves. What you will find is a young man, a *teenager perhaps, who left his home on a farm in New England or Virginia or Maryland, and with nothing but the shirt on his back. This young man volunteered to fight a powerful army because of a belief. An ideal. He will put his life on the line, and perhaps he won't survive. Look inside yourselves. That boy is inside you. That's who you are. That's who we all are.*

"I know that boy. I know him personally. He's afraid and he's lonely. His shoes are nothing more than torn stockings and shreds of fabric. He's ill equipped to fight such a well-trained, well-armed British force. But, he's there in camp, preparing to fight. That boy would be proud to know that what he fought for was real. That the United States of America of today, with your indoor plumbing and flying aircraft and moon rocket, is a world leader.

"Please don't let us down. Please don't let our fight for freedom be an effort in futility. America must stand for something positive. We all know the difference between good and evil. Please take the side of good, and do your part to ensure that America continues to stand for all that is good in the world."

Again, the audience broke into spontaneous applause. Washington stood there, and looked around the room. He was astonished to see, as he gazed at the people in the Chamber, that nearly every person was wiping tears from his or her eyes. Washington's words were truly a wake-up call for millions of Americans who, unfortunately, took everything that this country had stood for during its two hundred plus years for granted.

The anchors on the over-the-air and cable news networks were searching for the words to encapsulate what they had just heard from Washington.

CNN — ""It's amazing how one speech, which lasted by the way, twenty two minutes and eleven seconds, could work to completely change the mindset of Americans."

ABC News — "The last time Americans came together like this was after 9/11 — and we all know how long that lasted. But, it feels very, very different this time."

FOX News — "If I'm President Harp, I'm running — not walking — to get my hands on the latest poll numbers. There's no doubt the pendulum is in full swing — the other way."

Washington and the group made their way back to the SUV, which was parked under the Capitol Building.

"You were incredible, General," said Vice President Bashoff. "How can we ever thank you?"

"No need, sir."

"We will be staying here in Washington tonight," said Bashoff. "We'd like you to address a rally on the National Mall tomorrow afternoon — assuming you're up for it. We have to keep this momentum going. We'll fly back to New York on Saturday morning, and then you'll travel back. Of course, it will still be last Monday when you return. Instantaneous, remember?"

"Yes, that's fine," said Washington.

"Is there anything you'd like to do or see before your return?" asked Snyder.

Washington thought for a moment.

"I'd like to drive a car."

CHAPTER 36

The National Mall was packed. People began arriving as early as three o'clock in the morning. The news of Washington's planned address on the Mall broke at ten p.m. following his televised address from the Capitol, so it was unclear how many people would make the trip on such short notice. But, the opportunity to see and hear George Washington speak in person was just too great an opportunity to pass up.

Estimates indicate that attendance was more than two million, many of whom could not actually get to the Mall itself. Many of those who were in attendance had indicated it was the most important and moving day in their lives. Washington made another poignant speech, reminding Americans of their common bond.

After the rally, the group took the SUV to the Four Seasons Hotel at 2800 Pennsylvania Avenue. They moved into the Presidential Suite — West wing, and again, the entire floor was cleared.

"So, what did you think?" asked Jared.

"It was an extraordinary day," said Washington. "I have never seen so many people in once place in all my life."

"I agree," said Snyder. "I think it's the largest crowd the Mall has ever seen."

"Why, may I ask, is it called the Lombardi Project?" asked Washington.

"That was my idea," said Jared. "Vince Lombardi was an

NFL Football coach for the Green Bay Packers. That's Wisconsin."

"Wisconsin didn't exist during the General's lifetime," said Snyder.

"Wisconsin is one of the fifty States," said Jared. "Anyway, Vince Lombardi was the coach of the team. Not only was he a great coach, but he was an amazing orator and motivator. He didn't always have the most talented players, but he was able to motivate them to exceed their talent."

"I see," said Washington. "Did I live up to your expectations?"

"You blew my expectations away," said Jared. "You could teach Vince Lombardi a thing or two about giving motivational speeches."

President Harp sat at his desk in the Oval Office. Louise Turner, his Press Secretary, sat across from him on the other side of the desk. She handed him a stack of about fifteen pages of paper. Harp slid his reading glasses down from his forehead, and began perusing the documents. He looked at each page for about a minute, studying it. He made a face each time he flipped to the next page.

"This is terrible," said Harp. "They hate me. My approval rating is at seventeen percent. That's got to be a new record low."

"It's not good, but it will pass," said Turner. "This is all fresh on everyone's minds. George Washington spoke on National television last night for God's sake. But, luckily, people have short attention spans. They'll forget. They move on, they always do."

Harp stood up and began pacing. He pulled a tube of Chap Stick from his pants pocket, applied it liberally to his lips, and sat back down.

"It's not going to pass!" he said. "Seventeen percent!"

"They're calling for your resignation," said Turner.

"Who? Who's calling for my resignation, Louise?"

"Haven't you been watching the news? Everyone. The Democrats, the Republicans. Liberals and Conservatives."

Harp put his head down on his desk and placed his hands on his head. He looked defeated. But, when he sat up, the look on his face was pure anger.

"So, what do I do?" he asked.

"You wait it out. It will blow over, trust me. People don't stay angry forever."

"You're wrong, Louise. This time it's different. I pushed too far. I was arrogant, I thought I was Teflon. People are angry, and they won't rest till I'm gone. It's Bashoff's fault. This was all Bashoff's doing."

FedEx Field, the home of the Washington Redskins, is located in Andover, Maryland. It is just twelve miles from The Four Seasons Hotel, but nearly an hour's drive. Corkoran had arranged to give them exclusive access to the parking lots at FedEx Field. When they arrived, they searched for the largest, unobstructed section of the parking lot, which was off Hill Oaks Road. The driver pulled the SUV to a stop, opened his door and got out. Jared moved to the passenger seat, Snyder sat behind the driver's seat, and Agent Franco sat next to Snyder, behind Jared. Washington took his place in the driver's seat.

"The car is in park," said Jared. "You can move this lever to drive or reverse. When you do that, keep your foot on the brake pedal. You only use your right foot. The big one is the brake, and the little one to the right is the gas pedal. The gas pedal makes you go. The brake makes you stop. It's that simple."

"That sounds quite complicated," said Washington.

"It's not. You'll see. It's so easy you'll be shocked."

Washington pressed on the brake, and slowly moved the lever to drive. He let his foot off the brake, and the SUV began to slowly move forward.

"Is that usual?" asked Washington.

"Yes, now press down on the gas pedal slightly."

The SUV jolted forward, and began moving very fast.

"Lift your foot up a little," said Jared. Don't press so hard. Get a feel for it."

Washington quickly got a feel for it, and began driving around the perimeter of the parking lot. He was adept at gently pressing the brake, so that the SUV would come to a gradual stop. Jared wasn't looking at the lot, he was looking at Washington. The General had a smile on his face as he steered the SUV around and around the parking lot. Jared pulled his iPhone from his pocket, and began videotaping Washington as he drove. Pure joy. That's what it looked like. Yes, Washington had some difficult times while he visited 2018. He was busy with speeches, and he felt the pain and despair of existing alone, knowing all those who he loved were no longer living. However, as he sat behind the wheel of the SUV driving, all he felt was pure joy.

They spent a little over an hour driving, and then decided it was time to return to the Four Seasons. When they arrived, they went up to the suite, made sure Washington was comfortable, and then Jared and Snyder left. The suite at the Four Seasons had one bedroom, far smaller than the three bedroom suite at the Waldorf. Jared and Snyder decided it was time to give Washington some peace and quiet during his final night in the twenty-first century. They took a cab to the Club Quarters near Lafayette Square.

Aside from Agent Erdmann, who sat on a chair in the hall outside the door to the suite, Washington was finally alone.

Washington sat on the couch in the main living area, and turned on the TV. He came across a Baltimore Orioles baseball game, and stopped to watch. He found the game fascinating, and marveled at the number of people who filled the stadium to watch.

President Harp snuck out of the White House unnoticed. He went to the car park, and asked his driver to take him to the Four Seasons. He told his driver he felt badly about not greeting Washington while he was in the city, and wanted to say hello. Harp wore jeans, an untucked polo shirt, and a baseball cap so he wouldn't be recognized.

When he arrived at the Four Seasons, he went to the front desk and asked the attendant what floor Washington was on.

"President Harp!" said the young lady at the front desk. "Well, President Washington…"

"He's not the President, I am," said Harp.

"Yes, well he's staying in the Presidential Suite on the fourteenth floor. But, the elevators have been locked off, and the door on the stairway has been locked shut on the fourteenth floor."

"Is there any way to get up there?" asked Harp.

"You would need the elevator key, but I don't have one."

"Is there anyone who has the key?" asked Harp, in a soft tone which masked his utter frustration.

"Well, room service has a key. They take room service orders up there a lot."

"Can you get it for me?" asked Harp.

When the elevator stopped at the fourteenth floor, and made the 'ding' sound, Agent Erdmann was surprised. As far as he knew, no one was expected on the floor until the following morning. Erdmann assumed Washington called down for room service. However, when he saw President Harp get off the elevator, Erdmann was in shock and jumped to his feet.

"Mr President," said Erdmann. "Can I help you?"

"And you are?" asked Harp.

"I'm Special Agent Erdmann," he said, holding his badge out for the President to read it.

"Very well, Agent Erdmann. I'm here to see General Washington."

"I'm sorry, Mr President, but I'm under strict orders not to allow anyone into the suite."

"But, I'm the President," said Harp.

"Yes, sir. I understand that, sir, but my orders were clear," said Erdmann, as he slowly removed his pistol from its holster. "Again, sir, I apologize, but those are my orders."

Harp laughed.

"Come on, Erdmann, you're not going to shoot me! You took an oath to protect me. Don't be ridiculous. Killing a President is a capital offense. You'll hang.""

Harp was angry now. Who did this fucking kid think he was, pulling a gun on the President of the United States?

"Sir, if you would like to discuss this with Director Westhoff," said Erdmann, "please have him call me. Under his direction, I can allow you to enter the suite."

Harp reached into his pocket and pulled out a small automatic pistol. He pointed it at Erdmann.

"Open the door, Erdmann! NOW!" said Harp.

"I can't do that, sir."

"Open it or I'll shoot."

Erdmann didn't respond.

"I'm going in there, whether you open the door or not."

Harp reached past Erdmann with his left hand, while he continued pointing the gun at him with his right hand. He began knocking on the door. Washington, who was sitting on the couch, heard the knock and opened the door. Harp attempted to push past Erdmann, but the Agent pushed him back. Harp had his gun pointed at Washington. Erdmann couldn't imagine shooting the President of the United States, not because of his threat of a capital crime, but because he was the President of the United States. So, instead of shooting Harp, Erdmann pushed him back away from the door. He pushed so hard that Harp fell backwards and hit the floor. As his butt made contact with the floor, Harp's right arm banged down hard onto his own knee, causing his right finger to pull the trigger of his pistol. The bullet from Harp's gun hit Erdmann in the stomach, and he fell hard to the floor.

Harp and Washington looked at Erdmann, who lay there on the floor in the hallway, then they looked at each other.

"In the room," said Harp, directing Washington with the barrel of the gun. "Sit down and shut up."

"May I ask your name?" said Washington.

"Yeah, I'm President Harp."

CHAPTER 37

The woman at the front desk reported the gunshot to the police. They arrived at the hotel, and were immediately notified that Washington was staying in a suite on the fourteenth floor, and that President Harp had recently arrived at the hotel and talked his way onto an elevator. The Police Chief immediately recognized the magnitude of the situation, and placed a call to the Secret Service.

Corkoran arrived on the scene at the same time a dozen Secret Service agents arrived. They wanted to get Corkoran out of the way, but when he mentioned he was part of the Lombardi Project, they let him stay, thinking he might prove to be valuable.

The agents created a command center in a suite directly below the Presidential Suite on the thirteenth floor. They put Corkoran in a standard room, right next door on the thirteenth floor. Corkoran called Jared and Snyder on their cell phones, and they arrived by cab within fifteen minutes. Corkoran arranged for them to join him in the room on the thirteenth floor, having mentioned that they too were members of the Lombardi Project.

Vice President Bashoff was notified of the situation, but he was advised to stay far away from the Four Seasons. He was next in line for the Presidency.

A Secret Service agent called the Presidential Suite, and Harp answered. He spoke in a very quiet, monotone manner.

"Harp," he said.

"Mr President, this is Special Agent McNaught. Please tell

us the status of Agent Erdmann, General Washington, and yourself."

"I shot Erdmann, accidentally. I think he's alive. I shot him in the stomach and he's on the floor outside the suite. Washington is fine. Me? I'm totally fucked."

"Mr President, your wellbeing is of the utmost importance to us. Please, refrain from any behavior that might jeopardize your safety and that of General Washington's. Let me remind you, should anything happen to Washington, the future of our Nation could be in jeopardy."

"Maybe you should have thought about that before bringing him here," said Harp.

"Yes, sir, but that wasn't our decision. I am sending two men up to the fourteenth floor to try to help and recover Agent Erdmann. They will not attempt to enter the suite. They will attend to Agent Erdmann and then they will leave. Is that all right with you?"

"Yes, please do. I sincerely hope Erdmann is okay. It was an accident."

"I understand," said McNaught. "Please keep this phone line open. We will call back shortly."

Corkoran, Jared and Snyder sat in silence in their room. They had no contact with the Secret Service, so they had no idea what was going on since they arrived.

"So, what do you know?" asked Jared.

"I know Harp came here, forced his way up to the fourteenth floor where Washington is staying, then he shot the Secret Service Agent — I think it was Erdmann, not Franco. Now he's in the suite, and Washington is his hostage."

"What's he up to?" asked Jared. "What outcome is Harp hoping for?"

"No idea," said Corkoran. "Maybe he realized his Presidency was cooked. It's definitely cooked now."

"I guess we should feel happy," said Jared, "but with Washington in there with him, it's a pretty fucking bad situation. Harp has nothing to lose. That makes him extremely dangerous."

"We need to alert the media," said Snyder. "We can't help Washington right now, but we can help our cause. This story will spread like wildfire. Opinions will grow stronger. Everyone will see Harp for who he is — even the crazies who follow him."

The phone rang in the suite and Harp grabbed it.

"Yeah," said Harp.

"Mr President, this is Special Agent McNaught. We retrieved Erdmann."

"How bad is he?" asked Harp.

"He's in a serious condition. He's alive and on the way to the hospital. How is General Washington?"

"He's fine. I think he's in shock, but he's fine."

"Mr President, we are requesting that you release General Washington immediately."

"I can't do that," said the President.

"What do you want, Mr President?"

There was a pause. McNaught could hear Harp breathing through the phone as he considered the question.

"I don't know!" said Harp, quite loudly. "I need some time to figure this out."

"We don't have time," said McNaught. "Washington is scheduled to return to his time tomorrow morning. We need to resolve this now, and you need to return to the White House."

Harp laughed. He knew he'd never be returning to the White House. No sitting President can shoot a Secret Service Agent, kidnap the father of our country, hold him hostage, and expect to remain in office.

"I know I won't be returning to the White House," said Harp. "I know all the tricks, Agent McNaught, so don't bother flattering me. Give me some time to think. Call me back in thirty minutes, okay?"

"Yes, sir. Please take good care of Washington."

An email blast was sent out by Senator Janey Logan's Press Secretary to media outlets from coast to coast. The notice simply read:

NEWS ALERT

President Harp Shoots Secret Service Agent and Holds General George Washington Hostage at Four Seasons Hotel in Washington, DC. The Situation is Unfolding.

It seemed like a comic book headline, but considering the events of the past few days, everyone in America knew this was no hoax. Within minutes, television crews began to congregate outside the Four Seasons. News vans with satellite dishes on their roofs parked in the hotel lot along the driveway, and across the street. Dozens of reporters were doing their standups, lights on, cameras rolling.

Back inside the suite on the thirteenth floor, Jared, Snyder and Corkoran were completely in the dark with respect to the news. They turned on the television in the room, and saw coverage on virtually every channel. However, the coverage simply reported on the current status — that a man was shot by President Harp, and that he was currently holed up in the hotel with Washington. No one had information beyond that.

What nobody knew, including the Lombardi crew on the thirteenth floor, was that there was no further information, because Harp had no clue what to do next. He had no plan.

"How do you see this unfolding?" asked Jared.

"I think Harp takes his own life," said Corkoran.

"No way," said Snyder. "Harp is too proud to go out that way. He'll never do it."

"But he's not too proud to go to prison?" said Corkoran. "The man is going to prison. He shot a Secret Service Agent. I don't think Harp would last a week in Prison."

"He's not going to real prison," said Jared. "He won't be hanging with the crack dealers and rapists. He'll be going to cushy country club prison."

"So what do you think of the twentieth Century?" asked President Harp.

Washington was reclining on the couch next to Harp, watching the newscast on one of the local stations with no audio. Washington recognized the building behind the reporter as the Four Seasons.

"I was just watching the television screen, and was wondering how the pictures were being transmitted from outside? What a marvel. I'm sure you and everyone else take these things for granted, but it is truly an astonishing achievement. I find it quite sad to see, that with all the advancements mankind has made, he hasn't been able to solve the issues which have always plagued us."

"Like?" asked Harp.

"Like violence," said Washington.

"I know, it's terrible," said Harp. "I think it's biological. You are probably not aware of this, but it has been proven by Charles Darwin that man evolved from other animal species. We are related to apes, and apes are related to other species, and on and on. Animals, primarily males, are biologically programmed to fight and protect their turf. We are programmed to expand our territory and to defend it. It all ties back to our biological responsibility to procreate and keep our species alive and well. More land, more food, a better chance for survival. We can't change our biology."

"Is that why you led this Nation the way you did?" asked Washington. "Was it biology that drove you?"

"Partly, I think," said Harp. "I think I got carried away with the power. It's a strange thing to be President of the United States, leader of the free world. That's what they call the office of the Presidency — leader of the free world. My family came from Europe. My mother's family came from Germany, my father's family from Ireland. My dad worked in Real Estate, and was quite successful. He worked hard and provided for us. We weren't rich, but we were comfortable. My political attitudes came from him — conservative. Very, very conservative. He watched his own father make the most of the American dream. My grandfather didn't go to college in Ireland. But, he came here, worked hard and did well for himself. He was the superintendent of an apartment building in lower Manhattan. Five Points. A very rough neighborhood. My dad always felt that if our family could make it, without anyone lending a hand, others could as well. He hated all the social services this country offered the poor. He felt it was an incentive for people to sit back, put out their hands, and take a free pass."

Harp looked at Washington, eye to eye.

"That's how a lot of people in this country feel today. That we are giving people a free pass. They feel Americans have become lazy. They whine all the time. Many Americans want their old view of America back. An America in which nothing is given to us, except the opportunity to make it. What Americans wanted back then, was an opportunity to provide for their families, and to set their children up with an opportunity to do better than they did."

"It sounds a little like the attitude of the men who are fighting for liberty with me," said Washington. "They know they will not likely benefit, themselves, from their sacrifices during their lifetime. But they want a better life for their children. A life of freedom and opportunity."

"Yes, that's right," said Harp. "My message appealed to all those Americans who simply wanted an opportunity to succeed. They're not looking for handouts, and they don't want to pay for handouts for others. To me, it was a noble attitude. I got caught up in it. It felt like a movement. Like a return to good old fashioned American values. Work hard. Don't ask for handouts, and embarrass and shame those who do. You want a hand out, go to Canada, go to Sweden or Norway or Denmark. America is for fighters, and everyone has an equal chance to succeed."

"It sounds self-serving and mean-spirited to me," said Washington. "I don't have the answer, but I feel the country we envision, is made up of good people who have compassion for one another."

"That's a wonderful goal," said Harp.

The phone rang in the suite, and Harp answered it.

"Mr President, it has been thirty minutes," said McNaught. "What is your plan?"

"I'd like to see the Vice President," said Harp. "Can you arrange for him to come see me?"

"I'm sorry, sir, but I don't believe that is an option. Should something happen to you, Vice President Bashoff is next in line to assume the Presidency. The situation you have created — the environment is just too dangerous for the Vice President."

"Can you please get him on the phone?" asked Harp.

"Hold on one minute," said McNaught. "We'll patch him through."

Harp pressed the speaker button on the phone, placed the phone down, and sat back while he waited to hear from Bashoff.

"Mr President," said Bashoff, his voice filling the room.

"David," said President Harp. "Please call me Ron."

"Ron, what's going on? What on earth are you doing?"

"That's a really good question. I'm not quite sure what I'm doing. It's an exciting time for you right now, my friend. It appears you're going to be President of the United States."

"I'm not thinking about that right now," said Bashoff. "I'm worried about you. Don't do anything stupid."

"It's a little too late for that, don't you think?' said Harp.

"No, it's not too late. There are many options available to you. Come out of there, and let's figure it out."

"Actually, David, the way I see it, I have two options. I can walk out of here, turn myself in, and go down in history as the biggest fuck up in Presidential history. Or I can take everyone down with me. Erase history. Without General Washington, America might never exist, nor would any of us have ever existed. At the very least, it might create some alternate version of history which likely, would not have led to this moment."

"You can't do that," said Bashoff. "You have a responsibility…"

"Yes, I can. I'm sitting here with five more bullets in this pistol."

"I mean you shouldn't. Think about your family, Sydney and Taylor. Do you really want to wipe them off this earth? Wipe away their existence?"

"They might prefer it, rather than going through life as the daughters of Ronald Harp, Presidential joke!"

"No they wouldn't," said Bashoff.

In the Secret Service Command Center on the thirteenth floor, the Director heard the report through his headphones from a sharp shooter located in an apartment in a building across 29th Street NW.

"The angle is bad," said the sharpshooter. "Washington's location on the couch is directly in front of the target. I might be able to get a head shot if Washington reclines again."

"Hold off for now," said the Director.

CHAPTER 38

The phone rang in the Command Center on the thirteenth floor. Mc Naught answered it.

"Director Hayes, I have Vice President Bashoff for you."

"This is Hayes."

"Neal, what's the latest?" asked Bashoff.

"We have a sniper in an apartment across the street. He's got a good view of the suite, but the way they're situated on the couch, Washington is in the way. We can get a head shot, but we're hoping to avoid that."

"I understand," said Bashoff. "I'm worried about Harp. Did you hear our conversation?"

"Of course, and I'm worried as well," said Neal Hayes.

"He's unstable, and I wouldn't be shocked by anything he decides to do at this point. I think I need to go in there."

"That's out of the question," said Hayes. "You are next in line for the Presidency, sir. We can't risk it."

"There may be no Presidency after tonight," said Bashoff. "There may be no United States of America. We don't know what Harp will do, and we don't know what might happen if he takes out Washington. I'm partly responsible for Washington being here. I never considered the possibility we might put his life in danger — certainly not at the hands of the sitting President. We wanted to put pressure on Harp, but we backed him into a corner and now he's snapped! I need to do this. I need to help resolve this."

"Come down to thirteen and we'll work on a plan."

McNaught called Harp in the suite on the fourteenth floor.

"Mr President, Vice President Bashoff would like to come to your suite to talk," said McNaught.

"I thought you said it would be too dangerous?'

"In my opinion it is," said McNaught. "However, the Vice President insists. He is worried about you based on your recent telephone conversation with him."

"You mean he's worried about Washington."

"Yes, of course, but he's also very worried about you. He's worried you might hurt yourself."

Bashoff knocked on the door, and Harp opened it. The Vice President walked in, and turned towards Harp, who was still standing at the door, looking at the ground outside the door which was covered in Erdmann's blood.

"I think the kid is doing okay," said Bashoff, when he saw Harp staring down at the blood soaked carpet in the hall.

"It was an accident," said Harp. "I never intended…"

"I know," said Bashoff. "We all do."

"I need to frisk you, David," said Harp. "I need to check that you don't have a weapon on you."

"That's fine," said Bashoff. "But, I must inform you, I'm wearing a bullet proof vest. The Secret Service guys insisted."

Harp held the pistol in his right hand, while he used his left hand to pat down Bashoff's legs, his back, and around the vest.

"I feel like I'm on some TV show," said Harp. "This is all so surreal."

"I know," said Bashoff. "The least surreal part of it is that George Washington is sitting over there. It tells you something about the day we've had, right?"

Bashoff was preparing himself for a gun shot at any moment.

He wasn't sure when the sniper would take his shot. He tried to block it out of his mind and concentrate on the plan.

Harp walked to the couch and took a seat in the same location he was sitting prior to Bashoff's arrival. Bashoff sat between Washington and Harp as Hayes and McNaught directed.

"Come on, Ron, let's end this now," said Bashoff. "We can figure it all out. Let's not make things worse."

"Don't say 'let's figure it out', David," said Harp. "You make it sound like we're going to the same place, but we're not. You're going to the White House, and I'm going to prison."

"That may be for the short term, but don't forget, I am a member of your administration. Yes, we differed on many things — everything, recently. But, I'm not sure the American people see it that way. I may be guilty by association. My future is very uncertain. They can't hang me, but they may try to tear me a new one."

"No," said Harp, "they know you're one of the good guys. They know you were never really on my bandwagon. You'll be fine."

"Come on, Ron, let's go. Let's just walk out of here. I promise you, I'll do everything in my power to help you. Go home, hug your family. Get a good night's sleep. We'll deal with everything in the morning. We can figure it all out then."

Hayes and McNaught were listening in on a transmitter Bashoff was wearing in an inside pocket of his blazer. They were also watching on a screen which was being fed video from the sniper's location across the street. In case the audio went out, or if it was muffled and intelligible, Bashoff was to remove a red handkerchief from his jacket pocket and rub his forehead, an indicator that Harp was prepared to give up and walk out of the suite. At the same time, he was to say the code word 'revolution', to notify the Command Center and the sniper that they should stand down. Bashoff was praying that would be the outcome.

"I'm just so ashamed and embarrassed," said Harp. "You say I should go home and hug my family, but I don't think I can face them. You don't know what it's like to be in my shoes right now, David. I wish the floor would open up and take me down."

"I do," said General Washington, interjecting. "During our war with the French and the natives, I experienced several dismal failures. In July of '54, a large contingent of French and native forces reached the Great Meadows, where we had been encamped. I retreated with my men to Fort Necessity, where we were surrounded and were fired upon. The situation was hopeless, and I was forced to surrender to the French. I unintentionally agreed to sign surrender terms in which I unwittingly admitted to assassinating Ensign Jumonville, which was not true.

"The following year, I traveled to Boston to meet with Governor William Shirley, who had been the acting commander-in-chief after General Braddock's death. My efforts were unsuccessful, and I heard whispers that I was deemed unfit to lead due to my handling of the Great Meadows encounter."

"I appreciate that you are trying to help," said Harp, "but, while I'm sure that must have been embarrassing for you at the time, look at you now. You are the General in command of the Continental Army."

"That's my point, precisely," said Washington. "This episode will pass, as did my experience at Great Meadows. You will move on and past this point in time. You will overcome this unfortunate experience in your life, as I did mine."

"Wait a minute," said Harp, excitedly. "David, could I utilize Pangea to go back in time, and change some of the things I've done?"

"I'm sorry, Ron, Pangea is shut down. It will be used one more time — to send General Washington back, and then it's done."

"But think about it," said Harp, "I can go back in time — two days, and change everything. I can support Washington's efforts here, get onboard, and try to fix the things I've done. The decisions I've made. We wouldn't be here right now. I could work to fix all the bad I've done. I could repair my image, I could spend the next two years making amends. Maybe I wouldn't get a second term. Maybe I'll piss off all those ultra, right-wingers who loved me so much, but who cares? I could work to fix things. In fact, I could go back two years instead of two days, and I can change everything."

"Can't do it," said Bashoff. "It's too dangerous. We are not sure how events in the past are being impacted by all of this. I can't go into detail right now, but we are aware of at least one major impact — something we don't understand and can't explain."

"That's bullshit, David. I have an opportunity to change everything, to save my life and my political career. You have your eyes on the White House, no wonder you don't like the idea."

"It's not that," said Bashoff. "I promise you. No one would love to go back and re-do all of this more than me. My future is up in the air as well, don't forget."

"Bullshit! You'll be fine. Maybe you'll be a little uncomfortable for a while. But, you'll be fine. I'm looking at several years in prison."

Harp reached over to the phone sitting on the table next to the couch. He dialed the Command Center.

"McNaught here."

"Agent McNaught, This is President Harp. You asked me what I wanted a few hours ago. Well now I know. I want Pangea."

McNaught had been listening through the transmitter, so he

knew what Harp was seeking.

"I'm sorry, Mr President, but Pangea has been shut down. It's been deemed too dangerous."

"That's bullshit," said Harp. "Must I remind you that I am sitting here with a loaded weapon? If you want to keep Washington alive, I suggest you bring me Pangea."

"Mr President, give me a minute to discuss with my superiors, and I will call you back."

"Okay," said Harp. You have five minutes."

In the Command Center on Fourteen, McNaught and Hayes pondered the situation. They hadn't really considered it, but should something go wrong and Washington lose his life, they could use Pangea to reset and try again. However, the unpredictability of time travel on past events, led McNaught and Hayes to want to avoid that option at all costs. They decided to keep the Pangea option in their back pocket — just in case.

"Mr President, this is McNaught. We have decided to honor your request for Pangea, under two conditions. One, you go back two days — not two years. We believe traveling back a shorter distance will help limit the degree of impact we have on the past."

"I can live with that. I don't really love the idea of reliving two years of my life anyway. I'm okay stepping down if it means I can avoid prison time. What else?"

"You let Washington go now."

"No way," said Harp. "Without Washington, I don't get Pangea. You know that and so do I."

"Then we need your word that he will experience no harm. Before you step through, you drop the gun."

"Agreed."

CHAPTER 39

Jared, Corkoran and Snyder went next door to talk to Hayes and McNaught in the Command Center. They reviewed the plan. Pangea would be set up in the suite. Worried that Harp might jump the gun and pass through the hoop before they were ready, Hayes and McNaught did not want the uranium cylinder included in the set up. But, without it, the hoop wouldn't spin or light up as it normally did, and they felt Harp would be suspicious. They decided to insert the uranium tube, but they'd be on high alert with Harp.

The hoop was retrieved from Secret Service headquarters on N Street. Corkoran and Jared knocked on the door of the suite on the 14th floor. Harp came to the door, pistol in hand.

"I need to frisk you guys," said Harp.

They were both wearing bullet proof vests. Jared placed the duffle on the floor, unzipped it, and began putting the arches together. Luckily, the ceiling in the suite was fourteen feet high and able to accommodate the twelve foot tall hoop. Corkoran helped Jared stand the hoop upright, while Harp remained on the couch, gun pointed at Washington.

Jared connected the laptop to the base arch, and pulled the uranium case from the duffle. He removed the uranium cylinder, and gently slipped it into the slot in the base. He pressed the 'on' button on the laptop, and the unit came to life.

"Date and time?" asked Jared.

"Eight o'clock, two days ago," said Harp. "That would be

Wednesday."

The hoop began to spin, much slower as compared to the trips back and forth from 1776, since it required less gravitational force to make the trip.

"It's really too bad this technology is so dangerous," said Harp. "Think about how much money we could make with it! A guy cheats on his wife, gets caught, and wants to go back and fix it? We could charge him ten thousand bucks. Some other guy embezzles money — like Bernie Madoff? We could charge him fifty grand! And they'd pay it, too."

"That wasn't my vision when I discovered Pangea's time travel capability," said Jared. "I thought it could be used for something good. Perhaps stopping wars from occurring. To learn about history. I didn't set out to make money."

"Of course not," said Harp, suddenly trying to appear more Presidential.

"Okay," said Jared, "we're all set. Pangea is set to Wednesday at eight a.m."

Harp slid across the couch to where Washington was sitting, and wrapped his arm under his. As he stood up, he pulled Washington up with him, keeping the pistol aimed at him. He pulled Washington with him as he stood four feet in front of the hoop.

"You said you'd drop the gun," said Bashoff.

"No way," said Harp. "I wasn't born yesterday. I drop this gun, and you guys will tackle me in two seconds."

"But you can't bring the gun through the hoop," said Jared. "The metal of the gun will interfere with the gravitational force — it will impact the force of gravity and you might not end up where you want to go."

He was lying, of course. When Jared traveled to and from

1776, he carried a musket and other metal objects.

"I'll take my chances," said Harp.

If things went Harp's way, he would pass through the hoop and would still be in the suite when he emerged, instantaneously, on the other side. The others would not be in the suite, since they weren't in the suite two days ago at eight a.m. It would just be Harp and Washington.

But, that wasn't going to happen. Harp stepped arm-in-arm with Washington towards the hoop, then another step and then they went through. As they emerged from the hoop on the other side, Corkoran lunged at Washington, and pulled him to the floor. Then a shot pierced the window, and hit Harp in the shoulder. The gun immediately fell from Harp's hand, and he fell to the floor. Two Secret Service Agents came through the door, and pounced on Harp. Within seconds, he had handcuffs on his wrists as he lay on the floor on his stomach. A team of EMS workers entered the suite, and began attending to Harp's bullet wound.

"What happened?" asked Harp.

"We set the travel date and time to this exact minute. You didn't go anywhere. That's why the hoop was spinning so slowly."

Washington got to his feet, and brushed his clothing, which had bunched up at his midsection as he was pulled by Corkoran to the floor.

"Who shot President Harp?" asked Washington.

"We had a sharpshooter in an apartment across the street," said Neal Hayes. "Pleased to meet you, General Washington. I'm Director Hayes with the Secret Service. We were just waiting for the right opportunity to take him out. We didn't want to cause serious injury, so we needed a good angle on his shoulder. He'll be fine."

"We can certainly use some talented sharp shooters like that against the British," said Washington.

"Houston, we have a problem," said Jared.

"What is it?" asked Vice President Bashoff.

"When President Harp hit the ground, he landed on the bottom arch — knocked out the laptop input and he damaged the cylinder slot," said Jared.

"Can it be repaired?" asked Bashoff.

"I think so," said Jared, "but, it may take a day or so."

CHAPTER 40

With Pangea out of commission, Washington stayed the night at the Four Seasons — in a different room on a different floor. He agreed to stay as an honored guest of the President of the United States, David Bashoff.

Harp officially resigned his presidency in the suite at the Four Seasons, while lying on the floor in handcuffs. Bashoff was officially sworn in as the forty-sixth President of the United States in the suite at the Four Seasons, after Harp was taken away.

The official swearing in ceremony was to take place the following day, in the Rose Garden at the White House. Bashoff asked Washington to attend, and asked that he say a few words. Washington happily accepted the invitation.

Washington, Jared and Snyder arrived at the White House at eight thirty a.m. They entered in their SUV through the Northwest Gate. They toured the first floor, entering through the vestibule, before visiting the East Room, the Green Room, the Red Room, The State Dining Room, and the Family Dining Room. The highlight for Washington was when they passed through the Yellow Oval Room, and stepped out onto the Truman Balcony. The view took his breath away — the elegant columns, the wrought iron railing, the South Lawn with its fountain. Beyond the fountain, the Ellipse. And beyond that, the Washington Monument.

"What a breathtaking sight," said Washington. "It is magnificent."

They walked down to the West Wing, visited the Oval Office, and walked outside to the Rose Garden. It was almost ten a.m., so everyone was in place.

Jared saw Janey standing in a cluster of people beside Bashoff. He was immediately paralyzed, and hoped he would not be forced to speak to her. The Chief Justice of the United States Supreme Court presided over the ceremony. They used the Washington Bible, the actual book that was sworn upon by George Washington when he took office as the first President of the United States on April 30th, 1789. Ancient York Masons are the custodians of what is known as the George Washington Inaugural Bible. The Bible is the King James Version, and the Ancient York Masons were thrilled to make it available, especially when they were notified that Washington, himself, would be in attendance.

At the conclusion of the ceremony, President Bashoff made an announcement.

"Ladies and Gentlemen, and all distinguished guests, I would like to announce that I have selected Senator Janey Logan as my Vice President. Senator Logan has served dutifully in the U.S. Senate for more than four years, and her track record is both distinguished and noteworthy. She is beloved by her constituents in the State of Connecticut, and she was one of the first to express her concerns with the direction our Government was heading under the previous administration. At the time when she began to speak up, two years ago, there was no way of knowing how the situation would end up. Certainly, no one could foresee the events as they have played out over the past few days. For all she knew, Senator Logan might have been playing a game of political

suicide, speaking out fervently against policies she disagreed with strongly. Senator Logan wasn't concerned about that — she only concerned herself with what she felt was right, and what she viewed as wrong. Wrong for the American people, and wrong for the country. We need more politicians who are willing to put their necks out on the line and do what they feel is right, as opposed to what they feel is popular. Congratulations, Senator Logan, please join me at the Podium."

The First Congress passed an oath act on June 1st, 1789, authorizing only Senators to administer the oath to the Vice President (who serves as the president of the Senate). Later that year, legislation passed that allowed courts to administer all oaths and affirmations. So, on this day, the Chief Justice read the Oath to Vice President Janey Logan as well.

And, so it was done. President Bashoff was one of just three Presidents who were unmarried when they entered office — the other two being James Buchanan and Grover Cleveland (however, Cleveland married while in office). It has been debated whether an unmarried President could be elected these days. Of course, Bashoff wasn't elected by the American people.

Jared had two thoughts. First, while he didn't love Janey, perhaps he should have remained with her. It would have been pretty cool being the husband of America's first female Vice President. Second, he wondered if there might have been something going on behind the scenes between Bashoff and Janey? They seemed awfully close and chummy at times. Jared wondered if someone could be both Vice President and First Lady at the same time? Talk about a "power couple".

President Bashoff returned to the podium, and introduced General Washington.

"I'd like to ask General Washington to step to the podium to say a few words."

Washington was wearing his full Revolutionary War uniform, and the image of him standing in the Rose Garden, with the West Wing of the White House in the background, was just too much for the electronic media to bear. Cameras and flashes burst at a furious pace as he took his place at the podium. He began to speak.

"The events of the past several days have been interesting indeed. My introduction to twenty-first Century life has been interesting as well. As you know, I come from a quieter and simpler time, and I give all of you credit for working at such a frenetic pace while doing the job of Government. The system isn't a perfect one, but you are all clearly committed to making the United States of America great. I will be returning to my time shortly, and I will return knowing that our fight for independence is a noble and important one. We are fighting for liberty, justice and fairness. It is comforting to know that Americans who live during the twenty-first Century continue to appreciate and fight for those values today. What I witnessed here during the past few days, was the culmination of a civil war. No, this war was not fought with guns and cannon on America's battlefields. It was fought with words and ideas. It was fought with healthy debate and varying opinions. In the end, Americans came together for the betterment of the Union. I will never forget my visit to your world. Thank you."

President Bashoff and Washington shook hands. Again, the roar of cameras clicking filled the Rose Garden. Bashoff waved for Jared to join them, which he did reluctantly. While up near the podium, he saw Janey and gave her a kiss on the cheek.

"Congratulations, Janey," said Jared.

"Thank you. I'm sorry about what I said to you. But, please know how much I appreciate what you did. You are a hero."

"You're welcome, Ms Vice President."

The flight back to New York, this time on the much larger Air Force One jumbo jet, was uneventful. Knowing it would likely be his last flight on an airplane, Washington soaked it all in. He sat with his face glued to the window during the forty-five minute flight, even continuing to stare out the window when there was nothing to see but clouds.

In the back of the plane, Jared and Snyder discussed the puzzle of Benjamin Tallmadge's account of Washington's farewell address to his officers.

"Will you say something to him?" asked Snyder.

"I don't know. I feel like I have to, but I have no idea what piece of advice I could possibly give him to help win the war. I could tell him what transpired during the various battles. I could try to share the strategies they employed during the battles, but I'm not sure that's what he'd be looking for from me. Is it strategy-related? Could it be some sort of life lesson? Maybe something about the weather? I have no clue."

"I know, it's truly a needle in a haystack."

CHAPTER 41

Jared had called JPL to have the needed Pangea parts shipped overnight to Bell Labs in Murray Hill, New Jersey. Today, Bell Labs is called Nokia Bell Labs, but the place has a very rich history as a research and scientific development company.

The historic laboratory originated in the late nineteenth century as the Volta Laboratory and Bureau created by Alexander Graham Bell. Researchers working at Bell Labs are credited with the development of radio astronomy, the transistor, the laser, and the operating system Unix, among other significant breakthroughs. Eight Nobel Prizes have been awarded for work completed at Bell Laboratories.

When Jared was an undergrad at Princeton, he had a summer internship at Bell Labs, and remained close to several people who still worked there. He arrived at eight thirty on Saturday morning, and began unpacking the spare pieces he needed to rebuild Pangea. He laid Pangea out in the middle of the floor of a large laboratory, which was the size of a basketball court. The bottom arch, which accepted the laptop and cylinder inputs, was an older model, and a little thinner than the rest of the hoop. The width of each arch on the current model is ten inches, while the older model was just six inches. The bottom arch slid into place fine, and Jared slid it forward to align with the front of the hoop. On the back side of the hoop, it was obvious that the bottom piece didn't align with the rest of the hoop. The laptop intake jack was fine, as was the cylinder input.

The new laptop, which replaced the old one damaged by Harp as he fell, was actually the original laptop used during initial demonstrations. The Pangea program was pre-loaded, and appeared ready to go. Jared powered up the repaired Pangea apparatus, and after the uranium cylinder was inserted, he entered Monday, July 9th as the target travel date. The hoop slowly began to spin, and in approximately twenty seconds, a green light illuminated on the laptop which indicated that the target date was established successfully. Jared felt a sense of relief, and reported the good news to President Bashoff.

Despite the fact that he was beginning his first day in office and had numerous pressing agenda items, Bashoff made it clear that any call from a Lombardi Project member was a priority.

"Bashoff here. Is this Jared?"

"Mr President, it's Jared. I have repaired Pangea using some old parts, and it appears ready to go."

"Okay. Do I feel a 'but' coming?" asked Bashoff.

"Sir, this is in essence, a new version of the Pangea apparatus, it's never been tested. The old version, the original version that I created, utilized six inch wide arch pieces. For the current version, I went with ten inch arch pieces to add stability to the hoop when it was placed upright. The version we have now includes eleven pieces that are six inches wide, and one that is ten inches wide. So, it's a brand new configuration."

"Will it work?" asked Bashoff.

"It should," said Jared, "but we have no real way of knowing if it is precise. Is the gravity regulator precisely tuned to travel distance? Will Washington return exactly to his departure point? Will it be instantaneous?"

"So, you want to test it?"

"I think it would be a good idea."

"I'm concerned, Jared, about making additional trips to the past. We discussed putting Pangea away for good, remember?"

"I know, sir, and I am completely onboard with that. My concern is Washington — what if we're not precise? What then?"

"What do you have in mind?" asked the President.

"I go back to the precise time we left. I traveled with Washington, so I will return to the exact time we left — assuming Pangea is operating correctly. Then I'll find someone who can tell me the date and time. Assuming it's accurate, we'll have confidence that Washington will return to the exact date and time as well."

"Okay, but make it quick," said Bashoff. "Limit the amount of interaction you have with people — ask someone for the date and time, that's it. Then get back here."

While Jared worked at JPL, Washington and Snyder took the subway down to lower Manhattan. Washington was once again dressed in his polo shirt and khaki's, and wearing a NY Mets baseball cap. The men were surrounded by Secret Service Agents as they left the Waldorf and headed to the E Train subway at 53rd and 5th Avenue. It was a picture perfect day — sunny, blue skies, with just a few puffy white clouds passing by. They descended the stairs to the subway platform, and a train immediately arrived clanging and hissing as it stopped at the 53rd Street Station.

The doors opened and all five men got on the train.

"What do you think of the subway?" asked Snyder.

"It's a marvel," said Washington. "It's an amazing advantage. To be able to travel from one end of the island to the other, and across from river to river so quickly is miraculous. And, so many vessels traveling in so many directions at once. It's amazing that they're not constantly smashing into one another."

When they reached the Chambers Street station, the men exited the train and made their way back up to the street. They saw the Freedom Tower, and walked towards it. They were greeted at the main observation tower entrance, and guided straight to the elevator for the ride to the hundred and second floor. They took the escalator down to the observation platform, and Washington gazed out at the view in amazement.

"That's astonishing," said Washington, as he gazed out towards Brooklyn. "That's where we're constructing our defenses right now. What an interesting perspective. Ah, yes. The Heights and the Gowanus, I see how we can fortify that area, but we have so much ground to cover."

"Yes, indeed," said Snyder. "It's a mighty task, especially when you consider the size of your forces as compared to theirs."

Washington walked over to the south-facing window bank, and peered out at the harbor.

"The harbor is so large. How can we stop the British from assembling their massive navy off our shores? I have often said that controlling New York is the key to controlling the continent. But, how?"

The men walked around the observation floor, and Washington noticed the large green rectangle in the center of Manhattan Island as he gazed north.

"It's Central Park," said Snyder. "It's nearly eight hundred acres of fields, ponds and streams. As the population expanded north during the 1800's, New Yorkers had the foresight to protect a large amount of green space so that the people had a place to congregate and enjoy the outdoors. It's a truly beautiful place."

The men headed to a small cafeteria which was on the one hundredth floor. The place offered cook-to-order burgers, hotdogs, and pre-made sandwiches. Washington ordered a cheeseburger and fries. The men sat at a small table for two.

"What do you think of the burger?" asked Snyder.

Washington wiped his lips with a napkin.

"It's quite tasty," he said. "It's unlike anything I've ever tasted before."

"It's a very popular food item," said Snyder. "We have many restaurants called fast-food, which specialize in burgers. They sell millions — maybe billions of them every year."

"I appreciate the water in bottles," said Washington. "To have so much readily available water for all to consume is quite an advantage."

"So tell me," asked Snyder. "How do you like 2018? Do you think you'd do well here?"

"If I had been born in this year, I do believe I would have done well. My life would have been far different, of course. I don't know what my calling would have been. Would I have been in the military, or would I have been driven in a different direction entirely? However, as a person traveling from 1776 to 2018, I don't think I'd do very well here on a long term basis."

"That's interesting," said Snyder, "why do you feel that way?"

""My personality and sensibility has been formed over many years during my life in the 1700's. It is quite difficult, I've found, to become accustomed to a different version of the world."

"People are often born in rural parts of America — North Dakota, Wyoming, Idaho — and they move to New York, or other cosmopolitan cities, and they do very well."

"I could see that," said Washington. "However, in my case it's more than just a move from a rural area to a large city like New York. Everything is so different — transportation, electricity, plumbing, the way you eat and drink, television, moving pictures, cameras. And, that's only the things I've been introduced to. I'm sure there are many things I'm not even aware of. I'm curious about modern war tactics. I'm certain your armies are no longer using muskets and bayonets. I'm certain I'd be amazed by the weaponry which exists today."

"Yes, you would be," said Snyder. "But, I'd prefer you didn't know too much. It's a pretty horrific thing when you consider the magnitude of destruction and pain man can levy against his fellow man today. And, unfortunately, he often does. We have the capability of wiping mankind off the earth. We can end civilization by pressing a few buttons and dropping a few bombs. Thankfully, clearer heads have prevailed, but we live our lives knowing that a few madmen have the power to change things in an instant. In the end, the best use for Pangea, perhaps, might be to turn back time in order to change history should Armageddon ever occur. Pangea might save mankind one day."

"That's my point," said Washington. "The technology which exists today is beyond my comprehension. I would spend my lifetime becoming acquainted with everything that exists today, and I'd have to learn about all of the issues, all of the history. These are things that people born in this century know or learn as they grow older. I would have to learn it all very quickly, and I don't believe I'm capable of doing that. As I mentioned earlier, had I been born in this century, it may very well be different."

"I think you give yourself too little credit," said Snyder. "I believe you'd catch up quickly and your intellect would position you as one of the great minds of our time. But, don't worry, either way, you're going back."

Washington sighed.

"Now that I think about it, perhaps I should stay," said Washington. "The task that I'm facing back home seems monumental."

"It is, indeed," said Snyder. "Are you feeling optimistic at this time?"

"There has not been a single moment in which I have felt optimistic," said Washington. "I know quite well the odds we are facing, and I am intimately familiar with the magnitude of the force we are facing. However, we are a desperate army, made up of men who seek justice and freedom. Life hasn't changed for the men and women of Great Britain. They go about their lives as they always have — a world away. To them, this conflict is nothing more than a story they read about in the British news. But to our men, it's about life itself. That is what I am counting on to make the difference, and to drive a favorable outcome for our side. When it comes to battle, heart and will are powerful motivators, and good predictors of outcome. The side whose drive and determination comes from deepest within the heart, will most often prevail."

"General, obviously I cannot share anything with you that might adversely impact the outcome of your battle," said Snyder. "However, I will only say that your words have impressed me here today, and they explain many of the things I have read and learned about America's war of Independence. America could not have had a better, more talented, more formidable leader than you, General."

"I thank you, sir. I have enjoyed my day here with you."

"As have I," said Snyder, still pinching himself.

Washington, Snyder and the Secret Service Agents took the subway back up to midtown, and returned to the Waldorf Suite. When they entered the room, they found Jared on the couch, eating a cheeseburger from room service.

"How's your cheese hamburger?" asked Washington.

"How do you know about cheeseburgers?" asked Jared.

"I had one for lunch."

"Don't get too used to them," said Jared. "You're going home tomorrow, so unless you intend on cooking one yourself when you get back, you've likely had your last burger."

"Is Pangea fixed?" asked Snyder.

"It is."

"Well," said Snyder, "there's always time for one more room service burger for dinner."

Snyder winked at Washington. Washington smiled.

The following morning, Jared got dressed in his Connecticut Regiment uniform. He didn't wash it, so the odor emanating from it was quite strong. Jared and Corkoran transported the newly configured Pangea apparatus in its duffle to Prospect Park, and set it up at the Mount Prospect clearing at exactly six a.m. Jared input the target date and time, then stepped through the hoop. The flash occurred once again, and they were gone — Jared and the hoop.

Once in 1776, Jared packed the duffle, and buried it beside the same Dogwood Tree — the white fabric still tied to it as an identifying reminder of its location. He made his way down the hill to the Flatbush Road. Once again, it had taken approximately thirty minutes to bury the apparatus, so he estimated that it was approximately six thirty. The sun was up, and it was a clear and cool morning.

As he reached a farmhouse along the road, he saw a man feeding chickens beside a small barn. He walked up to the man, and introduced himself.

"Good man, my name is John Ross, with Mott's Militia of the Connecticut Colony. I am a Corporal, and serve under

General Gates at Fort Ticonderoga. I am traveling to the island of Manhattan to personally deliver a letter to General Washington on behalf of General Gates."

"How can I help you?" asked the farmer.

"I've been traveling for several days — I'm not certain how many. I was wondering if you could tell me what day it is?"

"It's Saturday, July the 9th."

And, now the hard part.

"Can you tell me the year?" asked Jared.

"The year?' asked the Farmer. "Just how long have you been traveling, Corporal?"

"I know it sounds, strange," said Jared, "but, if you could just tell me the year."

"It's seventeen hundred and seventy six."

"Thank you, thank you, sir!"

Jared ran down the road, heading west towards Manhattan. When he reached the ferry, he paid his fare over to the Manhattan side of the river. When he arrived at Pearl Street, he ran to Beaver Street, and knocked on the door of the inn. His heart was pounding. All he could think about was seeing Becky again, hugging her close, and kissing her.

Mrs Miller opened the door. ""Mr Ross, what a surprise it is to see you," she said.

"I'm sorry to show up unannounced, Mrs Miller. Is Becky available?"

"No, I'm afraid she's not."

"Do you have any idea when she will return?" asked Jared.

"I'm afraid not," said Mrs Miller.

"I see," said Jared. "Well, would you please tell her that I stopped by, and that I'm sorry I missed her?"

"Yes, I will."

Dejected, Jared turned and walked back towards Pearl Street. He wanted to stay — he wanted an opportunity to see Becky again. But, he was under direct orders from the President to return immediately and to whatever degree possible, to avoid interaction with people. There were just too many unknowns.

Back at the inn on Beaver Street, Becky had been sitting on the stairway leading to the second floor. She was blocked by an open door, out of view of Jared. She had heard the conversation between Jared and her mother, and when the door was closed, she got to her feet and hugged her mother while sobbing.

"Did I do the right thing?" asked Becky? "I miss him so much."

"You did the right thing, dear. It's difficult now, but it will get easier over time. You said it yourself — there's no future for the two of you, so why make matters more difficult. It is better you move past this now, rather than living a lifetime of sadness."

"I don't know, mother. I may experience a lifetime of sadness either way."

Once again, Jared's instantaneous return was startling from Corkoran's perspective.

"It works fine," said Jared.

"Great. I guess we send Washington back tomorrow."

CHAPTER 42

It was Sunday morning, July 10th at four thirty a.m. It was dark outside, and Washington was standing in the living area at the Waldorf Suite. He was dressed magnificently in his full general's uniform.

"I'll miss those clothes," said Washington, pointing to the khaki's and polo sitting folded neatly on a chair.

"Those clothes don't do you justice," said Snyder.

Washington grabbed a breakfast burrito from the room service tray.

"I'll miss these as well," said Washington, holding up a small, thin burrito.

"Those things will kill you," said Jared. "You'll be way better off without them."

The men headed out the door, to the elevator, and down to the lobby. The Sprinter was waiting at the curb on Park Avenue, and they all filed in. Jared placed the Pangea duffle in the back and slid in next to Washington. The driver slid the door shut, and hopped in.

The Sprinter headed south along Park Avenue, circled Grand Central Terminal, and then headed east along 36th Street. They passed the Morgan Library, where Washington's identity was confirmed against his life mask, and then they entered the Queens Midtown Tunnel. It was Washington's first trip through one of New York's many tunnels.

"How was this tunnel built?" asked Washington.

"They use huge tunnel boring machines — it's a slow and tedious process," said Corkoran.

"An absolute marvel," said Washington. "It takes several ferry trips to transport an army across a river — what an amazing advantage a tunnel or bridge would be."

"For obvious reasons, they're targets during wartime," said Snyder. "They are heavily defended, but often they are blown up using bombs."

"I can imagine, considering the strategic value of such structures," said Washington.

Jared pulled an envelope from his jacket pocket. The envelope was sealed, and in blue ballpoint pen was written, 'General Washington — Please Open When You Return'.

"General Washington," said Jared. "I have a note for you. Please read this when you return home. I think it is quite important."

"Thank you, Jared."

The driver stopped the Sprinter next to the Brooklyn Public Library. Washington, Jared, Snyder and Corkoran slid out of the van. Jared grabbed the Pangea duffle from the back of the van, and they ascended the stone stairway up to the clearing at Mount Prospect. Jared and Corkoran began assembling the arch hoop, while Snyder pulled the laptop from its case. When the pieces of the hoop were in place, the three men lifted it upright. With the thinner arch at the bottom, the hoop was less steady, so Corkoran held it upright.

"General Washington, may I have a word with you?" asked Jared.

The two men walked off toward the center of the clearing, about fifty yards from the location of the hoop.

"General, here is the extra cylinder of uranium. Please keep it in the carrying case until you need it. I already programmed the return date and time into the laptop, so all you'll have to do is hit the tab key as I showed you last night. The return date and time will move to the 'target' column, then you'll just need to hit 'enter'. If there's no return trip, break down the hoop and dispose of it in a safe spot."

"I know a safe spot — it will not be found," said Washington.

"If there's a return trip," said Jared, "the hoop and other equipment will return here so you will not need to be burdened with it."

"I understand," said Washington. "I am happy to help."

"Thank you, General," said Jared, as he extended his hand to shake Washington's. Then, he put his left arm around Washington, and gave him a man hug. This surprised Washington, but he didn't flinch.

The two men walked back over to the hoop, and the others said their farewells. Snyder asked Agent Franco to take a picture of the four men — Jared to Washington's left, Corkoran to Washington's right, and Snyder crouching in front.

Then Jared entered the date and time, and pressed the enter button. The hoop began to spin, first slowly, and then very quickly. When the green light illuminated on the laptop, Jared gave Washington a thumbs' up, and he stepped through. In a flash, Washington and the hoop were gone.

CHAPTER 43

Washington was back and he recognized the differences immediately. It was peaceful and serene. No noise from trucks or airplanes, just the sound of birds chirping in the trees. The hoop was standing as he looked back at it. He decided to lay the hoop on the ground, so that it wouldn't topple over and get damaged. He placed the laptop in its case, as well as the used cylinder. He placed the case behind a thick oak trunk which was a few feet into the woods. He knew he was taking a chance leaving the hoop intact in the clearing, but that spot at the top of Mount Prospect was out of the way and didn't receive much foot traffic.

Washington headed down the short slope of Mount Prospect towards the Flatbush Road. He saw the same farmer outside his barn feeding his chickens. The farmer didn't notice him as he passed, so Washington kept walking. About a half a mile down the Flatbush Road, he heard the sound of a horse and wagon coming up behind him. He turned to see a gray horse pulling a short wagon bed packed with buckets of fruits and vegetables. The driver stopped.

"General Washington," said the man, "would you like a ride? I'm heading towards the ferry, takin' my crop to the market."

"Thank you, sir."

The wagon was narrow, and the two men sat sat-by-side with their shoulders touching. Washington pulled the envelope that Jared gave him from his breast pocket. The man looked over at it, as it looked like nothing he had ever seen before. Washington looked at the man, who immediately looked away, and continued driving the wagon.

Washington opened the envelope, and withdrew the letter. He looked at it and began to read:

Dear General Washington,

If during your engagement with the British on Long Island, the situation turns perilous, you will have an opportunity to escape with your men under the cover of night and heavy fog across the East River."

Best of luck to you and your men.

Yours faithfully,

John Jared Ross

Washington's escape across the East River during the Battle of Long Island was nothing short of miraculous. Had a large percentage of the army been killed or captured, the Revolution might have ended there and then. Washington and the army were surrounded on Brooklyn Heights with the East River to their backs. As the day went on, the British began to dig trenches, slowly coming closer to the American defenses. Fearing the end was near, that evening, Washington's men escaped to Manhattan — many under darkness, but many after the sun had risen the following day, only to be shielded by a dense, heavy fog. Washington, the last man left, crossed on the last boat. At seven a.m., the last American troops landed in Manhattan. All nine thousand troops had been evacuated with no loss of life

Washington returned the letter to the envelope, closed it, and placed it back in his vest pocket. When they reached the

Brooklyn ferry dock, Washington was transported by boat over to Manhattan, while the driver of the horse and cart waited for a flat top ferry.

Once on Manhattan Island, Washington walked along Pearl Street, peering back over his shoulder at Brooklyn, where he believed the British would land. Washington began moving troops to Brooklyn in early May so that, within a short time, there were a few thousand of them in Brooklyn. On the eastern side of the East River, three forts were under construction to support Fort Stirling, which stood to the west of the hamlet of Brooklyn Heights: Fort Putnam, Fort Greene, and Fort Box. Each of these defensive structures were surrounded by a large ditch, all connected by a line of entrenchments and a total of thirty-six cannons. From where Washington was standing, he could see parts of each fort. He pictured the geography of Brooklyn in his mind, as he viewed it from the Freedom Tower the prior day.

Washington had assembled more than twenty thousand troops on Long Island, and was authorized by congress to reach twenty-eight thousand five hundred and one troops in total. Washington knew it would be a difficult battle, but the letter from Jared suggested it might be even more treacherous than he thought.

Washington continued his walk south, and turned right onto Broad Street, then left onto Beaver Street. He walked to the front door of the inn, and knocked. Mrs Miller came to the door.

"General Washington!" she exclaimed. "My goodness, to what do I owe this honor, sir?"

"I would like to have a word with your daughter, Becky, if she is available."

"My Becky, is she in trouble?"

"Oh no, not at all. I simply have a message to deliver."

Becky poked her head around the door, and stood before Washington.

"So nice to see you again, General Washington," said Becky.

"Becky, may I have a word with you in private?" asked Washington.

"Of course, come in please."

Becky and Washington walked down the hall to the parlor, and she closed the door. They each took a seat, across from one another.

"I am here on behalf of John Jared Ross, with whom you are acquainted. Over the past several days, I have become quite friendly with him. I believe him to be a man of great integrity and utmost sincerity. He shared with me, at my request, some of the details of your relationship with him. He has become quite despondent since he returned to his home, which as I am aware, you know to be quite far away."

"Yes, I am aware, General."

"He shared with me his position, that due to the strength of his feelings for you, he felt it was his duty to consider what was best for you, and he determined it would be in your best interest to remain here."

"Yes, he made that very clear," said Becky.

"I, in turn, suggested to Mr Ross, that he would be well served by not making a decision on your behalf, but to allow you to make said decision on your own. While his intentions were indeed noble and honorable, it was not appropriate given the circumstances."

"What, may I ask, was his reaction, General?"

"He agreed with me. Now, I must tell you, having spent five days in the twenty-first century, there is indeed, much to get accustomed to. However, I wouldn't describe it as bad, but merely as quite different from the world as we know it. There are many positives, in fact, not the least of which is indoor plumbing," said Washington with a laugh.

"So, he wants me to travel to the twenty-first century to be with him?"

"Yes, he does. Very much so. That is why I am here, to ask, on Mr Ross's behalf, if you would consider traveling to his time, to live there and marry. I must inform you, you will not be able to return. The method of travel, of which I am somewhat knowledgeable, will not exist after today. Therefore, if you agree to go, you must remain there forever."

"And if I decide to go," asked Becky, "how would I get there?"

"It's really quite simple, actually," said Washington. "The travel apparatus is set up across the river on Long Island. It sits atop Mount Prospect. It is there now, as we speak. If you say yes, I will travel with you to that spot, and I will help you travel to meet him."

"And, I must do it today?" asked Becky.

"Yes, you must," said Washington. "In fact, if you choose to go, you must go now."

"But, I need time to think, and I'll need time to prepare. I have to pack…"

"No, there's no need to pack," said Washington. "Everything you will need, everything you will wear, is in plentiful supply there. Nothing in your wardrobe will be in style when you get there."

"I'm just not sure I can make a decision of this magnitude so quickly."

"I understand how you feel, but you must," said Washington. "I will be outside your front door. I will wait for five minutes. If you don't come out, I'll know your decision and I will go."

Becky spoke to her mother. She tried to explain the situation, how she was going away to be with Jared, and that she wouldn't be able to ever return. She told her mother that, even though she wanted to go and be with Jared, if her mother objected, she'd stay. Mrs Miller told Becky she didn't understand why she'd never be able to return, but if Becky really loved him, she wanted her to go and spend her life with Jared. Becky assured her mother that she was, indeed, in love, and that she wanted to go. She came close to explaining the situation with the portal, and that she'd be traveling to the future. But, she knew this would only worry her mother, so she decided not to share the details. Becky and her mother hugged for a long time, and they both sobbed.

"Becky, I love you, and I want you to be happy. This inn is no place for you to spend your life. I imagined an exciting and adventurous life for you — I hope that's what you'll find wherever it is you're going, my dear."

"It will be an adventure, more so than you or I could possibly imagine," said Becky.

"Will you at least be able to send me a letter from time to time?"

"No, I won't," said Becky, and the tears returned.

Mrs Miller tried to hide her tears, and focus instead on practical matters.

"Now, Becky, you must run up to your room and pack a bag."

After packing a small bag with what she felt were a few necessities, she hugged her mother one last time. When Becky finally stepped outside the front door of the inn, holding her small satchel, Washington was nowhere in sight. Becky began to panic. Did she leave him waiting more than five minutes? Why didn't he give her at least a little leeway considering the gravity of the situation? Where did he say the apparatus was? Long Island? Mount Prospect? If she hurried, perhaps she could catch him before he boarded the ferry. Becky ran down Beaver Street with satchel in tow. She turned onto Broad Street, then north on Pearl until she reached the ferry dock. But, there was no sign of Washington. "Kind sir, have you recently seen General Washington?" she asked the ferryman. "Did you, perhaps, ferry him across the river to Long Island?"

"No, m'am" said the ferryman. "I ferried him to Manhattan Island earlier."

The man was drunk, no question about it. His breath was ripe with stale ale, and she detected a slight slur in his speech. But, could he possibly have been so drunk that he confused which direction he carried Washington? "Sir, I'd like to pay for passage to Long Island" said Becky. Becky climbed onto the boat, and took a seat on one of the benches facing Brooklyn. She worried about what she'd do when she reached the Long Island side. She had never been to Long Island, and had no idea where Mount Prospect was. Just then, she heard the clip clop of a horse's hooves. Becky turned and saw it was Washington, sitting atop his large white colt. Becky stood quickly. "General Washington, I was afraid I had missed you. When I stepped outside the inn, you weren't anywhere to be seen."

"My apologies, Miss Miller. I walked quickly to headquarters on Broadway to retrieve my horse. I fully expected that I'd return before you exited the inn, but I'm afraid it took longer than I had expected. I knocked on the door, and your mother indicated that you had headed in the direction of the dock."

"I understand," said Becky. "I have decided to go, General."

279

"Very well," said Washington, as he dismounted his horse. "Come join me. We will take the next flat top ferry to the other shore."

Becky stood, walked off the ferry, and joined Washington on the dock. The flat top ferry was making its way to the Manhattan side, carrying two horses and a large wagon full of timber. When the flat top arrived, the horses and wagon exited, and Washington attempted to hand the ferryman payment for the crossing.

"Oh no, General," said the ferryman. "You won't be needin' to pay for the trip."

"Thank you, sir," said Washington.

Washington turned to Becky.

"What changed your mind, dear?" he asked.

"I knew I'd never have peace in my life if I passed up this opportunity. My feelings for Jared are very strong, and I'd never stop thinking about him, and wondering if I'd made the right decision. I don't believe I'd ever have the motivation to meet another man, so I'd spend the rest of my life working in the inn. It seems like a very lonely existence, does it not?"

"It does, indeed," said Washington. "A woman as beautiful as you deserves a better fate."

The ferry reached the Brooklyn side, and Washington and Becky walked the horse off the flat top. Washington took Becky's satchel, and hooked it onto the saddle horn. Then Washington mounted the horse, and put his hand out for Becky to grab hold, and she mounted. Becky sat behind Washington, with both arms holding tightly around his waist. They headed off slowly up Ferry Road, then onto the Flatbush Road towards Mount Prospect.

"What did you like best about the future?" asked Becky.

"Aside from indoor plumbing," said Washington, "were the motor cars. People don't ride horses — they ride in carriages which are propelled by a motor. There are thousands of these things riding along the road. They can move extremely quickly, but they travel in an orderly manner. I had an opportunity to drive one of these motor cars. It is really quite an exhilarating feeling. I highly suggest you take a turn in a motor car one day."

"It sounds exciting."

"It was," said Washington, "it really was. They have flying vessels in the future. They are quite large, larger than a sailing ship. But these vessels fly through the air at great speed, and at great heights. They can fly over the ocean, and deliver people from New York to Paris in just six hours."

Becky began to laugh.

"No!" she exclaimed. "That's not possible."

"Oh, it is. I had an opportunity to fly in an air vessel more than once. It is an absolute wonder."

They came upon a farmhouse. The farmer, who was picking apples from a tree in his orchard offered one to Washington and Becky.

"General Washington, can I offer you and your friend an apple?" asked the farmer.

"That would be appreciated," said Washington. "The sun is quite strong today and my mouth dry. Becky, would you like one as well?"

"I would," said Becky. "Thank you."

Washington and Becky dismounted the horse, and took a seat under a shady tree. The farmer returned with two glasses of ale, which Washington and Becky consumed.

After a while, they remounted the horse and continued their journey east.

"Should I be wary of anything?" asked Becky.

"Yes, you should be wary of many things," said Washington.

"The pace of life in the future is much quicker than anything we're used to. Everything moves quickly. People talk quickly, walk quickly, think quickly. It's loud and the streets are quite crowded. But, it's all pretty orderly, so you will get used to it quickly. You should stay close to Jared when you get there. In time, you will develop the confidence to be on your own."

"That's very helpful, General."

"My pleasure, Becky."

"Why are you helping us, General Washington?" asked Becky. "I know Jared must have asked for your assistance, but why have you agreed to help?"

"I have developed a keen liking to Mr Ross. I believe him to be a good man, with high moral character. We spent a great deal of time together, and he shared much with me — particularly, his feelings for you. He has also helped me in certain ways with respect to the battles which lie ahead for our army. I feel I owe him a large debt. It saddens me to think that I will never see him again. I am happy to help him in any way I can."

Washington could see Mount Prospect ahead, and took a turn at the path which led up the hill to the summit. As they crested the top of the hill, Washington saw the hoop, but it was surrounded by three men in British uniform. The men hadn't noticed the arrival of Washington and Becky. They were staring at the hoop and at the laptop which sat on the bottom arch. The men were touching the apparatus, running their hands along the smooth metal surfaces. They were talking to each other, but Washington and Becky could not hear what they were saying from their distance on the other side of the clearing.

"Who are those men?" asked Becky.

"Red Coats. British. They are likely an advance team scouting locations ahead of battle. Mount Prospect is the highest point on Long Island, so it's not surprising, really, that they'd scout this location."

"What do we do?" asked Becky.

"I will attempt to get them to move on," said Washington.

Washington kicked and the white colt broke into a canter heading straight toward the hoop.

"Halt!" yelled Washington.

The men were startled as they turned to face Washington. They pointed their muskets at the approaching horse.

"We are members of the King's Army, Advanced Scouts with the fortieth Regiment of Foot. Who be you, sir?"

Washington stopped just in front of the hoop, as all three men stood before him.

"I am General George Washington, Commander-in-Chief of the Continental Army, and I say you have no business here. I respectfully request that you leave this spot immediately."

"If I'm not mistaken," said one of the British soldiers, "this land belongs to the King, which means we have every right to be here. Now tell me, what on earth is this contraption?"

"Then we have a difference of opinion," said Washington. "This land belongs to the people of America, and this contraption is a creation of the people of America. Again, I must demand that you leave immediately."

"Is that so?" said one of the British soldiers. "It's my duty as a member of the King's army to inform you that you are intruding on the King's land. You must leave at once, or else I will be forced to shoot you."

"Hold your fire," said Washington. "If you would like, I can demonstrate this apparatus for you."

"What does it do?" asked one of the other British soldiers.

"It's a time travel portal," said Washington. "You step

through the hoop, and you're transported to another time."

"What are you doing?" asked Becky, whispering in Washington's ear.

"I'm trying to save our lives," said Washington.

Washington's plan was to turn on the portal, set it for the day prior, and have them disappear with the hoop one day into the past. That would give Washington and Becky an opportunity to get out of there, even though they'd lose access to the hoop. Yes, they'd be alive, but they'd lose any opportunity to transport Becky to 2018. And, the hoop would be in the hands of the British. It's not as though they'd have the ability to utilize it — they wouldn't know how to operate the laptop, nor would they have access to the uranium cylinder Washington carried in his vest pocket. But, it would certainly be odd for the British to have this technology from the future in their possession.

"I will demonstrate by stepping through the hoop with my lady friend. We will disappear for a brief minute or two, and return to this spot."

Washington's new plan was to set the date to 2018, pass through with Becky — taking the hoop with them, then having Jared send Washington back on a different date and time.

"Hogwash," said one of the British soldiers. "That's not possible."

"Then explain to me," said Washington, "the nature of the equipment you are looking at. You must know these things could not have been produced in 1776. Admit that you have never seen anything like it, and you will know they were built at a time and place which could only exist in the future."

The three soldiers spoke among themselves in a whisper.

"All right then," said one of the soldiers. "Come down off your horse. Mr Washington, you will pass through the hoop, but

284

the woman will stay here with us."

"Out of the question," said Washington. "Based on the behavior you men have displayed, I will not leave a cousin of mine here with you brutes — not even for a few minutes. She will come with me."

"No she will not," said one of the soldiers, pointing his musket at Washington's head as he walked closer.

"Drop your weapons!"

The voice came from somewhere off in the distance.

Everyone turned and looked. At the far end of the clearing, where Washington and Becky had entered from the Flatbush Road, sat a man on horseback, dressed in Continental Army uniform. He was flanked on each side by five soldiers, who also sat upon their horses. All eleven men sat with their muskets trained on the three British soldiers.

"General Greene," said Washington, "your timing is flawless."

"Drop your weapons," said Major General Nathanael Greene. "You are severely outnumbered."

The three soldiers dropped their weapons. The Continental Army soldiers dismounted and approached the three British soldiers, and took them into custody.

"Are you all right, General Washington?" asked Greene.

"I'm fine. Thank you. Why are you here? Were you following me?"

"No, sir, we didn't know you were here. We were following the British soldiers. They arrived at Gravesend yesterday morning. We were tracking them. We assumed they were advanced scouts."

"Yes, they are. Please take them away, and make sure they don't reunite with their battalion. I don't want them reporting to their commander, the nature of what they saw here today."

"May I ask, sir, what is the nature of that thing?" asked Greene, pointing to the hoop.

"I'm not at liberty to say, Major General," said Washington. "I would appreciate it if you don't mention it to anyone, and I'd ask that you tell your men to do the same."

"Of course, General, I understand."

Greene and his men left the clearing with their prisoners in tow behind them. Becky and Washington were finally alone atop Mount Prospect, and Washington busily worked to get the portal working. He switched on the laptop, which had more than sixty percent of its power remaining. When the Pangea program opened, he typed in the travel date, just as Jared had showed him. Washington was not familiar with working a keyboard, so he pecked very slowly with one finger. When the date was finally entered, he pulled the cylinder from his breast pocket, and slid it into the slot in the bottom arch. Then he hit the 'enter' button, and powered Pangea on — for the final time.

"Jared designed and built this?" asked Becky.

"Yes, he did. He was attempting to build something else, and he accidently discovered that this contraption can cause a human being to travel through time. From what he told me, you can only travel backwards in time, or forward — but — only as far as from where you left."

"And, it's safe?" asked Becky.

"Yes it is," said Washington. "However, they have discovered that traveling into the past can cause dangerous issues that could impact the future."

"Can you provide an example?" asked Becky.

"Certainly," said Washington. "What if I had perished while I visited the year 2018? I would not have been able to return to s year, and I would not have been able to command the Continental Army in our fight for Independence. Perhaps my presence here will have no impact on the outcome of the war. But, if my presence were to make a difference, and I were not here to lead the troops, history could certainly be altered."

"Yes, I see," said Becky.

"For that reason, the authorities plan to destroy the hoop, and no further visits will be made. You will be the last person to make a trip through the hoop. That's why, as I mentioned, you will be unable to return to 1776."

"I understand."

The hoop was spinning at full speed now, and it was time for Becky to start her journey.

"Becky, it's ready," said Washington. "Are you certain you are still committed to making the trip to 2018?"

"I am," said Becky.

Washington walked to Becky, and gave her a hug.

"Good luck to you, and please send my regards to Mr Ross," said Washington.

"Thank you, I will," said Becky. "And, good luck to you. I wish you well in your fight for Independence."

Becky walked toward the hoop, slowly at first — then she picked up the pace. As she passed through the hoop she smiled at Washington, and then came the familiar flash of light. And, then she and the hoop were gone.

THE END